She moaned as he pulled her against him, scrambling her wits until she could barely think. His hands cupped her bottom to lift her closer yet. She hardly realized that he'd moved until he collapsed on a couch with her in his lap.

"Your skin is so soft," he murmured huskily, trailing kisses along her jaw until he reached her ear. Drawing the lobe to his mouth, he nipped it.

"Mmmm." She touched his cheek, surprised to find rough nubs sprinkled along the jawline. Hairs. Yet the hair on his head was as soft as hers, so why did this feel coarse? She slid her hand back and forth to test the different textures, but was distracted when the tip of her breast brushed his arm, exploding into more new sensations. She moaned again, then froze.

Dear Lord! This was not the time for lovemaking. There had been enough scandal for one night. Courting more could ruin them both.

"We had best return to the ballroom, Gray," she said, surprised that her voice was husky. "Not that I object to your kisses—they are quite remarkable. But people will be watching for us."

The Rake and the Wallflower

Allison Lane

A SIGNET BOOK

SIGNET
Published by New American Library, a division of
Penguin Putnam Inc., 375 Hudson Street,
New York, New York 10014, U.S.A.
Penguin Books Ltd, 27 Wrights Lane,
London W8 5TZ, England
Penguin Books Australia Ltd, Ringwood,
Victoria, Australia
Penguin Books Canada Ltd, 10 Alcorn Avenue,
Toronto, Ontario, Canada M4V 3B2
Penguin Books (N.Z.) Ltd, 182–190 Wairau Road,
Auckland 10, New Zealand

Penguin Books Ltd, Registered Offices:
Harmondsworth, Middlesex, England

First published by Signet, an imprint of New American Library,
a division of Penguin Putnam Inc.

First Printing, October 2001
10 9 8 7 6 5 4 3 2 1

Chapter One

"Th-thank you, sir." Mary Seabrook cursed the childhood stammer that had resurfaced in London, certain that it contributed to Mr. Timor's haste to be rid of her—now that the set was over, he was returning her to her sister at a near run.

The dance should have passed without incident, for he was hardly intimidating—barely eighteen, thin as a rail, with an Adam's apple that bobbed twice above a loosely tied cravat whenever he readied himself for speech. His shyness should have made him a kindred spirit. Yet this set had been her worst yet.

Her face heated with the memory.

On the very first pass, she had trod on his foot, making him stumble. Mortified, she'd then turned left instead of right so his outstretched hand slammed into her bosom. Two ladies laughed. Mr. Wendell, deeper in his cups than usual, murmured something about ladybirds, making Mr. Timor blush scarlet to match his hair. Mary had wanted to flee, but the door was too far away.

Mr. Timor's stuttered apology had made her feel even worse, because she knew it was all her fault. He did, too, remaining a full arm's length away for the rest of the interminable set.

Why had Catherine insisted that she attend Lady Debenham's ball? They both knew she had no chance of making a match this Season. Nervousness made her clumsy. Shyness tied her tongue in knots until she lacked even basic conversation—at least what society considered basic. While she talked well enough about birds, animals, and the natural history of Devonshire, the polite world cared only for fashion and gossip. But Mary paid little heed to fashion. And she had been the subject of too much gossip to ever repeat its endless scandals.

She would have been happier attending tonight's meeting of the Ornithology Society. Mr. Duncanson was sharing his research on the reedling, a bird found in reed beds along the east coast. But Catherine had refused, and Blake had backed her judgment.

Mary stifled irritation with her eldest sister. Where was the harm? It wasn't as if she'd expected the family to accompany her. Her sister Laura was a diamond of the first water and had to attend Marriage Mart events. Now that Blake was supplementing her meager dowry, she would find the brilliant match she deserved.

But even a large dowry wouldn't win Mary a match. She would have preferred to stay at Blake's estate or go home to her brother. But she had not been offered either choice. Instead, she was in London, forced to spend the Season in Laura's shadow.

Be fair, urged her conscience.

All right, they had only been in town for three weeks, and Laura needed to become established quickly. At two-and-twenty, she was already old for a first Season. And while Catherine's husband, Blake, was Earl of Rockhurst, their father had been an unknown baron. Once they settled into a routine, Mary could seek other entertainment.

Maybe.

Blake had promised intellectual soirees and societies devoted to her interests. But he was so involved in Parliament that he couldn't look after his wife's sisters. Catherine tried, but this was *her* first foray into society, too, so she had to establish her own place. Being unsure of the rules, she espoused rigid propriety, which kept Mary in ballrooms instead of with fellow intellectuals.

Catherine would mellow once she relaxed, though. The real problem was Laura.

Laura had changed since reaching London. Her sapphire eyes and blonde ringlets had always attracted every gentleman in the vicinity. They wrote odes to her porcelain skin and musical voice, comparing her to Aphrodite, Helen of Troy, and other mythical beauties. Laura had always accepted such praise as her due, but now she flaunted her looks and demanded constant flattery, turning petulant if she didn't receive it. And next to Laura, Mary's straight brown hair, freckled shoulders, and embarrassing penchant for doing and saying the wrong things drew unwelcome comparisons.

She sighed. She couldn't blame Laura for distancing herself, but her efforts too often focused attention on the very incidents she wished to ignore. And knowing that Laura's friends would laugh at every mistake made Mary even more nervous.

Mr. Timor deposited her with Laura, mumbled something under his breath, then retreated so fast he nearly tripped.

None of Laura's admirers noticed. As they vied for the next set, they inadvertently squeezed Mary against the wall.

A year ago, she would have accepted her invisibility with thanks—it was a normal condition when Laura was nearby. On those few occasions when neighbors noticed her, they accepted her shyness and her interest in natural history. She hadn't stammered since age ten.

Then Blake had hired Miss Mott to prepare her for London, believing polish would reduce her shyness. Instead, Miss Mott's rigid rules and perpetual disapproval had destroyed her self-confidence. Nothing she said or did or thought was acceptable. The harder she tried to conform, the worse she became. Her feet caught on phantom obstacles. Her tongue either froze or stammered embarrassing truths. She couldn't even hold a cup without rattling it against its dish these days. Thus she could only keep from plunging the family into scandal if she stayed out of sight—difficult when Laura was always the center of attention.

The next set was called.

Laura glanced around. "There you are, Mary. Mr. Griffin requested this set. Catherine knew no one else wanted it, so she accepted for you."

None of Laura's admirers noted the verbal jab. Nor did they recognize the lie. But Mary knew that Catherine had been gossiping across the room for nearly an hour. Laura had accepted his offer to avenge last night's insult.

This need for revenge was also new. Laura resented sharing her Season. Any attention to Mary irritated her, even polite greetings, for she expected gentlemen to see no one but her. So when Lord Whitehaven had led Mary out, Laura had been furious. As heir to the Duke of Cromley, he was the highest-ranking bachelor in town. But he wasn't ready for marriage. Instead, he used his charm to set the nervous and shy at ease.

Last night had been Mary's turn.

"You study birds, I hear," he said when the steps brought them together. The music was the most sedate of the country dances, allowing time to converse.

"I d-do, my lord. They are more interesting than people."

He ignored her stammer. "Less threatening, at least. A bird will never reveal your secrets."

"Unless it's a parrot," she riposted, amazing herself. "Our neighbor has one who is quick to learn and faithfully reproduces the speaker's voice."

"That could be embarrassing." He smiled.

"Very. Nemesis has criticized our leading gossip, revealed details of a smuggling venture, and repeated at least one amorous encounter."

"Remind me never to buy a parrot." His eyes sparkled. "Have you discovered any interesting birds in London?"

"Very few," she admitted. "Laura's social schedule keeps us busy."

He nodded, but he must have heard her wistfulness. "You might consider riding in Hyde Park in the morning. My groom mentioned a pair of—what do you call those tiny falcons with the white collars?"

"Hobbies?"

"That's the name. Thank you. He spotted them last week."

"Is he sure?" Enthusiasm animated her voice. "Hobbies are quite rare. Though they supposedly nest along the south coast, I've seen only one before. Could they possibly be nesting so near town?"

"I have no idea, but Trotter likes birds almost as much as horses, so I would trust his identification. He saw this pair beyond the Serpentine, near Kensington Palace." He shrugged—very elegantly—then turned the conversation to *on-dits*, entertaining her with a witty description of Miss Derrick's latest attempt to attract Lord Wroxleigh.

Mary had laughed, survived the set without a single stumble, then endured Laura's animosity for the rest of the evening. Laura wouldn't admit that an invitation from Whitehaven would have insulted her by grouping her with society's misfits. Instead, she felt humiliated by his indifference.

Now Mary had to deal with her revenge, and a fiendish one it was. Mr. Griffin was Lord Whitehaven's antithesis. Her skin crawled whenever he was near, as it did now.

"Come along, Miss Mary. The music is about to begin." His voice hissed.

She dreaded the next half hour. His malicious tongue eroded her confidence by criticizing her stammering, her awkwardness, and her education. And he repeated his observations to others, adding to her reputation as a laughingstock.

At least he wasn't courting her, though she was his primary victim just now. Since his eyes gleamed whenever she flinched, she deduced that he enjoyed inflicting pain. Perhaps he needed to feel superior, attacking society's antidotes because they made such easy targets. And maybe he would give up if she ceased reacting.

To distract her thoughts from Griffin, she studied the ballroom. Lady Debenham had one of the few private ballrooms in Mayfair. It was classically appointed, with Greek columns marching down each side, elaborate frescoes at either end, and heavily carved friezes framing an ornate ceiling. Tonight's decorations included an unusual number of palms massed in corners and lined up between columns. Perhaps she'd been striving for a garden effect, though flowers might have achieved it more easily.

Mary smiled as the music started. Lady Debenham's niece, who was calling the sets, must also be cursed with an unwanted partner, for she'd chosen an energetic country dance performed mostly with other gentlemen. Mary could enjoy this set after all.

The music stopped a scant quarter hour later, making it the shortest set of the evening—possibly the shortest at any ball this Season. But Griffin foiled her escape.

"We need fresh air," he said firmly, tugging her toward the terrace. "You look ready to faint."

"Hardly," she replied curtly.

He laughed.

Alarmed, Mary dug in her heels and jerked her arm free. "I have no desire for fresh air, sir. It is foggy and cold tonight. Either escort me to Lady Rockhurst, or I will go alone."

He narrowed his gaze, surprised by her resolution. But she saw no reason to flatter him. Nor would she give him time to argue. Perhaps those rumors she'd overheard last week had more substance than she'd thought. She had trusted Blake to warn her if they were true, but Blake might not know Griffin was plaguing her. Parliament kept him too busy for ballrooms.

When Griffin again reached for her arm, she backed out of reach, darted around four men arguing about last night's riot at the opera, then skirted a dozen dowagers speculating on Miss Derrick's next ploy. When a cluster of ladies screened her from view, she ducked behind a pillar near the refreshment room. There was some advantage to being shorter than half the ladies in town.

Breathing deeply, she waited for her pounding heart to settle, then peered through a palm. It was stupid to be afraid of a man when she was surrounded by people, but she wasn't sure she could scream, even if Griffin dragged her away. It would draw attention.

Eighteen months earlier she had stood in a similar crowd, shocked into paralysis at the hatred, disgust, and censure being hurled from all sides. Though she'd been innocent of all charges, her neighbors had turned on her, casting her out of local society—temporarily—but she would die if it happened again. So she effaced herself, avoiding attention, good or bad. It was safer that way.

Griffin was seeking her. She snapped her head out of sight, cringing farther into the shadows. Perhaps he meant to see her safely back to Catherine, but she doubted it. He wanted something from her, and it wasn't marriage. Unlike his namesake, there was nothing noble or protective about this griffin. Slyness lurked beneath his façade. His eyes watched her like a cat toying with a mouse.

So far he'd attacked only her obvious flaws, but eventually he would discover facts London didn't yet know— her years as governess to her niece, her solitary treks about the countryside to study birds, and the false accusations of eighteen months ago. Reviving that fiasco could throw the entire family into scandal. Laura would be furious.

But maybe she was doing him an injustice. Perhaps Laura had triggered this sudden urge to take her outside. Laura was a poor judge of character and might have laughingly suggested a romantic stroll in the moonlight as part of her retaliation—discovering Mary in a compromising position would remove her from town. It was an unworthy thought, but one Mary couldn't stifle. And if Laura was scheming with Griffin, she must tell Blake. Griffin was not right in the head. Encouraging him could only lead to trouble.

He was heading for the refreshment room, so she sidestepped to keep the pillar between them. But she forgot to check behind her. The pillar and palms screened a servants' door propped open by a cluttered table. Her skirt snagged a tray, knocking it to the floor. Breaking glass stopped conversation cold.

Mary cursed. This was her worst accident yet. Every eye was now turned toward this corner. If Griffin had heard the crash—and how could he not?—he would know where she was. Who but Mary Seabrook would cause such a disturbance? Only last week she had over-

balanced while making her curtsy to the royal Duke of
Clarence, bumping his arm so wine spattered all over
his coat.

She darted past the door, followed the palms along the
next wall, then paused to peer out. Griffin was rounding
her pillar. Praying he would think she'd escaped through
the servants' door, she sauntered past the terrace, then
slipped behind another row of palms near the card
room—a thick, double row that screened a shocking hole
in the wall.

She stared. A hole in Lady Debenham's elegant ballroom? It looked like someone had struck a heavy blow
with a club. But this explained tonight's plethora of
palms. They must be camouflage.

The hole reminded her of a truth she'd ignored until
now. London society was built on façades—hypocritical
matrons decrying vices they practiced in private, elegant
drawing rooms in houses falling into disrepair, ladies
fawning over people they savaged elsewhere, suitors dis-
guising poverty with fancy wardrobes. She could trust
nothing. But that very fact gave her hope. If she could
erect her own façade of competence, she might survive
the Season intact.

Leaning against the wall, she pulled a tiny sketchpad
from her reticule. Catherine wanted her to leave it home,
but Mary needed to escape nearly every evening, either
to recover her composure or relieve boredom. Its pages
captured scenes she wanted to remember and transformed disasters into humor.

Under her flying pencil a picture of Eden evolved—
lush plants, bubbling streams, mouthwatering fruits, and
a poisonous snake curled around the branch of an apple
tree. Its face bore a striking resemblance to Mr. Griffin.

Smiling, she turned to a new page and began drawing
a common chaffinch. It wasn't a particularly interesting
bird, but one had landed on her window ledge yesterday
and cocked its head as if amused, evoking a laugh.

Lord Grayson sauntered across Lady Debenham's ballroom, pausing frequently to exchange greetings with ac-

quaintances or flirt lightly with matrons. His path was far from straight, for he avoided a dozen disapproving dowagers and every unmarried lady—a habit honed over three years of society's censure. Avoiding innocents maintained an uneasy truce, keeping his name on guest lists. Sometimes he wondered why he bothered, for he had more than enough work to fill the hours, and he was always welcome in his clubs. But he couldn't stay away from the Season.

You're lonely.

He quickly suppressed the thought, though it was true that only in society could he meet ladies of quality. And despite everything, he still dreamed of one day marrying and setting up his nursery—not that he could imagine what that fantasy family might be like. He would cast himself into the Thames before reproducing his own. And no decent young lady could speak to him, let alone accept an offer.

He skirted a cluster of misses, then deflected an invitation from Lady Alston. She was renowned for entertaining gentlemen, but he had no interest in sampling her charms. Rumor had always exaggerated his raking. And even at his worst, he'd never bedded matrons. The last thing he wanted was to emulate his father.

Long practice hid his disgust at allowing Rothmoor into his mind. At least half of his reputation arose from the assumption *like father, like son.*

The Earl of Rothmoor had long pursued anything in skirts, ignoring rank, wedded state, or even desire on the unfortunate female's part. The man had three loves— horses, hounds, and whores. And in his view, if it was female, it was a whore. Ladies gave him a wide berth, and villagers hid their daughters when Rothmoor approached.

Gray felt Lady Cunningham's animosity as he passed her. She was one of his more vocal detractors, not that he could blame her. She'd whelped eight children, six of them girls. If his calculations were correct, she would be firing off daughter number three this Season. In her eyes, he should have been ostracized three years ago so he couldn't endanger her offspring.

The shield protecting his heart quivered, but he quickly steadied it. No one had promised that life would be fair. Those who followed the rules suffered as much as those who didn't. Yet honor demanded he at least try, so he did whatever was necessary, then hoped for the best. All in all, he managed a tolerable existence. If donning his public façade seemed difficult tonight, he could blame only himself. Attending a ball after six hours of skidding into muddy ditches and bouncing across ruts was one of his poorer ideas. But he'd wanted the latest news. Where else to get it but in Lady Debenham's ballroom? She was the second most formidable gossip in London.

"Gray!" A grin split Nicholas Barrington's face as he shook hands. They had been close friends since school. "When did you return to town?"

"An hour ago." He shuddered. "Horrible journey. All this rain." His eyes took in Nick's appearance, from the Byronesque curls, through the intricate cravat and wine-colored coat, to the highly polished dancing shoes. "New knot?"

Nick laughed. "New valet. I've not yet broken him in. He has delusions of dandyism, I fear."

"Not a bad idea. The affectation would mask your intellect to a nicety." Gray was one of the few who knew that Nick supported himself entirely on wagers based on his understanding of human nature.

"I would rather be thought intellectual than court comparisons to peacocks."

Gray laughed. "So who's in town this year?"

"Atwater is back, though it's barely six months since his wife died. He seems smitten with Miss Warren—Forley's sister."

"Forley?"

"This is his first Season in London, but you might recall his father. Died about six years ago."

"Ah. Fast parties. Ran with Cavendish, as I recall. Dissipated his fortune trying to keep up."

"That's the one." Nick scanned the room. "The latest Cunningham chit will do well—looks and a keen sense of humor. Rockhurst is back and supporting the reformists in Parliament. He's sponsoring his wife's two sisters. The elder Miss Seabrook is a diamond, though too aware of it. She uses the younger as a foil, which I deplore."

"Perhaps it would have been kinder to leave the younger at home another year."

"Perhaps, but Miss Mary is already twenty—the family was destitute until Rockhurst stepped in. Once she conquers her nervousness, she should do well." A shrug dismissed the Seabrooks. "The other diamonds are Miss Norton and Miss Harfield. As for the lesser lights, Miss Huntsley is beyond hope. I expect she will return home within the month."

"Why?"

"Clumsy, gauche, not overly bright, and looks that would make a bulldog seem handsome. Her dowry is too small to compensate. That's her talking to Lady Stafford."

Gray glanced across the room. Horse-faced and dressed in a gown so bedecked with ribbons and bows that she could pass as a display in a draper's shop. He would have to avoid Miss Huntsley.

Socially inept females were his bane, though he could blame only himself. As a stripling, he had sympathized with society's misfits. So he'd tried to set them at ease, drawing out the shy, relaxing the nervous, introducing originals to gentlemen who shared their interests.

No more. He'd been badly burned for his efforts and now stayed far away from eligible misses. Another scandal would ruin him. Only his fortune and expectations had kept him in London ballrooms after the last one.

"What are the latest *on-dits?*" he asked, his eyes scanning the crowd for potential trouble. Lady Alston playfully rapped a fan on Wigby's arm—arranging an assignation? Lady Cunningham had pulled her daughter behind a pillar, probably to warn her away from Lord Grayson. Griffin burst from the refreshment room with a face like thunder.

Nick smiled. "Shelford made a cake of himself last week. Fell off his horse in Hyde Park."

"Fell?" Shelford was a noted Corinthian and outstanding horseman who could prose for hours about horses, riding, and carriage construction. Gray found his lectures as boring as Rothmoor's discourses on hunting and shooting.

"At least fifty people saw him. He was so smitten by a young lady's beauty that he wasn't ready when his horse shied."

Gray shook his head.

Nick continued. "Renford and Garwood are suddenly at odds, though no one knows why. I suspect the complaint is Garwood's."

"Not surprising. The man's a prime prig."

"True. And in another dispute, Atwater may regret returning while in mourning. Blackthorn is trying to provoke a challenge."

"Atwater had best look out, then. Blackthorn has already killed several men."

"He won't be the next. I've never seen him in a temper, no matter what the provocation. The man is a saint—and just as annoying as one." Nick shrugged.

Gray chuckled. Nick always suspected those who were too perfect. "Anyone I should look out for besides Miss Huntsley?" Some girls were drawn to rakes. It made no sense, since such associations could ruin them. But every rake knew they existed.

"Miss Derrick. Her mother is dead, so her father hired Miss Pettigrew as chaperon."

"Damnation. The woman is too enamored of cards to watch anyone." He ought to know. One of her previous charges had made his life hell. "Does Miss Derrick court danger, or is she already unchaste?"

"Danger, certainly, but I doubt she is experienced. Her ultimate goal is marriage, and after a month in town, she's growing desperate. Her father can't afford a second Season. Doubtless she will ruin herself before long, but in the meantime, she is forward enough to be a serious problem."

"I won't be the one who ruins her. Maybe we should direct her to Devereaux or Lord Roger, and be done with her. Neither cares a whit for society or for convention."

"It wouldn't work. She's drawn to rakes, but demands wealth and position, too. Devereaux would never offer marriage, and Lord Roger lacks social standing. She cut my acquaintance when she discovered I have no fortune and am only remotely connected to a title. She's been after Wroxleigh for the past week. He set her down quite firmly yesterday, then cut her dead in the park this morning, so she will rejoice over your arrival. You also meet her standards."

"Heir to an earl who despises me. An exaggerated reputation that is often out-and-out false."

"But you are rich."

"From engaging in trade." He shrugged.

"I doubt she would care, and Rothmoor can't cut you out of the title. So watch out."

"Is she here tonight?" Gray frowned. Girls who craved danger were as bad as the greedy ones who had destroyed his credit. He would gladly throttle the lot of them.

"She's talking to Lady Beatrice. The white gown with rosebuds on the bodice. She always dresses in white. It makes her look angelic if you ignore her eyes. They are alive with scheming."

Nick would know. He could see beneath the surface better than anyone.

Gray casually glanced toward the corner. Honey blonde hair, light eyes, heart-shaped face. With a decent portion, she would have no trouble making a good match, so why did she risk a reputation that must already be tarnished? Only two gentlemen were paying her heed, and neither had marriage on his mind.

He shuddered when she turned and met his gaze. She must already know who he was, for her eyes lit like lanterns, and she coquettishly waved her fan.

"Is Justin here tonight?" he asked, turning back to

Nick. Lord Justin Landess was the other member of their trio.

"In the card room. Heatherford is trying to convince him to replace his team."

"I'd better rescue him, then. Once Heatherford starts talking horses, he never stops."

Nick nodded. "I'll see you at White's later. I've bespoken this next set."

Gray watched Nick move off, then headed for the card room. But he'd not gone three steps before spotting Miss Derrick headed his way. Damnation! She'd already crossed half the room.

He joined a group of gentlemen discussing the latest news from Spain, then ducked behind a screen of palms when they headed for the door. Since two of them wore jackets the same blue as his, Miss Derrick might believe he'd left with them. But his real destination lay in another direction.

He hugged the wall, careful not to brush the branches as he followed the palms toward the card room. He'd traversed half the distance before he realized he was not alone. A young lady was also hiding.

Curses exploded through his head. He was neatly trapped. Retracing his steps would draw Miss Derrick's attention, yet he must squeeze past this new threat to reach the card room.

But was she a threat?

She almost looked like a companion or governess, though she could not yet be twenty. Brown hair coiled untidily atop her head—or perhaps it was falling out of an attempt at curls. A plain white gown encased her slim body, a single ribbon beneath the bodice its only embellishment. The high neckline covered a lack of jewelry. One hand clutched a pad of paper.

A journalist?

He shook off that notion as she added lines to a picture, the tip of her tongue protruding past her teeth. She couldn't be sketching the ballroom, for she never looked at it. She might have been alone in a field for all the attention she paid her surroundings. Odd. Very odd.

Curiosity is dangerous, warned his conscience.

Ignoring it, he peeked over her shoulder, then inhaled in surprise. She was a talented artist and a student of natural history. Who else could draw so well from memory? A chaffinch perched in a gnarled apple tree, head cocked perkily to one side. A few lines evoked rough bark, soft feathers, and lustrous fruit. But he could see why she was frowning. The bird's beak was too thick, pushing it slightly off balance.

"Try this," he murmured, grabbing the pad.

"Oh!" She whirled, one hand to her breast. "I d-didn't know anyone was here."

"Not so loud." He rubbed out the beak. Brisk strokes reshaped the appendage, bringing the bird to life. "That's better. Are you from the west country?"

She nodded. "How did you know?"

"That is the only place you find apples that shape. Those in the east are rounder. You are an accomplished sketch artist."

"I—" She blushed. "I was hoping to see some different birds in town, but we have so little time to look about."

"If you walk in the park in the mornings, you will see hoopoes and bee eaters. And a magnificent purple heron visits the Serpentine at dawn most days."

"I heard a pair of hobbies was spotted near Kensington Palace recently."

"Interesting. I've not seen them here before." He smiled, leaning negligently against the wall. "Richmond is better suited for bird watching. Forest. Heath. River. Plenty of space and food."

"Perhaps Laura will consider an excursion to Richmond, then," she murmured, half to herself.

"You would enjoy it." Gray knew he should leave before someone spotted him—clothes notwithstanding, this girl was clearly quality, and unmarried quality at that. But he couldn't do it. Aside from the certainty that Miss Derrick still lurked, he was enjoying her company. Obviously she didn't recognize him. She was not flirting or swooning or regarding him as Satan. It had been too long since he had talked with a young lady—or relaxed while talking to anyone. His reputation overshadowed every contact.

He idly turned pages. A sparrow hawk, a hedgehog, a caricature . . .

"Egad, that is Wigby to the life. We were schoolmates." He chuckled. She had sketched him as a stork. Very appropriate, as the dandy was tall and very lean, with thin legs and a long pointed nose. No amount of padding could cover his defects. The next page depicted Lord Edward Broadburn as a charming pouter pigeon, so overburdened by a thrust-out chest that he teetered on his feet.

"Sir— My l-lord—" She stammered to a halt.

He knew his manners were outrageous—she was an innocent, for God's sake—but something about her drew him. Her presence behind the palms told him she was shy, though her sketches displayed a wicked sense of humor. Four years ago he would have set her at ease. And maybe he still could.

"My apologies," he said softly. "But I must wonder why so talented a lady is hiding in the shadows. London is not filled with ogres."

"Of course not. But it takes only one."

"An ogre? Are you sure? Did someone spurn your smiles? Surely you need not fear rejection." He turned the page and chuckled again. Griffin hung from a tree, his forked tongue hissing. "You've a delightful eye for character, my dear. He is pure poison, though too few see it. But except for ungentlemanly insults, you should be safe enough. He prefers country innocents of fourteen or so."

"I had heard rumors, though no one will confirm them to young ladies. Yet he clearly seeks me out. Though I try to avoid him, he is forever popping up."

"Like a weed?"

She laughed. "Exactly. Bindweed, most likely. One moment the room is quite congenial, the next it contains Mr. Griffin. One cannot root him out."

"So circumvent him. You might befriend Mr. Hempbury. Not only is he fascinated by birds and other natural wonders, but Griffin cannot tolerate the fellow."

"Th-thank you," she stammered.

When she was nervous she seemed quite young, and very unspoiled. Perhaps she had reason to fear the snake after all.

It might be instructive to check on Griffin's current activities. The man inhabited society's fringes. As long as he behaved, he was welcome at large *ton* gatherings, but even a mild scandal would banish him. Rumors suggested that he frequented a certain house of punishment, though not as a penitent. He was said to have a strong arm with a whip.

Gray returned her pad. "*Au revoir*, my dear artist. It has been a most delightful meeting. I needed a chuckle after a frustrating day. But be careful whom you parody. There are those who lose all humor when they are the subject."

Stepping past her, he grinned at the damaged wall her skirts had hidden. That explained this convenient excess of palms.

The set was over, with the usual confusion as gentlemen returned partners to their chaperons, then sought new ones. Thus it was easy to slip unnoticed into the card room.

But he felt an unexpected tug of regret. She had talent, intelligence, and eyes that saw beneath the surface. Quite different from the usual society miss. Were she a man, they might have become friends.

Chapter Two

Mary shrank against the wall as the gentleman squeezed past. The light brush of his body made her heart pound and dampened her palms—a ridiculous reaction. She didn't even know his name.

But he was a handsome devil, with a long, rugged face, dark hair, and quicksilver eyes—beautiful eyes fringed with long black lashes. The rest was equally intriguing. His lean body topped her by a head, muscular enough to fill his clothes without padding. And his taste was impeccable—elegant cravat that did not impede his movement, blue jacket, white waistcoat embroidered in silver, and dove gray pantaloons clinging to well-formed thighs. Simple elegance that made the dandies crowding the ballroom seem overdressed. He must turn heads wherever he went.

So why had she never noticed him before?

Not that it mattered. He would forget a plain miss like her the moment he was out of sight—especially if he spotted Laura.

But he did *notice you*, insisted the dreamer who lived in her head.

"Only because I was drawing," she murmured. And hiding.

She blushed. Catherine would be appalled that she had been caught. And if she discovered the caricatures, she would likely confiscate the lot. Even the gentleman thought them dangerous, though he'd enjoyed them. But his warning echoed Catherine's. And seeking solitude left her vulnerable. What if it had been Mr. Griffin who'd found her?

Shivering, she cast about for a distraction and found it in her own behavior. Amazingly, she had spoken naturally, with hardly a stammer. No embarrassing truths or brainless observations, either. Somehow, she had felt as comfortable with him as with her family.

The novelty reawakened dreams she had buried years earlier, dreams of marriage and children. Helping raise her niece had made those longings stronger, and observing the connection between Blake and Catherine reinforced the hope that she, too, could find love.

She pulled her mind back to the ballroom, cursing. Nurturing that fantasy served no purpose. Even marriage was unlikely. No man wanted her. If anyone actually did offer, it would be for the dowry she would bring or because a widower sought help with his children.

She shifted a palm branch so she could peer out. Griffin strode toward the stairs, the crowd drawing back to ease his way, as if they, too, were anxious to see the last of him. But he disappointed them, stopping to chat with Lord Hervey. Was he still seeking her?

Laura was dancing. Catherine and Lady Potherby headed for the refreshment room. Her stranger was nowhere in sight.

Her stranger? She castigated her dreamer for weaving absurd tales of love and white knights and happily ever after around a man she didn't know. Instead of teasing herself, she should concentrate on surviving this Season without shaming her family.

Voices rose as the music swelled, the loudest unmistakable. Lady Washburn had a voice like a buzzard, and her perfume could overpower a cesspit. She was avidly recounting her terror at being caught in last night's opera riot. Nearby, Lord Hartford lisped a humorous account of Blackthorn's latest insult to Atwater.

Ignoring them, Mary opened her pad to a blank page, then cringed when the palms shook.

"Stay away from Wroxleigh," hissed Lady Smythe-Gower to her daughter Hermione. Mary held her breath, but neither noticed her.

"We were only talking," protested Hermione.

"That doesn't matter. He is a rake—a charming one, to be sure, but he has no interest in marriage. Do you want Sir Leonard to think you fast? He will not offer for anyone he considers improper."

"If rakes are so awful, why are they allowed in respectable ballrooms?" Hermione's chin was set in a stubborn line.

"Many aren't. You would never find Blackthorn or Devereaux here. But most hostesses welcome amusing gentlemen, even if they are rakes. And Wroxleigh isn't the only one you must avoid. Grayson has already ruined several innocents. Sanders is growing bolder. And stay well away from Millhouse."

"But Mother—"

"Do you wish to find a husband?"

Hermione sighed.

"Once you are wed, you can befriend anyone you choose, but for now, avoid all rakes."

Mary gave silent thanks when Hermione capitulated and rejoined the other guests. They had not seen her.

Griffin still lurked.

She contemplated the sketchbook. How could she depict the stranger? Even on this brief acquaintance, he seemed more complex than the average gentleman. Almost as bad as Laura. Mary had done a series of sketches showing Laura as a haughty cat, a preening peacock, a stubborn mule, and a silly goose. Laura would undoubtedly accuse her of jealousy—or worse—if she ever saw them, for she would never admit that each depicted a facet of her character. Yet they were not comprehensive, even taken together. They didn't show Laura's generosity and need to help those in trouble, not did they depict how she could change from loving sister to furious judge in an instant.

Turning pages, Mary stared at the sketch of Lord Wigby. Her stranger had chuckled wickedly when he'd seen it. She still glowed from his approval, for her drawings had never seemed good enough to show to others— not that she would have done so anyway. People already laughed at her. She could hardly risk further censure.

Yet he had enjoyed them. And more. He had not only recognized her drawing of the chaffinch, he had improved it with a few brisk strokes. Was he an artist?

She choked down a laugh. Of course he wasn't an artist. Lady Debenham would never invite such a person to her ball. He probably dabbled with pen and brush to fill time, just as she did. Many gentlemen could produce decent watercolors. It was more surprising that he knew about natural history.

Returning to the blank page, she concentrated on his face—the intriguing eyes that turned silver when he smiled, the lock of hair tumbling over his brow, the hollows under prominent cheekbones, the grace that reminded her of a cat. Power and a hint of wildness lurked under that elegant façade. An intriguing combination. Did he ever feel an urge to do something outrageous?

She penciled a sleek panther, then frowned. While it radiated strength and grace, it also implied a haughtiness he'd lacked. Did he truly share her interests? It was a tempting thought, for it hinted that he might become a friend.

Shaking away such a ridiculous notion, she turned the page. Men did not form friendships with ladies. Especially handsome men gifted with talent and intelligence.

Who was he?

The question teased her harder this time. In three weeks of perpetual entertainment, she had met hundreds of people. She would have sworn only an hour ago that she had seen everyone of note at least once. Even the Regent had attended the Hartleigh ball last week. But she'd not seen this man. Who was he?

Someone on the fringes of society perhaps, like Griffin? A lord would have been shocked to find her hiding behind the palms. Of course, he'd been hiding, too—

Her eyes widened. Maybe that was why she'd felt comfortable with him, though the idea that he was hiding seemed ridiculous. But why else had he been back here? Did he also have something to fear?

Catherine begged every day that she not slip away. Laura was usually more emphatic. "Such cowardice will ruin you," she'd snapped in the carriage tonight. "Society will cut you, and me with you. I know they will. They will wonder if I share your disregard for convention. You must abandon these silly fears and talk to people. Flirt. Dance. Ignore your unladylike education and plain face. Prove to the world that Seabrooks know how to behave." There had been much more, including a vow to arrange a marriage for Mary once she settled her own future.

But this was no time to think of marriage. Mary knew what Catherine refused to admit. Staying out of Laura's way would keep people from wondering how the Seabrooks had produced such dissimilar daughters. Raising such questions could lead only to trouble that would impede Laura's chances.

Two sets later, Mr. Griffin finally left, so Mary rejoined Catherine. Laura was enslaving the very eligible Lord Seaton when the stranger returned from the card room. Lady Horseley snorted loud enough to be heard above the buzz of conversation, then administered the cut direct. Three others followed suit.

"Who is that?" Mary murmured to Catherine, nodding in his direction. "The man Lady Horseley just cut." The woman was one of the highest sticklers in London. Was he an artist after all?

Catherine bit off an oath. "I thought he left an hour ago. Lady Debenham swore he came only to speak with Mr. Barrington. Stay away from him, Mary. Any contact could ruin you."

"Why?" she asked, grimacing. Another faux pas, though how she could have avoided him she didn't know.

"If you had been here when he arrived, I wouldn't have to repeat the tale," Catherine chided. "Lord Grayson is the most dangerous rake in society. Worse even than Devereaux, for he preys on innocents and has already ruined several. Surely you can't find him attractive."

"Of course not," she lied. "But I thought I had met everyone."

Catherine relaxed. "Be careful. Not everyone in society is acceptable. Grayson is very wealthy and is heir to the Earl of Rothmoor. Almack's won't admit him, and he knows better than to enter drawing rooms, but he is welcome elsewhere. Few can afford to shun a future earl."

"Does he really ruin innocents?" The statement did not fit her impressions.

"Yes. I don't know all the details—and this is hardly the place to discuss them—but four years ago he jilted his fiancée. He might have recovered if he hadn't seduced a baron's daughter the following Season, leaving her with child. After she took her life, he had the gall to deny responsibility. Lady Horseley is determined to drive him from town."

"Why?"

"The man is too dangerous." Her voice cracked with emotion. "He spent a year on the Continent after the last scandal. Some think him a French spy."

"A spy?" demanded Laura, joining them. Her eyes shone with excitement. "Who?"

Mary cringed. Laura's greatest weakness was a quest for adventure that had led to trouble more than once. She had rejected a dozen suitors in Devonshire because they disliked travel. The family thought she'd settled down after the scandals of eighteen months ago, but the expression in her eyes made Mary wince. And it added a new perspective to last night's complaints.

"You'd think the cream of society would contain more than bores and idiots," Laura had snapped, slamming the door behind her. "But London gentlemen are no better than the farmers at home."

"Sir Bertram seems quite nice," Mary had said calmly. "And he dotes on you."

"He's impossible. His idea of excitement is perfecting a new knot for his cravat." She'd stalked to the fireplace to kick an andiron.

"So you don't like dandies." It hadn't surprised her. Laura wanted a beau who worshiped *her* beauty, not his own. "What about Mr. Carlson? He is seeking a wife."

"He plays faro until dawn most nights and will undoubtedly lose his estate at the table before much longer. That is not the sort of excitement I can condone."

Mary had nodded, grateful at this exhibition of sense.

Gamesters made poor mates. "Lord Biddlethwaite seeks excitement."

"But he defines it as emulating Devereaux. His list of conquests grows longer every day. Besides, can you imagine going through life with a name like Biddlethwaite? I would become a laughingstock."

"Lord Kemp? He will one day be an earl, and you can't deny he dotes on you."

"Perhaps, but he is boring. I've seen him near hysterics because his tea was weak or his coat wrinkled." Laura ripped the pins from her hair in frustration. "Is there no one who seeks more than gossip and cards? Why do men no longer travel?"

"The war," explained Mary succinctly. She had refrained from adding that men drawn to adventure were likely out seeking it rather than dancing and gossiping in London. And she had yet to meet any man who believed ladies could endure hardship. Even Blake embraced that view, and he was the most tolerant man she knew.

Now she shook her head at the gleam in Laura's eyes. All it had taken was the word *spy*. Laura had learned nothing from past mistakes.

Catherine must have also spotted that gleam. "Stay away from Grayson," she murmured, gesturing to Laura's court. "Making his acquaintance will drive away your suitors and ban you from respectable drawing rooms."

"I wouldn't dream of it," said Laura demurely. "But which one is he? I must know whom to avoid."

Catherine pointed him out, but Mary wasn't fooled. Laura's eyes gleamed brighter than ever, for Grayson dominated the room. Mary could almost hear her plotting. They would have their hands full if they hoped to keep Laura from making a cake of herself—again.

But perhaps all would be well. Catherine's report might be exaggerated. No one knew better than the Seabrooks how gossip twisted facts. And her own impressions did not fit an unscrupulous cad. The man she had met was honorable. No matter how she twisted his words, he could only have been setting her at ease.

So what had really happened three years ago?

* * *

Gray left before supper. The card room had offered little sport. He dared not dance even with his married acquaintances, especially after Lady Horseley cut him dead. Returning to the ballroom had been a stupid mistake arising from too much cold rain atop too little sleep. The cut resurrected gossip made more lurid by time—or by Lady Horseley. Though three years had passed, she still blamed him for Miss Turner's death, keeping the scandal alive.

Tonight's cuts had hurt just as badly as the first one and focused every eye on him. Unfortunately, nothing discouraged Miss Derrick. She seemed more interested than before. And she wasn't the only one. Miss Huntsley had smiled in a disturbingly predatory way, as had a blonde holding court near his artist. He had no idea why some girls loved rogues, but having intrigued three of them, he would have to be careful. So he had collected his cloak and left.

A shiver tingled his spine as he climbed into his carriage, almost as if eyes were digging holes in his back. Yet a glance over his shoulder revealed only servants. Lady Horseley was nowhere in sight. Nor were his other detractors.

Sinking into the squabs, he closed his eyes. It was harder to slip back into his London routine this year— as he had proved by talking to that artist. He should not have succumbed to temptation. If anyone had seen them, her reputation would now be tarnished. Yet he couldn't get her out of his head.

Incongruities teased him as the wheels rattled over cobbled streets. She wasn't a diamond, but neither was she an antidote. Average, he decided, with the potential to look better. Five-foot-three, but sturdy enough not to seem fragile. A hint of gold in her hair, though it was buried beneath those failed curls. Wit and intelligence that added vibrancy to her face when she forgot to be nervous. Quick, clever fingers that turned that wit into something substantial. And her view of society was intriguing.

Again he chuckled over her sketch of Griffin. The man was rotten to the core, though his earnest façade and treacly compliments fooled many. While in the card room, Gray had casually steered the conversation to Griffin. New rumors were circulating that hinted at questionable honor. No one could prove Griffin a cheat, but few would risk a game with him. And fathers steered their daughters elsewhere.

Gray pressed his lips together. Without evidence against Griffin, he could do little to keep his artist safe. So he would hire a runner to watch Griffin for a few days. It was the least he could do.

He did not question why he felt so protective. Or even why he did not turn the matter over to her father.

His carriage rocked to a halt in front of White's. As Gray emerged, malevolent eyes again sliced his shoulder blades, accompanied by hatred thicker than a London fog. It seemed to originate from the shadow between two buildings.

He glanced back. No one was in sight, but he couldn't shake the certainty that someone wanted him dead.

Imagination. He must be more tired than he'd thought. The encounter with Lady Horseley had unsettled him. But cards would improve his mood.

The watcher waited until Grayson disappeared into White's. Hatred choked him, twitching hands that wanted to squeeze the life from the blackguard. But that would be too easy. First Grayson must suffer as badly as his victims. A quick death would not satisfy vengeance.

Pulling a vial from his waistcoat pocket, he followed his quarry into the club.

Chapter Three

The next morning, Mary sat in the corner of Lady Beatrice's drawing room, doing her best to fade into the wall.

Lady Beatrice was London's most knowing gossip, a title she had held for forty years and one which gave her great power. It was said that she had spies on nearly every staff in Mayfair, which explained why she was the first to know everything. Thus her drawing room was the best place to hear the day's news.

Sitting in the corner allowed Mary to listen without joining the conversation. And it kept Laura from voicing her daily complaint in public. Today's concerned Mary's gowns. Mary hated wasting money on embroidery, lace, and other trims. Until Laura was wed, no one would notice her anyway, and it was more rewarding to use the funds Blake had provided for books and drawing supplies. Besides, donning fashionable gowns required a maid, but she shared Frannie with Laura.

As the elder, Laura had first claim on Frannie's services. Mary was too used to the situation to complain. Nor did she blame Frannie for devoting most of her time to polishing the Season's diamond. But since Mary often had to dress herself, it made more sense to use a special corset that laced up the front and to buy simple gowns featuring drawstring bodices. Unfashionable, but practical.

Blake would have provided a maid had she asked, but she disliked putting him to the expense when she couldn't make a match anyway. Catherine hadn't thought of it. Laura and Mary had always shared Frannie's services, and Catherine was too new to London to realize how much work was involved in dressing a society lady.

But Mary was beginning to wonder if she should raise the issue. Her favorite walking dress remained smudged from staggering against a carriage in Bond Street three days earlier. Frannie had not yet found time to clean it. And though only Frannie had accompanied her that day, Laura knew every detail of the incident, confirming that Frannie shared everything with her favorite mistress. It was another reason Mary kept her sketchpads well hidden.

But complaining would make her seem petulant. Blake had already given her so much, despite having no obligation to her. How could she ask for more?

She pulled her mind back to Lady Beatrice's drawing room. It was furnished in the French style that had been popular thirty years earlier, before revolution and war had pushed it out of fashion. It was also just a wee bit shabby, though no one would dare criticize. Lady Beatrice's power arose from information rather than from wealth.

To Mary's right a new scandal was brewing, this one concerning Miss Norton, another of the Season's diamonds.

"Her dancing master!" Miss Ingleside laughed. "No imagination at all. I swear half of society's beauties have formed attachments for their dancing masters."

"Not I," insisted Laura.

"Nor I," added Miss Cummings. "Mine was sixty if he was a day."

"I heard Miss Norton eloped with him," said Lady Catherine Crosby.

"No!"

"So Lady Wilkins swore."

"They weren't caught until morning," added one of the Caddis twins. Mary could never tell them apart.

"I don't believe it." Miss Ingleside glared. "Miss Norton is all that is correct. She might flirt, but she would never elope. And her father would have kept her home if it were true."

"Then maybe he abducted her," suggested Laura.

"You can't mean it!" The other twin paled.

"Of course not. I'm sure she went quite willingly. Lady Wilkins said—or maybe it was Miss Ormsby; I don't quite recall. Anyway, I heard she was in dishabille when her father caught up with them—hair down, clothing rumpled. And so was he."

"How dare she play the innocent after that?" demanded Lady Catherine.

"It's false, I tell you," repeated Miss Ingleside. But no one listened. Voice after voice condemned the Nortons, fury rising with each new detail.

Mary remained silent, though she was amazed at how silly Miss Norton seemed. Eloping with a dancing master! At least Laura had never put the family through *that* scandal.

To her left, the topic had moved to Lord Grayson.

"He's a bad one," swore Lady Horseley. "But what can one expect? The Dubonne family has always been unpredictable."

"But he's the worst." Mrs. Martin gripped her cup so tightly, it was in danger of cracking. "Rothmoor threw him out years ago and won't let him return."

"You exaggerate. He only threw Grayson out of the local hunt," countered Lady Sefton. "Grayson insisted on overriding the hounds." Gasps greeted this infamy. "Now he refuses to set foot in Yorkshire until he is reinstated."

"Nay," snapped Mrs. Martin. "I had the tale direct from Lord Granger, whose land runs with Rothmoor's. The rift had naught to do with hunting. Rothmoor cannot condone Grayson's reckless raking."

"Hah!" snorted Lady Horseley. "He's no saint himself. The only thing Rothmoor ever approved about the boy was his expertise in bed."

"Mildred!" Lady Cunningham gestured toward the innocents across the room.

"Facts are facts."

"Whatever his reasons, Rothmoor cut him off without a shilling, proving Grayson's dishonor. A man don't throw out his heir without reason," said Lady Marchgate, accepting another biscuit from a footman. "I'd hoped he would stay in Sussex this year or go off on another of his adventures. How can I protect Eleanor from his ruinous attentions? The man has a positive genius for enticing girls to clandestine meetings."

"Lady Eleanor would never listen to him," said Lady Wharburton soothingly. "She is all that is proper. You are fortunate in your daughter. Miss Derrick is already showing a dangerous interest in the fellow. I thought she'd come to her senses when Wroxleigh cut her dead. For all he's a rake, at least he is honorable. But now that she's after Grayson, I must withdraw the invitation to my masquerade. I cannot abide impropriety."

Mary flinched. Being stricken from Lady Wharburton's guest list was almost as bad as losing vouchers to Almack's. Her annual masquerade was the highlight of any Season, but it was open only to those of the highest *ton*, meaning those who adhered to Lady Wharburton's very strict standards. Losing that invitation was little better than being put in stocks.

"I have no patience with Miss Derrick's behavior," said Lady Horseley. "But the blame lies with her father. What was the man thinking to consign her to Miss Pettigrew? I wouldn't hire the woman to shepherd a dog through the Season, let alone an innocent. She lets her charges run wild. Miss Derrick will be ruined in a month."

"Miss Derrick won't be the first she's lost," confirmed Mrs. Martin. "Wasn't she chaperoning the Foster girl last year when Jacobs eloped with her?"

"And the Falmouth chit two years ago?"

"And Miss Turner the year before that," confirmed Lady Beatrice. "Why don't people check references anymore?"

Several voices recalled Miss Turner's suicide after Grayson abandoned her, predicting a similar disaster for Miss Derrick.

"Grayson won't be the one to ruin her," protested Lady Westlake. "He was never as bad as rumor claimed."

"You always were blind," said Lady Marchgate. "Just wait until your own daughter faces society."

"I am not blind." Lady Westlake's face darkened. "It is easy to condemn, and rumor does so quite harshly. But where is the evidence? Miss Irwin's father swears that betrothal existed solely in her head. If Grayson never offered, how could he have jilted her? She was little better than Miss Derrick, flirting outrageously, then lashing out when he ignored her."

"It is true that Miss Irwin was scandalously forward," agreed Lady Wharburton. "But I will never believe that the affair existed solely in her head. Where there is smoke, one always finds fire."

"Do you claim the most honorable Mr. Irwin lied?" asked Lady Westlake, frowning.

"Irwin's father may be a baron, but there is nothing honorable about him or his daughter," snapped Lady Marchgate.

"Very true," agreed Lady Wharburton. "He gloated quite vulgarly when Grayson began courting the girl. And everyone knew he had plans for Grayson's fortune. But he only clamed his daughter had fabricated a betrothal because Grayson paid him to do so. Irwin would do anything for money."

"Still does," added Lady Marchgate. "He fleeced young Gower-Jones last month, using an altered deck of cards. If he returns to town, the clubs will deny him entrance."

"Which shows where Miss Irwin learned to lie and cheat," put in Lady Westlake.

"It suits you ill to defend the man," warned Lady Marchgate. "And whatever the truth about the Irwins, you cannot ignore the Turner affair."

Lady Westlake remained silent.

"He drove her to her grave," intoned Lady Wharburton. "And to this day, he denies remorse."

Lady Marchgate nodded. "Abominable. To seduce and abandon a lady of quality—" She snapped her mouth shut in disdain.

"There has to be more to the story," insisted Lady

Westlake. "Think about his history. He was the kindest gentleman in society, always ready to partner an overlooked miss or introduce girls to those who shared their interests. He arranged at least a dozen matches over the years. And he is devoted to his estate. I cannot believe he would deliberately harm anyone."

"He is in trade." Lady Horseley's voice shook.

"What else was he to do when Rothmoor cut him off?"

"We all know that he introduced you to Lord Westlake," said Lady Wharburton. "But do not let gratitude blind you to his faults."

"I don't. But I knew him well eight years ago. He was a good friend to society's misfits, drawing out the shy and relaxing the nervous. He danced with us regularly, playing mentor and alleviating embarrassment until he could pair us with the perfect suitor."

"I doubt his purpose was selfless," snapped Lady Marchgate. "He probably made sport of you in his clubs."

"If so, not one man has ever mentioned it, though most gossip as freely as ladies. I do not believe he seduced anyone. It is not in his nature."

"Blind as a bat," muttered Lady Horseley. "His magnanimous gestures mask his spying. Too much French blood in the Dubonnes. Not only was his mother French, but his grandmother and others before her."

"Not one of them would have favored the current regime." Lady Westlake gestured toward the Channel. "Every French Dubonne perished on the guillotine. Only the English branch survived."

Mary let them argue it out. Her own observations supported Lady Westlake. Lord Grayson had recognized her shyness, for what else would have driven her into the palms? He had tried to set her at ease, praising her sketches and suggesting others who shared her interests. He had made no advances, adhering strictly to propriety. And he had confirmed her opinion of Mr. Griffin.

She could believe him a rake, for he exuded a blatant masculinity that must attract women. But most men his age enjoyed the courtesan class. Even her brother William visited a willing widow on occasion, though he'd so often denounced those who succumbed to lust that he tried to hide that fact.

But that was her dreamer speaking, she acknowledged as the argument continued. Her dreamer liked Grayson and pounced on any evidence in his favor. Her dreamer wanted Lady Westlake to be right, for it believed Grayson was honorable. But could she trust it? London was different from the quiet countryside she knew. Her judgment might not work here.

On the other hand, people were much alike wherever they lived, especially when it came to gossip. Most of them twisted events to fit their preconceptions. Gossips preferred simplicity. A man was a rake or a sportsman or a prime catch. Ladies were proper, silly, or wanton. There was no room for complexity.

But Grayson was complex. In less than a day, she'd heard him described as a rake, a scoundrel, a benefactor, a traitor, and a man with a golden touch. Only better acquaintance would reveal how much of that was true.

Of course, she could never judge for herself. Labels might be simplistic, but society adored them. And no innocent could befriend a scoundrel without ruining herself.

"Mary!" Laura's voice sliced through her abstraction. "Answer Miss Ingleside."

"What?" Mary jumped, rattling her cup and dropping a biscuit on the carpet.

"I asked if you were attending the Wharburton masquerade next week," said Miss Ingleside.

"I b-believe so," she stammered, embarrassed to be caught dreaming. A blush crept up her cheeks. The image of Grayson was so clear in her mind that she feared others could see it.

"I have the most delicious costume," said Lady Catherine. "Diana, the huntress. It is short enough to expose my ankles halfway to the knee." Everyone gasped. "The headdress is made of leaves sprinkled with diamonte to

glitter like starlight in the ballroom. How about you?"
She stared at Mary.

"A T-tu . . . A lady." Mortified, she stared at her
hands.

"A Tudor lady-in-waiting," said Laura, with a laugh.
"It covers her clear to the neck. Freckles, you know.
They blanket her shoulders like a rash."

"Haven't you heard of cucumber wash?" demanded
Miss Cummings.

"I prefer oil of talc," said Miss Ingleside.

"Mustard ointment," announced Lady Catherine. "It
is the only remedy that never fails."

Mary wanted to sink through the floor.

Rescue arrived in the form of Lady Wilkins, who was
so excited that she burst into speech before greeting
Lady Beatrice. "The most shocking news!" Her eyes
sparkled with pleasure. "Lord Grayson was accosted by
footpads and beaten to within an inch of his life!"

Beaten? Mary barely stopped her hand from flying to
her mouth.

"I'd heard." Lady Beatrice sounded bored as she
handed Lady Wilkins a cup. "If you wish to replace me
as a reliable source of news, you must not exaggerate."

Someone tittered, bringing a flush to Lady Wilkins's
face.

Lady Beatrice gestured her to a chair. "Grayson fool-
ishly chose to walk from White's to Albany last night
instead of summoning his carriage. Quite absurd, of
course, but gentlemen do not always behave with caution. The Lord Mayor really must expand the watch. The
footpads grow bolder every year." She shook her head,
the folds in her neck wobbling.

"Was Grayson badly injured?" asked Lady Westlake.

"Bruised, but nothing broken," replied Lady Beatrice
dismissively. "The culprit stole his purse. No doubt he
expected a fat profit, but Grayson's game had been
quite off."

"I heard he was much the worse for wine." Lady Wilkins could not keep the pique from her voice. Being

first with a story garnered admiration—an honor usually reserved for Lady Beatrice.

"No doubt." Lady Wharburton snorted. "It would not be the first time."

"Nor will it be the last."

"Enough about Grayson," said Lady Marchgate, nodding toward her daughter. "What is this new tiff between Brummell and the Regent?"

Mary ignored them. Brummell's posturing seemed eminently silly. She was more concerned about Grayson. How badly had he been hurt?

Silver eyes hovered before her face. His chuckle upon seeing her sketches had been from enjoyment rather than ridicule. She hoped he was not in too much pain. Even were he worse than rumor declared, she would not have him suffer.

She shivered. Catherine's first husband had endured endless hours of pain before his death. As had her father, who had died by the same hand. Grayson did not need that.

Gray set down his knife and flexed his shoulders, vainly trying to ease their stiffness. But comfort was impossible. The pain was worse than when he'd crawled home last night.

Jaynes, who doubled as valet and butler, returned with a calling card in one hand.

"Show him in," said Gray with a sigh. He was in no condition to receive guests, but Nick was hardly a guest.

"I hear you had a spot of trouble," he drawled from the doorway.

"A trifle." Gray gestured to a seat. Jaynes had already produced a second plate.

"What happened?"

"I'm not sure. I was turning from Piccadilly into Albany when a footpad attacked." He shook his head to clear it. "The details are hazy. I would have defended myself, but my arms wouldn't move."

"Wouldn't?" Nick accepted ham and scones.

Gray shrugged, cursing himself for saying too much.

No one knew his innermost secrets, especially his tendency to freeze when danger threatened. "Besides stealing my watch and purse, he entertained himself by beating me."

Nick paused with his fork midway from plate to mouth. "Even though you weren't resisting."

"That much I do recall, though my head was as muzzy as if I'd drunk two bottles of brandy."

"You are rarely the worse for drink."

"I said *as if*. I'd consumed two glasses at most. The drive from Shellcroft must have fatigued me more than I thought." In truth, he had chosen to walk home because his stomach had been roiling so badly a carriage would have made him ill. Perhaps Lady Debenham's lobster patties had gone bad.

"I don't believe your journey fatigued you. Could you have been drugged?"

"Absurd!" Gray slammed his fork down, then winced. "Is it?"

"Of course. I was playing whist with Shelford, Atkins, and Alderson. None of them have any reason to drug me, and we had no audience—everyone was watching Brummell and Alvonley in deep play across the room." He'd watched that match himself for a time.

"Alderson laces his wine with laudanum." Nick chewed thoughtfully.

Gray pondered. "I suppose it is possible that I drank his by mistake. He is left-handed, so our glasses were together. Bad luck."

"Why did the footpad decide to attack?"

"Perversity, I suppose. He left when the watch approached." The man had kicked him to see if he remained conscious. Gray had been too groggy to respond, though he thought the man asked if he'd had enough. But that might have been imagination. He'd been reviled so often in recent years that he sometimes saw antagonism where none existed.

Yet he could not shake the feeling that the footpad had been waiting specifically for him, not just for easy prey.

"Nothing makes sense," he said aloud. "My purse contained only a few shillings—not even enough to garner transportation should he be caught. And he could have lifted it without my knowledge. So why attack? That could send him to the gallows."

"Most perplexing," agreed Nick. "I heard Lady Luck deserted you last evening."

Gray shrugged. While it was true he'd not won, neither had he written any vowels.

"Have you annoyed anyone more than usual?" asked Nick.

"No. Why?"

"Don't be obtuse. A beating is out of character for the average footpad. He might knock you on the head to make robbery easy and identification difficult, but no more. Thus we must consider the possibility that he was hired. So . . . Who is annoyed with you?"

Gray gritted his teeth, but Nick was tenacious. "No one is annoyed enough to injure me—except possibly Lady Horseley, but I can't see her hiring a ruffian."

"Nor I." Nick grinned at the image of the very proper matron prowling the stews, seeking footpads. "What about those inventors you collect? Who have you turned down lately?"

"Givens. He wants to adapt steam engines for hauling freight long distances, but Stephenson and Trevithick are far ahead of him. He wasn't happy, but he found funding elsewhere within the week, so I doubt he would repay me with a beating."

"Any others?"

"I've turned down half a dozen since Twelfth Night, but none of them would retaliate. They would more likely attack someone I've backed, though I can't see them doing that, either."

"Competitors? Some don't like you moving into the world of trade and besting their own efforts."

"If they wanted to hurt me, they would look for me on the docks. Besides, how would they know I was in town? Until yesterday, I'd planned to return next week."

"Good point. But I'm not convinced you drank

Alderson's wine. Mistaking the glass is not like you. Nor is poor play. If Albright's description is valid, a schoolboy could have beaten you last night. Laudanum might put you to sleep, but it wouldn't affect your mind."

"What are you suggesting?"

"According to Albright, you seemed three sheets to the wind when you left White's. Since you didn't drink much, you must have consumed something else."

"Are you claiming someone poisoned me?" Again he felt the eyes burning into his back.

"It fits. Your behavior was abnormal. You felt sluggish. Your attacker went beyond necessity to hurt you. What would you call it?"

"Preposterous. I'd worked twelve hours before leaving Shellcroft. The drive took six more. I should have stayed home last night, but I overestimated my stamina."

It had to have been an accident, he assured himself, even as breakfast turned to lead in his stomach. Laudanum affected people in different ways, even producing illusions on occasion. The beating might have been pique because his purse was empty. Not everyone was put off by the threat of punishment. Some believed they were too clever to be caught.

Chapter Four

Gray stayed home that night, lighting a fire in his sitting room to ease his stiffness, though fires in May were an extravagance. Reading business reports proved impossible, for he couldn't concentrate. Light reading was no better. His mind kept wandering to the laudanum he was taking for the pain. Surely he would have noticed drinking something that bitter at White's.

Yet he couldn't be sure. Alderson might use sweeteners to mask the taste. And he could no longer trust his memories. The longer he considered the matter, the surer he became that the wine had tasted odd. Certainly something had been amiss. He'd joined the game because he'd wanted to sit down, and he'd been unable to recall which cards had been played from the very first hand. By the time he'd left, he had been seriously ill.

Again his mind lost track of his book, forcing him to back up. His reflexes were sluggish—and this from only a small dose. He could understand picking up the wrong glass when in this condition, but how had he done so the first ti—

Idiot! Alderson was responsible. The man had already been badly foxed when Gray joined the game, and he'd refilled his glass several times afterward. With their glasses sitting so close together, it was no surprise that Alderson had poured laudanum into the wrong one.

The explanation relaxed him.

Last evening had been a comedy of errors arising from his own poor judgment. He'd attended Lady Debenham's ball when he was too exhausted to think straight, then broken his own inflexible rule against speaking to innocents. Something about that artist intrigued him, so she'd remained in his mind long after he'd joined the card game—a fact he'd not told Nick. Distracted, he'd played poorly and failed to notice Alderson's mistake. He had best clear the lady out of his head before it happened again.

Relief eased his tension, proving how much Nick's fears had bothered him. An enemy willing to poison his glass in a private club was worrisome. The footpad already made him feel too vulnerable.

By the next day Gray felt well enough to attend the Oxbridge ball. According to Justin, rumors that he was dying gave Lady Horseley an excuse to revive every exaggerated tale and offer new ones as well. She was as adamant as ever, determined to drive him from town.

So he must appear before she convinced people that he was Satan incarnate. Ostracism would unbalance his life. His estate provided peace and the privacy to pursue his interests. His business offered challenges and occasional excitement. But he also needed contact with his own class, beyond what he could find at the clubs.

Of course, going out would be embarrassing, he conceded as he chose a jacket that wouldn't clash with his mottled eye. The men would make sport of his bruises and offer to teach him the manly art of self-defense. Some ladies would disapprove him flaunting the injury in public. Others would shower him with unwanted sympathy.

But half an hour later, he handed his greatcoat to a footman. Countering Lady Horseley was more important than pride.

"On your feet already?" Connelaugh laughed, slapping Gray on the back. He was a bear of a man, as jovial as a drunkard and with the manners of an ill-trained dog. "Rumor has you at death's door."

"Rumor exaggerates, as usual." Gray suppressed a wince as Connelaugh's hand slammed into one of his deeper bruises.

"You mean you weren't robbed of your entire fortune?"

"Hardly. The rogue caught me by surprise"—he pointed to his eye—"then stole my purse, but it contained only two shillings, sixpence and a modest vowel he has no hope of redeeming." His tone implied that the joke was on his attacker. But he'd been fond of the watch he'd lost. It had been a gift from his grandfather shortly before the man died on the guillotine. Rage burned in his breast. When he found the culprit, he would see the man transported.

But for now he made light of the incident, enduring endless questions about the encounter. Some joked, others offered sympathy, and a few seemed disgruntled that he appeared none the worse for the experience. Since those were the same people who wished he'd left the country after Miss Turner's death, he ignored them.

An hour later, he regretted his decision to face society. A thousand candles burned overhead, flickering in the breeze raised by a hundred dancers. The uneven light made his head swim until only leaning negligently against a pillar kept him upright. Echoes of voices and music melded with his pounding heart, producing a dull roar. Sweat soaked his cravat.

But weakness wasn't his worst problem. He'd been so intent on hiding his pain that he'd forgotten his other danger. Miss Derrick and Miss Huntsley were at the theater tonight, which was why he'd chosen this ball. But they weren't the only threats.

That blonde stood twenty feet away, her lids fluttering enticingly over the top of her fan. He hadn't considered her a problem, for she was a beauty with a large court of admirers that should have kept her too busy to bother him. Now she swiftly dispersed her court, then headed in his direction.

He swore.

"Who is the beauty in the yellow gown?" he asked Nick. A name would let Jaynes discover her plans in the future.

"The blonde passing Lady Jersey?"

"That's the one."

"Miss Seabrook. I mentioned her yesterday. Her brother is a baron with an estate in Devonshire, and her older sister married Rockhurst. He is sponsoring her and a younger sister this Season." He glanced around. "I don't see Lady Rockhurst at the moment. Do you need an introduction?"

"No. Diamonds are usually too selfish for my taste, so wrapped in their own wishes that they care little for others."

"You always were partial to bluestockings."

Gray shrugged. "At least they can converse intelligently." Miss Seabrook drew closer. Her mouth stretched into a practiced smile, but her eyes gleamed with avarice. "No doubt about it, she has her eye on me. Would you distract her? I refuse to tarnish another reputation." When Nick nodded, Gray headed for the card room. He was too dizzy to deal with problems tonight.

Lord Oxbridge was in deep play with a dozen other gamesters, none of whom noticed him. And just as well. His vision was fading in and out, his head whirled, and sounds had merged into the pulsing echo that presaged a swoon. He should have heeded the doctor's advice and stayed abed for a week. But it was too late—for everything. He had to lie down before he collapsed. His carriage would not do. He would never find it in time.

He left the card room by the other door. The hallway led to the ladies' retiring room and then to the family quarters. They were not open to guests, but he no longer cared. He would never hear the end of it if he collapsed in public.

Black spots were crowding his eyes by the time he staggered into Oxbridge's library. Moisture beaded his brow. With his last ounce of strength, he closed the door and collapsed on a couch.

Time passed. The dizziness gradually faded, steadying the ceiling fresco. Not until he shifted into a more comfortable position did he realize that the room was occupied. His artist was sitting at a table.

He swore.

"You should have stayed in bed another day, Lord Grayson," she said càlmly. "Skipping a ball would damage your credit less than swooning in public."

"Hiding again?" He kept his tone light. She knew his identity now, though she made no move to flee.

"Not exactly. Lord Oxbridge mentioned a folio of animal prints, but he was interrupted before I could ask to see them. I hope he won't mind."

Gray raised his head. The table was littered with natural history books and prints. He recognized the folio. The hand-tinted drawings showed animals in their natural state, with more detailed backgrounds than most artists used, more detailed even than the bird illustrations his friend John Selby drew—he'd urged the fellow more than once to publish a collection.

He dropped his head back on the couch. "He won't mind, but your reputation will suffer if anyone finds you here. This part of the house is closed."

"Which is why you came here to swoon." She nodded.

He started to deny it, but closed his mouth without a word. She knew the truth. How could she not? He'd staggered in half dead and continued to recline despite her presence. She was right. He should have stayed home. All of society would know the tale by morning.

She shook her head. "You are in terrible shape, Lord Grayson. Your face reveals every thought. But relax. I won't mention your foolishness, though you should return home as soon as you can remain on your feet."

Embarrassment heated his face. "You have the advantage of me," he said through clenched teeth. "We've not been introduced."

She blushed. "Forgive me. Miss Mary Seabrook, Lady Rockhurst's sister."

A jag of fear produced another surge of dizziness. Was she also stalking him? But reason quickly returned. She could not have planned this meeting—or the one behind Lady Debenham's potted palms. No one could have predicted he would turn up in either hideaway.

Nor was she like her sister. Average looks. Simple gown. Matter-of-fact tone. And a bluestocking, unless his instinct was completely gone. One of the books she had gathered was a natural history of Kent. Another was a volume on birds, written in the most turgid prose he'd ever encountered.

"Surely they warned you to stay away from me." The

moment the words were out, he cursed himself. The beating must have loosened his brain.

"Of course." A smile lifted the corner of her mouth as she faced him. "You are an ogre of the first water, sir. Merely speaking with you will tarnish my reputation, cancel my voucher to Almack's, and call my virtue into question. You are a hairsbreadth from being cast into eternal perdition with only Blackthorn as company."

"Ouch."

"The view is not universal, of course. Lady Westlake defends you with great vigor—she is grateful for a past kindness—and others suspect the tales are exaggerated. I prefer to judge for myself—not a difficult chore since fate seems eager to throw us together."

He nodded. "You could always leave."

"I see no need."

"Why?"

A small frown crossed her forehead. Intrigued, for she seemed to be giving his question serious thought, he rolled onto his side, propped his head on one hand, and waited.

"Curiosity, I suppose," she said at length. "My instincts are usually accurate, and you do not strike me as a blackguard. I know that gossip usually exaggerates and is sometimes downright false."

His jaw dropped in astonishment. "You are young to have learned such wisdom."

"Lessons can come at any age." Pain flashed in her eyes. "My eldest sister once suffered a malicious attack on her credibility. The resulting censure spilled onto the entire family. Only luck and considerable effort saved her reputation. The incident taught me the folly of believing everything one hears."

"Are you speaking of Lady Rockhurst?"

She nodded. "Rockhurst unmasked the perpetrator. It is how they met."

"When was this? I've heard nothing of such a campaign."

"Not surprising. It was a country matter that did not

reach town." She shrugged. "But what is the truth in your own case? You seem kind."

Even more surprising than the question was her tone. No condemnation. No fury. Only curiosity and the surety that he could explain. He shocked himself by answering.

"Like Lady Rockhurst, I did nothing. I suppose you've heard the stories."

"Of course. Those who enjoy scandal delight in warning newcomers to avoid people like you—strictly for our own good; any pleasure they derive from the exercise is purely incidental."

Her tone made him chuckle.

"You are accused of jilting Miss Irwin, then ruining Miss Turner, who ultimately did away with herself. I presume that last claim is true, for no one suggests suicide lightly."

He nodded.

"Everyone agrees on those charges. Other tales are more nebulous—the unnamed innocents you supposedly ruined, suspicions that your fortune was acquired dishonestly, hints that you are a French spy."

"None of those have any basis in fact," he snapped.

"So I thought. I distrust any tale that does not include specifics or that changes significantly from one teller to the next. But what of the others?"

"Miss Irwin arrived in London with little training in the ways of society. Thus she managed to annoy or insult a great many influential ladies, including Lady Beatrice. She was poised to do the same to Lady Jersey when I deflected her."

"How?"

He cautiously sat up. The room swung twice, then steadied. "Lady Jersey can be delightful if you show her proper respect, but she does not tolerate criticism, particularly of the subscription balls at Almack's."

"Rockhurst warned us about that. Even Laura dares say nothing about stale cakes and uneven floors." She shifted in her chair. "So you prevented Miss Irwin from taking the lady to task?"

"Exactly. It was a minor incident, but it drew her attention. Over the following month, I danced with her three times and exchanged greetings on two other occasions. Each meeting took place in a large gathering at which I spent time with a score of other females, so I was astonished to open the *News* one morning and see our betrothal announcement."

"Good heavens! What on earth was her father thinking? You cannot have approached him."

"Of course not. I was barely four-and-twenty and had no interest in settling down. I had never called on her or sought her out in any way." Fury still burned whenever he thought of Irwin's treachery. However, Mary's face held so much compassion that an unfamiliar ache settled into his chest.

She shook her head. "It must have been a terrible shock. What did you do?"

He ran his hands through his hair. "I immediately called on Irwin to demand an explanation. He had the nerve to call me a liar. That's when I realized the greedy bast— He and his daughter were conspiring to attach my fortune. They had hoped to compromise me, but I had refused to leave a ballroom with her. So they concocted a bolder scheme."

"Everyone understands his greed," she reported calmly. "He was recently caught cheating at cards. But the current theory is that you paid him to deny a betrothal."

It was a twist he'd not heard before, not that it helped much. "I did, in a way," he admitted, "though not a farthing changed hands. When I demanded details of our supposed courtship, he tried to bluff, reeling off a list of secret rendezvous. I made him write them down—places, dates, exact times—then informed him that I could prove his list false. He could either retract the announcement or stand trial for extortion. I could produce plenty of witnesses."

"So you paid him by not filing charges?"

He nodded.

"He cannot be very bright," she noted.

"Definitely not. To hide his own complicity, he blamed everything on his daughter and vowed to send her home. But she attended one more ball, where she enacted her own retribution by accusing me of seduction."

"She sounds less bright than her father."

He actually laughed. "True. Irwin was furious, creating a scene that became the talk of the Season—he probably feared I would have him arrested for breaking our agreement. The incident ruined her beyond repair, of course. Both father and daughter disappeared the next morning. I heard she married a farmer not long afterward."

"So why do people blame you?"

"That began the following year." He sighed. "Miss Irwin convinced me that protecting people from their own stupidity was dangerous—and impossible anyway. Until then I had tried to set the nervous and unprepared at ease."

"Like Lady Westlake?"

He nodded. "Her brothers held all but the dullest gentlemen at bay. The few they approved despised bluestockings, but she wanted a husband who accepted her studies."

"Surely her brothers wanted her happy." Her hands gripped the bird book.

"But on their terms. They distrusted intelligent females—even their own sister—and believed she needed a firm, controlling hand to correct her odd habits."

"So you introduced her to Westlake. She remains grateful. But why did you do it? Matchmaking is not usually a gentleman's activity. Nor is saving the gauche from embarrassment."

"It bothers me when people are ill at ease," he admitted, shrugging. It wasn't something he'd ever analyzed. Nor did he wish to start now. Thinking about it recalled confrontations he wanted to forget, so he resumed his tale. "After Miss Irwin, I distrusted innocents and never danced more than once with one. It didn't help."

"Miss Turner?"

He nodded. "I met her the following Season at Lady Debenham's ball." The irony was obvious. He had first spoken to Miss Irwin at Lady Debenham's ball, first danced with Miss Turner, first met Miss Mary hiding behind the palms. Perhaps he should avoid the event in the future, though it was too late to undo this latest acquaintance. And he wanted to believe this one was harmless. Mary triggered neither sympathy nor compassion. "Beyond that evening, I never spoke with her, but she pursued me relentlessly. No matter where I went, she followed. She even tried to force entrance to my club."

"Good heavens! She sounds like Lady Caroline Lamb."

"Very like, though this happened before Lady Caroline met Byron. Most people can laugh over Lady Caroline's antics because she has credit Miss Turner could never achieve. Society might check the facts more closely if Miss Turner pursued me today, but three years ago, they blamed me for encouraging her."

"No smoke without fire. How I hate that phrase."

"As do I." He met her eyes and smiled. "I finally left town to escape her. That's when she killed herself, leaving a note that blamed me for seducing her. The family confirmed she was with child."

"She actually named you as the father?"

He nodded. "I've been a pariah ever since."

"How unjust. I wonder whom she was protecting."

"It no longer matters."

He leaped up when he heard footsteps in the hallway, but no one entered. Yet it recalled him to their danger. "You had best leave. If anyone finds us together, your reputation will be in tatters. I've no interest in igniting another scandal." His head spun, so he resumed his seat.

"Nor I. My family barely survived the last one. But few would care about me. Laura attracts all eyes."

"Your sister?"

"And a diamond of the first water. She outshines the sun."

Her tone contained pride, but also a hint of pain. Anger flared as he recalled the avaricious blonde in the ballroom. Like too many self-absorbed beauties, she had probably sucked the life from her younger sister—unfairly.

"Be glad that she deflects the tulips to her side," he said lightly. "You wouldn't enjoy their company anyway."

"How would you know?"

"You are too intelligent to like posturing, but those who share your interests would flock to you if they could find you."

"You underestimate her impact. Surely you've seen her." She snorted. "Of course, you have. Everyone notices her the moment they enter a room. I am invisible when she is around."

"Not true. I admit I've seen your sister, but I cannot like her. She is the sort who is never satisfied with what she has. I left the ballroom just now because she fixed her sights on me."

"She wouldn't be so foolish!" Agitated, Mary paced to the window and back. "Of course, she would," she muttered. "The rumors appeal to her. Drat her, anyway. I'd hoped I wouldn't have to bother Blake with this."

"Bother him how?" Gray demanded.

Mary jumped. "I'm sorry. For a moment I forgot you were here. Laura is usually sweet and caring, but she can sometimes be headstrong."

"If she thinks to attach me, she must be mad."

"Not mad. Bored." She blushed. "Laura longs for the sort of excitement described in tales of adventure and exotic lands. Unfortunately, no real man can compare to the heroes of those books, a truth she sometimes forgets. It leaves her dissatisfied with those who would court her."

"God help me," he muttered.

Mary seemingly didn't hear as she paced the library. "She rejects ardent suitors, then trails after those who avoid her. She is particularly drawn to anyone who might show her the world. Someone mentioned that you toured the Continent despite the hostilities that still rage. And another tale claims you often travel about England."

"More exaggeration. The only touring I undertook was six years ago when I inspected four estates before buying Shellcroft. I did visit Brussels after the debacle with Miss Turner, but that was strictly business. I returned in a week."

"But avoided London until the following Season, I suppose."

"Do you blame me?"

"Of course not."

He rested his chin on his hands to contain a new bout of dizziness. "If she thinks I am an adventurer, then all I need do is tell her the truth."

"I wouldn't advise it. When she turns headstrong, Laura ignores facts that contradict her assumptions. That is another lesson she seems to have forgotten." She sighed.

"Then how do you expect Rockhurst to talk sense into her?"

"Blackmail. He holds the purse strings since he is financing this Season—our oldest brother's estate barely covers his own expenses. Blake can also ruin her if he chooses." She blushed. "Please do not repeat that, my lord. I don't want to harm her if I can help it, but you have a right to the truth. Blake was another who ignored her."

"Do you mean she tried to force Rockhurst into marriage?" What the devil had he done to deserve this? And why did unstable girls always target him?

"She considered it. William discovered the plot before she could put it into operation. There was a rather ugly scene that should have taught her a lesson—and did, for a while. But she seems to have forgotten it. Like too many diamonds, she expects every man's regard, and when she takes the bit between her teeth, there is no stopping her. Perhaps you should take advantage of your injuries to avoid society for a few days. Spend time at your clubs while that bruised eye heals."

"I won't allow anyone to dictate my life." The reaction was automatic and contradicted his own history of avoiding dangerous people.

"Men!" She shook her head. "Then at least remain in company for a week or so. I'll not have her add to your problems."

It took him a moment to recognize she was protecting him rather than arranging his life as his father had tried to do. No one had ever protected him. Even his family considered him hopeless. "I will consider it if you will stop skulking in corners. You would attract your own court if you remained in the ballroom."

"Don't flatter me, my lord. What would I do with a court anyway? I've no chance of making a match in town. I wish to wed for love—Catherine has done so twice—but I'll not find such a man here."

"Why?"

"London gentlemen are superficial, which is why they gravitate to beauties like Laura. The few willing to talk to someone as inept and clumsy as I spout bad poetry and false flattery as if I hadn't the wit to converse sensibly."

"Surely there is someone who cares for you."

"No one." She grimaced. "Except possibly Mr. Griffin, but I cannot like him. Nor can I believe he is truly infatuated."

"The snake." He nodded toward the reticule holding her sketchpad. "You caught his character perfectly."

"I know. But he is persistent, which is another reason I prefer to remain out of sight."

Gray said nothing. The runner he'd hired had not yet turned up anything useful. There was no point in mentioning his interest until he had evidence. But he could ask Nick and Justin to keep Griffin from annoying young ladies. No girl should be forced into seclusion because a gentleman made ballrooms unsafe. "Is there no other?"

She shrugged. "If I cannot wed for love, I would prefer to remain single."

"A barren life for a woman."

"For some, but I had expected no other choice until recently. What little Father left was set aside for Laura, so I accepted a role as governess to my niece. Only Catherine's marriage to Rockhurst changed my prospects. But I sometimes wish I could go back. Life was simpler then—more enjoyable in some ways."

"Really?" The question was rude, but he couldn't help himself. He'd heard the conviction in her voice. She was unlike anyone he'd ever met. "Why would you say that?"

"It would have been different had I held a post with strangers. But with family, I suffered none of the indignities of service. And Sarah—my niece—is a joy. Bright, happy, smart . . . It broke my heart when Rockhurst hired a real governess."

"Surely the woman is capable."

"Very. In fact, she is a warm, loving lady. Intelligent, well educated, and she'll be able to prepare Sarah for society. We'd all feared that Sarah would end as a governess." She rubbed her arms. "But I miss our time together. Since Blake hired Miss Mott for Laura and me, my days have been filled with manners and court curtsies. I've had no time to study anything of interest."

"That is part of life, my dear."

"I know, but it is frustrating. Rockhurst is determined to find me a husband. My only consolation is that he will never force me to accept someone I do not approve."

"What about your brother?"

"He is rebuilding his estate, so Catherine took charge of Laura and me—to no one's surprise, for she'd raised us. Mother died when I was four."

Approaching footsteps cut off further confidences.

Gray stifled a curse. He should have insisted she leave instead of succumbing to the pleasure of talking to her. If anyone found them together, she was doomed to spend the rest of her life as his wife. He would not tolerate another scandal.

But would that be so bad?

The thought distracted him. Before he could gather his wits, Mary had shoved the bird book into his hands, swept the folio out of sight, and ducked into the window seat behind heavy velvet draperies. She must have made contingency plans the moment he staggered through the door.

And just as well. The draperies had barely closed behind her when the drunken Earl of Clifford stumbled into the room.

"Sho this is where you went, Grayson," he slurred. "Did the beating shcramble your brains? Always knew you were prissy, but never took you for a scholar." He stared pointedly at the book open in Gray's lap.

Clifford was a self-righteous prig, far too like Rothmoor for Gray's liking. Both men considered reading a waste of time. Rothmoor preached that the only knowledge a gentleman needed was how to choose horseflesh, hunting dogs, and bed partners. He left everything else to solicitors and stewards. Gray had started his shipping business as much to thumb his nose at Rothmoor as to support himself—he'd been living quite nicely from his investments.

But Clifford's real complaint was Gina Wren. The earl had never forgiven Gray for winning the delectable courtesan. Clifford had offered a larger house and more extravagant allowance, but she had turned him down. He never forgot slights.

"Birds?" the earl continued in incredulous tones, catching sight of an illustration. "You won't find your next bird of paradishe in that dusty old tome."

Gray donned his social mask, surprised that it had slipped with Mary. A glance identified the illustration as a pied flycatcher. "Just settling a wager," he said mildly.

"Wager?"

"Precisely. One party claims a pied flycatcher appeared outside his window last evening. The other swears it is found only in the country. They were working up to pistols at dawn when I offered to discover the truth—for a fee."

Clifford sneered. "You always had a nose for profit. Sho who wins?"

"Neither. The bird prefers woodlands, but sometimes visits Hyde Park. Since the window in question is in Albany, a lost flycatcher might have flitted by. Thus I judge both men correct."

"Sho you lose."

"Hardly. My fee stands. Arbiters never lose."

A sound from the window told him Mary was battling laughter. Fortunately Clifford was too foxed to notice.

"Since when do you unruffle ruffled feathers?" asked Clifford, resting one hip on the corner of the table.

" 'Tis an innocent lark. And a service to society. Those hen-wits were ready to meet over a bird."

"Abshurd. Now a dog or a horse? Good wagering there. But never a bird."

"Not even a wren?"

Gray enjoyed Clifford's scowl. After losing Gina, the earl had added new exaggerations to Gray's reputation. In retrospect, Gray wished he'd bowed out of the competition. Gina's passion was as fiery as he'd expected, but she was a demanding little witch—one of the reasons he'd delayed his return to town. He would have to dismiss her, but she was the sort to throw things, and he hated violence.

"If you've settled your wager, you'll be on your way." Clifford swayed. It was clear he wanted privacy to sleep off the wine. He was so far beyond foxed that it was a miracle he'd retained the sense to leave the ball. But the man would never risk becoming an *on-dit*.

Any other time, Gray would have left, but he could not abandon Mary. Until Clifford passed out, she would be trapped. And Clifford was looking rather green. Gray didn't want Mary subjected to the sights and sounds of illness. So Clifford had to go—voluntarily, lest he wonder why Gray wanted him gone.

"I'll not leave just yet." Gray stifled a yawn. "Lady Stafford was chirping about a reed bunting last evening, but I'm not sure what the beast is. As long as I'm here, I might as well look it up." He cocked his head as if puzzled. "You look a bit green around the gills, Clifford. Do you feel all right?"

"Are you implying that I can't hold my wine?" Clifford straightened so fast he nearly toppled over.

"Of course not. Only the veriest greenling would fall ill from a little wine, and you are far beyond that age. But it appears that supper did not agree with you. Oxbridge rarely serves decent food, but tonight was the worst I've tasted. The lobster patties were so greasy, I was bilious after only four. And I could swear the pickled herring was spoilt. Who serves herring at a ball, anyway? So *déclassé*. It positively reeked, and one piece was actually green." He heard Mary choke. "Of course, Oxbridge's catering is ambrosia compared to that inn I was stranded at last month. The fish had gone quite off, and I swear the stew was at least a week old. Mutton and lumps of rancid fat. Three men shot the cat in the taproom. Horrible mess. And the smell! I nearly lost my own dinner."

Clifford's face had turned greener with each word. He swallowed rapidly, then tried to speak, but a loud belch erupted. Snapping his jaw shut, he bolted. Gray hoped he made it outside.

"Time for you to return to the ballroom," he told Mary. "It is dangerous to slip away as you do."

"Clifford would never hurt me."

"No. He is far too proper to seduce an innocent. But being found alone with him would force marriage, whether you liked it or not. And believe me, with him, you would not."

"That was most unsporting of you," she complained, but her eyes twinkled.

"It was the fastest way to be rid of him."

Her scowl dissolved into peals of laughter. "Oh, but you were brilliant. He is so very stodgy. However did he become foxed at a ball?"

"Probably evading his mother. She is pressing him to settle the succession. Have you met Lady Clifford?"

"I don't believe so."

"She makes Lady Horseley seem frivolous. More rigid than Clifford and a Tartar as well. The man will be shackled by summer. But come. You must return." He cracked the door to see whether the hallway was clear, then hustled her toward the ladies' retiring room.

The strains of a waltz floated from the ballroom, allowing him to relax. The dance was still so controversial that everyone gathered to cast envious or censorious looks at the participants. Thus no one would notice them.

The moment Mary was safe, he sought his carriage. She'd been right. He should have stayed in bed. Even this short walk was making him dizzy.

Chapter Five

Mary curled into the corner of the carriage as it zigzagged through late evening traffic. Ladies weren't supposed to slump, but she didn't care. She was exhausted. Even stealing an occasional hour of privacy didn't alleviate the strain of the Season. Of course, tonight's private moments had not exactly been alone.

She smiled. Grayson was fascinating. And she could talk to him. Not once had she considered whether her words might offend. Nor had he. Only friends could be so open without censure. She basked in that thought for several minutes, hardly believing it was true. Even Blake, who usually set her at ease, remained intimidating at times. But Grayson did not—hadn't from the moment he'd grabbed her sketchpad to fix the chaffinch's beak.

He invited confidences, extracting information she never shared with others.

A shiver rippled down her spine. If she had misjudged him, he could now ruin her just by speaking the truth. She had twice met him alone, the second time far from others. Both times she had remained in his company for a considerable period.

But it was the threat to Laura that was the most serious. Again, he need only speak the truth. Laura had indeed plotted to trap Blake, but if that fact became public, society would turn on her. And it would be Mary's fault. Forgetting to guard her words could extract a greater toll than all her other mistakes combined.

He won't talk, her dreamer insisted. *You know he won't.*

She had to believe that. Grayson was kind, intelligent,

and very much a gentleman. It broke her heart that a pair of schemers had harmed him. Being innocent must make the cuts even harder to bear, for his only crime had been sympathy.

But there was nothing she could do. Gossips rarely admitted fault, and never at the urging of a nobody like her. Championing his cause would call censure on her own head—not that she would mind personally, but it would redound on Blake and could revive the false charges against Catherine. Her behavior already reflected poorly on them, as Catherine was again reminding her.

"You must stop running off, Mary," she said sternly. "Even Lady Jersey noticed that you missed three sets tonight. Three sets! It does your reputation no good at all."

"I was feeling faint," Mary claimed, thankful that she had been in the retiring room when Catherine found her. Barely. Not that she regretted meeting Grayson, but explanations would have been awkward. "The ballroom was horridly stuffy."

"All ballrooms are stuffy," said Laura. "It gives us an excuse to walk in the garden."

"Tonight was worse than usual," insisted Mary. "Lord Delwyn's scent was so powerful, it dominated the entire room. I've never smelled anything that made breathing so difficult."

"He does overuse perfumes," agreed Catherine. "But that is common in men of his age, as is his choice of heavy musk. It does not justify avoiding company."

"Nothing does, so stop seeking excuses," added Laura. "I know men ignore you, but manners are more important than pleasure. Cowering in the retiring room announces that you are hopeless and don't care who knows it. You don't see Miss Huntsley hiding, and she's even clumsier than you."

"Enough, Laura," snapped Catherine. "You are not helping."

Laura scowled. "She should have stayed at Rockburn. But since she is here, she must behave. Flaunting her vulgarity shames the whole family. Even louts like Griffin feel compelled to correct her. And her insults have discouraged half my suitors."

"Hardly," snapped Mary.

"Well . . ." She drew out the word in satisfaction. "It is true that gentlemen trip over their feet in their rush to admire me. Since society learned of Miss Norton's elopement, I've gained four new suitors. And Sir Randall switched his devotion from Miss Harfield," she added, naming another of her rivals.

"Puppy," murmured Mary in disgust. Sir Randall was eighteen and had already joined and abandoned four courts this Season. Why Laura craved the fulsome fawning of such cubs was beyond her comprehension.

"He is charming. Even Lord Whitehaven danced the last set with me."

Mary snorted. "Since he dances only with misfits, one must ask what you did to draw his attention."

"That is not—" began Catherine.

Laura ignored her. "That may be why he danced with you, but having done his duty to propriety, he is now able to seek his own pleasure. And I am his pleasure. I could see it in his eyes. He was smitten by my beauty." She sighed dreamily.

"That makes no difference," declared Catherine. "His—"

"You said exactly the same thing about Blake," Mary interrupted. "And Harry Fields and John Drummond. But it was never true."

"How dare—"

"Stop this, both of you," ordered Catherine. "There is no point in arguing over Whitehaven, for Cromley would never allow his heir to wed you, Laura, no matter how great your beauty. He will accept no one below an earl's daughter and would approve that only with a fortune in settlements."

Laura sputtered.

Mary nodded agreement. "You know that he treats every partner as though she were Helen of Troy. It's part of his charm, but it means nothing."

"How would you know?" demanded Laura nastily.

"No man would look twice at you. Why else do you hide at every opportunity? Not that I'm complaining. Your antics embarrass us all."

"Laura!" Catherine had not sounded so furious since the day she'd caught fourteen-year-old Laura embracing a groom, her gown open to the waist.

"What? Must I pretend she makes us proud? I'm tired of having people commiserate with me every time she mortifies us. You know their real purpose is to gloat at my discomfort. Too many of them expect me to be as gauche and untutored as she. I've lost three suitors to her insolence. And others stay away because they are afraid to ally themselves with a family that includes her. She's ruining my Season. It's not fair!"

"You will apologize at once," ordered Catherine. "If you've lost suitors, blame your own insufferable arrogance. You talk only of yourself and pit admirers against one another, insulting any who annoy you. No gentleman likes acting the fool, so it is no surprise that the more discerning ones avoid you." She continued over Laura's protest. "Yes, avoid you. Like Mr. Hawthorne. He cannot tolerate your vanity. And men aren't the only ones you irritate. Lady Oxbridge complained that you cut her daughter just because Lord Seaton asked her to dance. And if Lady Wilkins were a man, she would have called you out for insulting her. Instead of criticizing Mary, you should consider your own behavior."

Laura's face mottled, but the carriage drew to a halt, forestalling any retort.

Mary escaped into Rockhurst House, hoping to reach her room without further argument. Laura was in a strange humor tonight. She had achieved triumphs that would delight most girls, yet she was furious because they weren't bigger. Grayson's words suddenly seemed ominous. *She is the sort who is never satisfied with what she has.*

He was astute. She had noticed the problem before, though she'd not put it quite so succinctly. Laura was beautiful, but there was a devil deep in her soul that reared up whenever a dream shattered. It had done so eighteen months ago when scandal heaped censure on all Seabrooks. Mary feared it was happening again. London was the biggest dream yet, but the reality could never match Laura's fantasy.

Laura had always expected a triumphant London Season. Through all the delays, she had honed those expectations, building London into a modern Mount Olympus that offered glamour, excitement, dashing men, dazzling ladies, and adventure beyond imagining. Her dream always ended with her sailing away to explore the world with a man who would fulfill her every desire.

Nothing could live up to that image. While London was bigger, fancier, and more exciting than anything in Devonshire, it was not mysteriously exotic. Balls might occur daily, but the dances were the same, as were customs and manners. Theaters might employ better actors and more opulent sets, but the scripts hadn't changed, and most people still attended only to see and be seen. Gossip still dominated every gathering. Ladies still flirted, and men retired to their clubs for wine and cards. Life was no more alien than in Exeter or Bath. Thus Laura was bound to be disappointed.

Mary saw that disappointment in the growing petulance, the imagined slights, and the increasingly desperate flirting. Laura wanted more than London could provide, which endangered them all.

"You are right. Most of my suitors are pitiful puppies, and Whitehaven is too obedient to his father's will," said Laura, making one of her inexplicable reverses as she joined Mary on the stairs. "Society bores me. My suitors are no better than the squires and farmers at home. Their clothes may be more elegant, but behind their dash, they care for exactly the same things."

"Why does that surprise you?" Mary asked cautiously. "The gentry and aristocracy have similar interests. But don't make the mistake of thinking everyone dull. Town conversation revolves around gossip, clothes, and the latest wagers. Other topics are unfashionable. Even Blake adheres to that custom, though he has many interests."

It was another reason Mary knew she could never find

a husband in town. Society chatter disguised a man's character. She might have met some interesting gentlemen at literary gatherings or intellectual soirees, but she had no time to attend. Thus the only intriguing man she knew was Grayson.

But she could hardly count him a friend. He would hate knowing she had seen him at his worst. No gentleman admitted weakness.

Laura lowered her voice. "That wasn't what I meant, and you know it. I enjoy gossip as much as anyone. But I cannot tolerate a husband who remains on his estate, or even in London. He must be a traveler. An adventurer. Someone who ignores convention."

"Like Lord Byron?" Mary shook her head.

"Of course not," snapped Laura. "Byron is too conceited to ever interest me. I don't know what Lady Caroline sees in the man. He ignores her every wish."

Mary bit her tongue, though she knew that a man with the confidence and determination to explore the world would never devote his life to satisfying Laura's whims.

"But I've finally found the perfect husband," Laura continued, excitement threading her voice. "I suspected as much earlier, and now Lady Wilkins has confirmed it."

Mary grasped the handrail more tightly. Lady Wilkins was vindictive and had a grievance against Laura. It would not take much intelligence to plan the perfect revenge. Laura's penchant for coveting anyone not in her court was already known.

Laura didn't notice her agitation. "He has traveled extensively, both in England and abroad. He is titled and wealthy, is fascinated by China and the West Indies, and would welcome a wife on his journeys. She was interrupted before she could introduce us, but I caught him watching me a short time later. The look in his eye was obvious. I expect he'll contrive an introduction tomorrow."

"Who is he?" Maybe her fears were groundless.

"Lord Grayson."

"Don't be ridiculous, Laura. You know better than to take Lady Wilkins's word for anything. She would love to ruin you. But even if her claims were true, Grayson will never do. You can't even speak to him. Every matron in society would cut you, and your entire court would flee."

"Her claims are certainly true. I heard the same ones at Lady Beatrice's yesterday."

"What difference does that make? You of all people should know how rumor can exaggerate, twisting truth into something utterly false. Have you forgotten Jasper Rankin?"

"Jasper was a consummate liar. The chances of it happening again are so remote as to be impossible."

"I doubt it. I heard another version of Grayson's so-called travels from someone in a position to know. There was only one trip—to Brussels on business. He splits his time between his London office and his Sussex estate."

"That sounds like Lady Westlake. I swear she must fancy the man to champion him so consistently. But it will avail her naught. I'll not tolerate liaisons."

"You won't have a say in the matter."

"Of course I will. We will be wed before the Season is out. I saw the spark in his eye. He is already madly in love with me."

Shock turned Mary speechless. And fury. It was bad enough when Laura formed sudden *tendres* for men she barely knew. This time she hadn't even met the man, yet she was planning a wedding.

She must deflect her attention. Grayson already considered her a pest. The last thing he needed was another Miss Turner.

Yet what could she do? Claiming that Grayson wasn't interested would raise questions, and Laura would deny anything she said anyway. It would do no good to reveal that Grayson had fled the ballroom to escape her. Laura would twist his actions into concern for her reputation. She'd done exactly that with Blake.

Laura seemed to read her mind. "Don't you dare mention Blake again. I never would have misjudged him if he hadn't pretended a courtship to cover his investigation," she swore in blatant untruth.

Mary drew in a deep breath. "If Grayson cares for

you, then he will contrive to meet you. Let him handle everything, Laura. Showing undue interest could ruin you. Society is not ready to forgive him."

"Brilliant idea!" Laura beamed. "I will prove my love by redeeming his reputation. I have more than enough credit to do so. How grateful he will be."

Mary's mouth fell open. She should have expected this twist. Laura would naturally seek to heal. Yet the suggestion created a new dilemma. Laura's credit was already under fire if Catherine's complaints were any indication. Fashion might proclaim her a diamond today, but that could change in a trice. Yet that was another reality Laura would ignore.

"Laura, think! Some of Jasper's rumors reached town. While his banishment laid most of them to rest, too many people believe there is no smoke without fire. Thus we must avoid any hint of scandal. If you so much as smile at a man society dislikes, they will turn on you." *Listen to yourself*, her conscious warned. *You should also take heed.* "Speaking to Lord Grayson can ruin you—and not just you. None of us can weather another scandal. Do you wish to be ostracized? Surely you remember how it felt to be denounced by people we had known all our lives. If Blake hadn't discovered the truth, we would be outcasts."

Laura bridled. "While it is true that you must be careful, that restriction does not apply to me. Society worships beauty. I could ride naked down St. James's Street with impunity. If you stayed in company instead of fleeing at every turn, you would know that."

"I do know the difference between your situation and my own." Mary kept her voice steady with difficulty. "Acclaim has perched you on a pedestal high above the rest of us. But that means you have farther to fall, making you more susceptible to scandal. People watch your every gesture and drink in your every word. Your rivals will pounce on the slightest indiscretion, trumpeting it to the world. Public opinion can shift in an instant, especially about a diamond. You need look no further than Miss Norton."

"You sound like Miss Mott. Governesses often spout such nonsense to coerce blind obedience from their charges. But it isn't true. You know little about society and nothing about love. You've never seen a man gaze at you with his heart in his eyes or communicate across a room with a single glance. Grayson loves me. It is as clear as the words in those books you devour. And he knows that he cannot approach me until his reputation is restored. He will suffer unbearably until we can be together, so it is up to me to save him."

Mary nearly swore. "At least let him come to you instead of chasing him. If you even look at him, your reputation will suffer."

Laura shrugged. "It matters not. We will not be in England long enough to notice." Her expression hardened when Mary raised a hand to protest. "I will wed him. Make no mistake about that. He is everything I seek in a husband—exciting, adventurous, and determined to have only the best, as his refusal to wed his mistress proves." She glared. "And if you try to stop me, I'll destroy you. It is bad enough that I must share my Season with an antidote, enduring pity and suspicion whenever you draw censure. But I won't tolerate interference. I had nearly given up hope, but this match is perfect." She stalked into her room and slammed the door.

Mary stared, appalled. Would Laura never grow up? She might be two years the elder, but she had no more sense than a child. And her craving for adventure was as powerful as ever. She hadn't changed a jot in eighteen months. Her arrogance had led to trouble then, and it would do the same now. Unless she was stopped, her antics would drive Grayson from society for good. And she could irreparably harm Blake and Catherine.

Mary woke early, despite lying awake for hours trying to choose her course. Laura's new obsession threatened them all. This was hardly a country backwater in which indiscretions could be covered and forgotten. Lady Beatrice knew everything that happened, most of it within the hour. And what Lady Beatrice knew, everyone knew.

But perhaps Laura was not as reckless as she sounded. She was far from stupid. In addition to adventure, she also craved adulation. Thus she would not risk losing her court until she grew desperate. So Mary had a day or two before she must carry tales to Blake.

That was the point at which she'd fallen asleep. But dreams had kept her tossing. Not of Laura, but of Grayson. He had been tied to a stake, with angry lords and ladies thrusting blazing torches into the wood heaped about his feet. She had tried to stop them, to convince them he was innocent, but no one saw or heard her. Finally her mounting frustration had awakened her.

Rain drummed against the window, promising a dreary day.

Mary treasured these early morning hours. No calls or callers. No ladies frowning at her for slips of the tongue. No criticism to increase her tension and make matters worse. If only she'd remained in the country. Laura would certainly be happier.

But that option was even less possible today. Laura would destroy Grayson if she wasn't stopped. Unfortunately, Mary was the only one who could protect him. Blake would take the threat seriously, but he rarely attended Marriage Mart parties, so would not be at hand. Thus any action he took would be after the fact. Catherine would dismiss the complaint as exaggeration. Even after the plot against Blake, Catherine did not truly understood Laura.

Mary shook her head as she slipped into a muslin morning gown. Catherine had married their vicar when Laura was twelve. Thus she had not witnessed the lengths to which Laura would go to win a man's favor. The incident with the groom two years later had not been an aberration. There had been similar scenes with a footman, two tenants, and a neighbor. And those were just the ones Mary knew about. She thought Laura's virtue remained intact, but there was no guarantee. Laura craved affection and sought every possible sign of it. So if she wanted Grayson's hand, she would take steps to claim it. Patience had never been her forte. Thus Mary must remain nearby, ready to deflect any schemes that might harm the family.

But for now, she would go to the bookstore.

Shopping was something she rarely enjoyed, for Laura usually took charge of expeditions, spending hours—and fortunes—in hat shops, modiste shops, and bazaars. After a lifetime of pinching pennies, Laura was determined to make a name for herself as the best-dressed, most beautiful miss of the Season. As a result, she had long since overspent her allowance.

Catherine made an equally tiring companion, complaining constantly that Mary's wardrobe was inadequate. She even offered to buy gowns out of her own money so Mary needn't feel beholden to Blake, but Mary always refused. She had enough gowns. It was more important to expand her library, for there was so much she did not know. That was today's errand.

She had just arranged for a maid to accompany her—Frannie had to be available when Laura awoke—when the knocker sounded. A footman accepted the first of the day's flower deliveries. Mary shrugged. Laura received many such offerings, though they meant nothing to her beyond a way to keep track of her popularity.

She was heading upstairs when the footman stopped her.

"For you, Miss Mary." He handed her a posy of delicate violets.

"Me?" There had to be a mistake.

But her name was scrawled across the attached card. It was unsigned, save for a sketch of a pied flycatcher.

She nearly laughed. Grayson was so very different from rumor. Without risking her reputation, he had thanked her for their time together and assured her that no one would learn of the incident. A true gentleman.

Smiling, she set the violets on her dressing table, then set out for Mason's Book Emporium, a smallish shop that specialized in the sciences. If the day were truly magical, she might find a copy of that folio.

That hope soon died, but an hour later, she was engrossed in a book on the natural history of Cornwall.

Despite its proximity to Devonshire, the duchy supported a different mix of birds, animals, and plants, some of which Mary had never seen.

"The carriage is here, Miss Mary," reported the maid.

"Already?" But the clock on the counter verified that it was time to go. Catherine would be furious if she was late for morning calls.

"Tell Briggs I will be out momentarily," she instructed. At least the rain had stopped. If her gown remained dry, she wouldn't have to change.

But she nearly dropped her parcel when she stepped outside. Despite the early hour, Lord Grayson was strolling along the street, looking healthier than last night except for his purple eye.

No one from society was in view—not surprising at this time of day—so she could thank him for the flowers. And she could also warn him about Laura. If he avoided any balls the Seabrooks attended, Laura could do nothing rash, and Mary wouldn't have to tell Blake about this latest start. But as she raised a hand in greeting, Grayson darted across the street, narrowly avoiding a carriage.

"Stop!" His command was clear above the clatter of traffic, though the rest of his words were drowned by shouts and curses from a dozen drivers. He looked furious as he pulled two boys upright by their collars and shook them. Whatever he said was effective. The moment he released his hold, they fled.

That's when she saw the dog cowering against a building. The boys had been tormenting it.

Grayson scooped it up, holding it against his chest as a hand soothed its fears. He jumped into a carriage and slammed the door. Only then did Mary recall her own carriage.

Her throat tightened.

Grayson protected girls from social disaster, studied natural history, and rescued animals from harm. He was a kind man with a sensitive nature, as she'd suspected from the first. How had he tolerated the scorn heaped on him by a judgmental society? His only crime was helping people like her who didn't fit. And for that he was reviled, distrusted, and misused by unscrupulous girls who knew nothing about him.

No matter what Lady Horseley and her ilk claimed, Grayson was not a cold, callous man who cared only for pleasure. It might be a façade he used to cover pain, but it wasn't real.

She owed him a stronger warning about Laura. Maybe a let—

Her carriage suddenly stopped in the middle of Piccadilly. Merchants, peddlers, and a dozen wagons blocked the way. Beyond a narrow arch stood a crowd of gentlemen, many attired in dressing gowns. Smoke poured from a window above them.

Fire.

It was a most fearsome enemy.

The gathering had also blocked Grayson's carriage. He jumped out and hobbled into the building, leaving the dog behind. To help?

Blake's cousin, Jacob Townsend, spotted the Rockhurst crest and hurried over. Blake had introduced them a year ago, hoping they might make a match. That hope had rapidly fizzled, but they had become friends.

"What happened?" she asked.

"Mischief." Jacob shook his head. "Two lads stole one of those rockets they use for the Vauxhall fireworks displays. I don't know what they expected when they set it off, but it broke loose, crashed through one of Albany's windows, and set fire to the room."

"Goodness!"

"Fortunately, no one was there. Servants and neighbors are battling the blaze, but it could have been disastrous. Jenkins claims it landed in a bed and ignited the linens." He nodded toward a gentleman standing at the curb.

"What will happen to the boys?"

"We have to catch them first." He grimaced. "They fled. Several people followed, but the lads probably escaped. It has been half an hour with no sign of them."

She gazed again at the building, where the smoke was

lessening. Whoever lived there would suffer considerable damage. "Poor man."

"Who?"

"The owner. Even if the furnishings survive, they will never be the same. One of our neighbors once suffered a chimney fire. You could still smell smoke in her drawing room a year later."

He nodded. "Our local inn had the same problem. They finally refurnished the private parlor because too many customers complained." He shook his head. "But don't lose your soft heart over this one, Mary. By all accounts, the damage is slight and easily repaired. Grayson will hardly notice the expense. His fortune puts Golden Ball to shame."

"Lord Grayson?"

"Those are his rooms, though he wasn't here. He just returned from his evening revelries." Jacob nodded toward Grayson's carriage, then mumbled something about the Delectable Wren. Probably his mistress if Jacob's blush was any indication.

She stifled a burst of pique at Jacob's assumptions, but didn't bother correcting him. Grayson could not have remained out all night. He had been too faint after the ball to do aught but stumble home, and he had changed his satin evening jacket for a superfine morning coat before reaching Coventry Street. He was also wearing boots today. But defending him would raise questions, and Jacob would never believe her anyway. He was a prig who probably thought Grayson split his nights between multiple gaming hells and a dozen courtesans.

Men were clearing the street, allowing traffic past. But she couldn't get the image of flames from her head. First her dream, and now this. Coincidence or warning?

At least Grayson had been away, for stiff bruises would have hampered his escape. If he'd been in bed—which most gentlemen were this time of day—he would have been badly injured. Or worse.

Or perhaps not. People often accomplished the impossible in emergencies. One of William's tenants had escaped a furious bull by running a quarter mile despite a broken ankle.

She frowned, then realized that Grayson had triggered that last memory. He'd been limping badly when he raced inside, most likely from the beating. Last night's saunter had hidden the extent of his injuries. Today's dash had made concealment impossible.

Chapter Six

Gray took the stairs three at a time and raced down the hall, coughing from the smoke. His door stood wide open, belching more smoke. He'd had to count windows twice to believe his eyes. But there was little doubt. His bedroom was ablaze. The neighbors would blame him for any damage to their rooms. He should have stayed at Shellcroft for another week. Luck had been against him from the moment he'd returned to town.

And it could worsen. Laura Seabrook was serious trouble. If he interpreted Mary's warning correctly, her sister's obsession could precipitate a worse scandal than Miss Turner, banning him from ballrooms as well as from respectable drawing rooms. He must keep Nick or Justin near at hand to deflect trouble.

But he could address that problem later.

A footman carrying two empty buckets ducked into a servant's stair, returning a moment later with full ones. Jaynes must have organized a line to pass water up from the kitchens.

Gray followed him inside.

Lord Sedgewick Wylie and Terrence Sanders, his nearest neighbors, were tossing water on the fire. They were the last men he would have expected to find here. Granted he barely knew them, but both had struck him as fools. Wylie was a consummate dandy, slavishly following Brummell's dictates. Sanders had spent the last five years cutting a wide and very public swath through the muslin company, provoking even more notice than Gray had done ten years ago.

They weren't the only men battling the blaze. Jaynes

wielded a rug, as did two servants Gray didn't recognize. But there was no sign of firemen.

"We're making headway," reported Lord Sedgewick, nodding a welcome before wiping his face on the sleeve of a sooty dressing gown.

Sanders handed his empty bucket to the footman, then mopped his face with his cravat. His evening coat lay in a heap by the sitting room door.

"You've made excellent progress," acknowledged Gray. "Thank you." Tossing his own coat in the corner, he dipped a rug in a pool of water and attacked the fiercest flames.

Smoke stung his lungs. Sparks burned his hands. Shouts funneled through the broken window from the drive below. But victory seemed to dance just out of reach.

Water hissed angrily every time it lost a battle with the heat. Though each blow of the rug snuffed the fire for an instant, it always returned, greedily reaching for new fuel. Gray's bruises screamed, but he kept fighting—stooping, swinging, gasping for air.

He was wavering from dizziness when Lord Sedgewick's victory shouts revived him. New energy surged through his shoulders. His rug swung faster.

"Toss those draperies out the window," he ordered. Jaynes could finally reach the smoldering fabric.

"Behind you, Grayson," warned Sanders.

Gray turned. Flames had found a dry line of carpet. "Water!"

Lord Sedgewick hurled a bucketful at the new blaze. Gray followed up with the carpet.

Half an hour passed in growing elation until the final flame flickered and died. But the room was not a pretty sight. The mattress had followed the draperies through the window. Puddles stood in corners and saturated the carpet. Charring blemished the walls, ceiling, bed, shaving stand, and one end of the wardrobe. His bootbox and bureau were in ashes. The acrid stench of burnt leather bit into his nose.

Gray staggered into the sitting room and collapsed in

a chair. Now that the crisis had passed, he could barely move.

The loss and violation were beginning to hit. He had occupied these rooms since the day Albany opened ten years earlier. Though he now spent half the year at Shellcroft, in the early days he had lived here year around. But at least the fire had damaged only his bedroom. The library, with its five thousand volumes, was intact. As was his office. He hoped the smoke had not reached his birds.

Lord Sedgewick and Sanders joined him. Jaynes opened windows, passed brandy, then disappeared to serve the servants who had helped.

"What happened?" Gray asked once they had eased their parched throats.

Sanders stretched his legs and examined his ruined shoes. "I had just returned from my evening revelries when someone shouted *fire!* I'd heard nothing until then, but when I reached your rooms, your man mentioned a rocket."

"A rocket?"

"I know it sounds preposterous, but that's what he said."

Lord Sedgewick nodded. Today was the first time Gray had seen the dandy less than impeccably dressed, yet the man even appeared elegant clad in a filthy dressing gown. His Hessians shone despite soot and ash. "When I arrived, the bed and wall were ablaze," he reported. "This fell from the coverlet when I pulled it off." He produced a flattened metal cone.

Gray turned the piece in his hands. Though damaged, he recognized it as the cap-piece of the military rocket designed by one of his inventor friends. Reports indicated that it sent the French troops scrambling for cover whenever it rained blazing gunpowder across a battlefield. The effect was lessening with custom, but it had caused considerable chaos at first.

"The servants claim that two boys ignited a rocket in the street," continued Lord Sedgewick. "Perhaps they planned to pick a few pockets in the resulting confusion. They did not expect it to crash through a window."

"But where would pickpockets find a rocket?" Gray asked.

"Probably stole it from Vauxhall." Sanders shrugged. "They use them in the fireworks displays. Strap two to a wheel so it rotates in a shower of sparks. Quite a show."

"I know," agreed Gray. "But Vauxhall won't open for another fortnight. And their rockets are small. More to the point, fireworks rockets don't use this sort of cap."

Lord Sedgewick frowned.

Sanders straightened. "What are you saying?"

"I've seen this piece before, because I know its designer. It is found only on military rockets. God knows the army's supply problems are notorious." Many shipments went missing, and others substituted inferior goods for those contracted. "But if rockets are in the hands of street urchins, we need to know. Can you imagine one of these loose in Seven Dials? It could ignite another Great Fire."

"Devil it!" Sanders gulped brandy.

"No one has fire insurance in the stews, and the streets are too narrow to stop a blaze," said Lord Sedgewick, frowning.

"Not that fire insurance helped here," grumbled Gray. "I appreciate your assistance."

"It was nothing."

Sanders echoed the view.

"Nevertheless, I thank you," repeated Gray. "I will call at Bow Street. We must discover where this rocket came from. Do you know who saw the boys?"

Sanders shook his head.

"I can ask," offered Lord Sedgewick.

"Thank you. Too many would ignore my questions."

The dandy nodded. "Fools. The shortsighted rarely grasp the larger view. This endangers us all."

Gray thanked them again, expressed hope that smoke had not damaged their quarters, then bade them farewell.

"Have you anything to add?" he asked Jaynes, who had been lurking outside the door for some time.

"Nothing, my lord. By the time I set the volunteers to work, we were too busy to ask questions."

"Neither fire company appeared."

"Perhaps they were at another scene," suggested Jaynes. "The porter dispatched a footman to summon them."

Gray nodded. Finding both services occupied fit the way his luck was running lately. Albany subscribed to two companies to avoid this very situation and to assure enough men to fight a serious blaze. Fire was an ever-present danger in London, where buildings crowded against one another and entertainments usually lasted until dawn. The new lights along Piccadilly added to the danger, for the gas lines were prone to leakage.

"How long will the repairs take?" he asked.

"A week, perhaps two. I do not know the extent of the damage. Perhaps cleaning will remove the smell in here, or perhaps not. I dare not open the wardrobe to inspect your coats until the bedroom is aired. And—"

"That is the least of my problems. Weston is nearly done with this Season's clothing. Have him deliver the finished items today."

"Where?"

"Funston's." He'd stayed at the club for several months when he first arrived in London, newly estranged from his father and with barely enough funds to cover a week's lodging. If Medford's ship hadn't docked . . . "They keep rooms for members."

"What about the birds, my lord?"

Gray sighed. "The titlark is ready for release, but the hoopoe will have to remain here. Its wing will not be fully healed for another week. Where are they?"

"The pantry." Jaynes didn't like it. Birds were insignificant in his estimation, though he had learned to care for them properly.

Gray followed him to the butler's pantry. A dozen sketchbooks Jaynes had rescued from the bedchamber were heaped beside the bird cages. A pain eased in Gray's chest.

The hoopoe's black-tipped crest was fully raised, indicating agitation, but it did not seem to be suffering. It was a striking bird, a foot tall, with a clay-colored body, startling black-and-white-striped wings, and a white stripe chevroned across a black tail. The long curved beak had been known to fend off predators.

"Easy, fellow," crooned Gray, slowly extending his hand to check the splint he had contrived for a broken wing. The bird had lost a fight with a hawk—unusual for hoopoes; their skill at evading birds of prey was legendary. Gray had brought the creature to town with him, trusting only Jaynes to properly care for it. If the bones knit badly, it would never again fly free.

The hoopoe gradually relaxed. Two wing feathers were out of line, but the splint remained intact, and the fragile bones had not shifted. Its recovery remained on schedule.

The titlark was a simpler story. Gray had rescued it from a cat two days earlier, keeping it under observation in case it had suffered hidden injuries. It had showed normal hunger that morning, so it was time to release it.

"Free this one in the yard," he ordered Jaynes. "And keep your ears open. I need evidence of how the fire started. The rumors do not ring true."

"You know it was a rocket."

"Yes, but street urchins?" He shook his head. "As soon as I change, I'm for Bow Street, then the War Office. Perhaps they know of a theft. If more are at large, the entire city is in danger."

He wondered briefly if someone had attacked him because of that idiotic rumor that he was a spy. But it didn't seem likely. Only a few people, like Lady Horseley, still believed it. And these rockets had very erratic flights, so could not be aimed. Their main purpose was to light battlefields after dark, allowing artillerymen to see their targets. Frightening the enemy was a useful side effect.

Jaynes summoned a footman to fetch hot water from the kitchens. Then he drew in a deep breath and opened the wardrobe. "Not too bad," he said in relief. "These should clean up quite nicely."

"For now I'll wear the green coat and fawn pantaloons," said Gray. "Smoke will add urgency to my tale."

* * *

"Where the devil is he?" Laura smoothed her skirt. "I saved the supper dance for him."

"Who?" demanded Mary. "Your court is all here, and then some."

Miss Norton stood alone tonight, despite heated denials from family, friends, and even two neighbors. Most of her former admirers now clustered around Laura, with the rest doting on Miss Harfield. Even her bosom bows hesitated to approach lest they be tarnished by association.

"Grayson, of course. I expected him to manage an introduction by now."

"Why?" Mary stifled a sigh. Laura was as stubborn as ever—and as shortsighted. "He rarely dances, and then only with matrons. Lady Debenham reports that he has not spoken to an unmarried miss in three years. She should know. She's as avid a gossip as Lady Beatrice."

"But he was not in love with anyone else. He cannot help but dance with me."

"Laura!" Thank heaven they were alone in the retiring room. She played one of her trump cards. "Even were he to request a set, you could not accept. It would destroy any chance that Lady Jersey would approve you for the waltz. She is considering it. But if she suspects you have a *tendre* for Grayson, she will forbid you the waltz and might even revoke your voucher. Dancing with him could ruin you."

"I can't believe you are so stupid," hissed Laura. "Speaking to Grayson would ruin a nobody like you— you only received vouchers as a favor to me anyway— but my credit is too high. Even sticklers love titillation. They still receive Lady Caroline Lamb despite her scandalous pursuit of Byron."

"But she will never set foot in Almack's again. And her situation is entirely different. She is wed; you are not. You are chasing a notorious scoundrel rather than a dashing poet. Despite your beauty, suitors care that Father was merely a baron. And you lack a powerful patron like Lady Marlborough. Blake is related only by marriage, and he would never support you through a scandal—not after you tried to compromise him."

Laura swore. "How dare you—"

"I dare because I do not want you hurt," said Mary. "If Grayson truly cares, he will find a way to approach you. But chasing him will give him and everyone else a disgust of you. Blake would pack you off to the country in a trice. You know it took Catherine more than a year to convince him to sponsor you. He won't tolerate impropriety."

"You would love to see me packed off, wouldn't you?" demanded Laura. "But it won't do you any good. Even if I leave, no man will notice you. There are too many choices for them to waste time on an ugly, manipulative bluestocking. I doubt Blake could pay a farmer to take you on."

"This has nothing to do with me," protested Mary, though Laura's venom hurt. Even knowing it arose solely from temper did little to ease the pain. "I want you to succeed, but you have to follow the rules. Haven't you learned that ignoring convention never works?"

She might as well be speaking to a wall. Laura peered this way and that in the long mirror, pulling her bodice lower to draw attention to her bosom, puffing her sleeves and teasing tendrils loose from her curls to frame her graceful neck. With a last pat on her hair, she flounced out.

Mary shook her head. She should not have allowed passion into her voice. The more adamantly she protested, the more likely Laura would do the opposite. Besides, this was a bad time to argue. Grayson would not be here tonight. Aside from the fact that his evening clothes were probably in ashes, he knew Laura was stalking him. He had apparently taken her advice to heart. Or so she hoped. It was also possible that the fire had worsened his injuries. If he couldn't hide his pain, he would stay home.

She wished she could see him—just to verify that he was well—but it was better this way. They could never be friends. Anyone who saw them together would assume the worst.

Regret stabbed her chest. Heaven knew he could use a friend.

Three young ladies entered the retiring room, laughing. With the peace shattered, Mary left, passing Lord Hartford and Mr. Turlet outside an antechamber. Those two gossiped as avidly as Lady Debenham.

As Mary started down the steps into the ballroom, Laura laughed, then drew Griffin's attention to the stairs. He immediately started forward.

Mary cursed, plunging into the crowd. Laura was becoming as vindictive as Lady Wilkins. She must speak to Blake in the morning.

In the meantime, she ducked into the refreshment room, circled through the card room, then slipped behind the draperies that formed a backdrop for a mass of flowers. It was a tight squeeze, but she was flat enough to leave no bulge, and the flowers would mask her slippers. Hugging the wall, she prayed that no one had seen her. Especially Mr. Griffin.

Three matrons were talking nearby, too intent on discussing the fire at Albany to have noticed her.

"Mr. Sanders said it was started by a lad playing with fireworks," reported Lady Wilkins.

"Absurd," snapped Lady Horseley. "Grayson probably knocked a lamp over in a drunken stupor. A shopkeeper in Upper Bolton died in just such a fire last month."

"You may say what you like about Grayson, but he is rarely the worse for drink. And he was not home at the time," said Lady Wharburton.

"According to whom?"

"Lord Sedgewick Wylie. He helped fight the blaze."

Mary smiled, though it was hard to imagine Lord Sedgewick battling a fire. He was one of Brummell's followers, oozing ennui as well as style. But Lady Horseley could hardly deny his credit.

"Why would he risk his coats in a fire?" demanded Lady Wilkins.

"His rooms are adjacent to Grayson's, so he was first on the scene," said Lady Wharburton. "Grayson arrived half an hour later."

"Spent the night with his mistress, I suppose," snapped Lady Horseley. "That Wren person—or so I've heard."

"Cut Clifford out to win her favors," murmured Lady Wharburton. "Their competition caused a stir in the clubs. She's been all the rage ever since."

"Men!" Lady Horseley snorted.

That explained Clifford's animosity in the library, Mary realized. More than Grayson's reputation and Clifford's priggishness stood between them. Competing for the same courtesan often created bad blood—or so Blake had admitted when she'd wheedled details of London life one night when he'd been the worse for wine. He'd been appalled to recall the conversation the next morning.

"Will he move in with the Wren while repairs are in progress?" asked Lady Wilkins.

"Even Grayson would never consider it," replied Lady Wharburton. "He is staying at Funston's."

"Why not the Pulteney?" grumbled Lady Horseley. "He is wealthy enough to command the best suite, and the service is better in a hotel. Funston's attracts vicars and the like."

Mary wondered why Lady Horseley disliked Grayson. Granted, she was one of the more rigid dowagers, but she criticized everything he did, whether good or bad. Other gossips distrusted him, but took avid pleasure from discussing his affairs. Lady Horseley simply hated him.

"It does seem odd," admitted Lady Wilkins. "The rooms at Funston's are small and dingy—or so Wilkins claims. Why would a wealthy man consider it?"

"Why not retire to his estate? It is near enough, and he hasn't enjoyed much luck this year. If he returned home, he could start over once his rooms are repaired."

Mary ceased listening as the ladies debated this point. A window alcove a few feet away offered space. Moonlight streamed in. Since it did not overlook the garden, no one would see her. She pulled out her sketchpad.

Her pencil fashioned a trio of bullfinches perched on

a fruit tree, their heads huddled together as they chattered about the latest news. Greedy bullfinches stripped trees of buds, destroying fruit and sometimes even killing saplings. Not much different from gossips stripping reputations.

Their voices washed over her, sometimes clear, sometimes muted by music. "Clarkwell picnic . . . Lady Atkins . . . Sanders visited Lady Darnley . . ."

The set concluded. She peered through a crack in the drapery. Catherine would be looking for her, but Mary would not return while Mr. Griffin was in sight.

People milled about the room as ladies returned to their chaperons and gentlemen sought new partners or the card room. Griffin stood ten feet away, head craning to see everyone.

Frowning, she retreated to finish her sketch.

"I always knew Lady Flint would meet her comeuppance," declared Lady Marchgate, joining the trio.

"What happened?" Lady Wilkins's eyes would be avid.

"You know what a pinchpenny she is."

"Insists on using that appalling modiste on Hay Market," complained Lady Wharburton.

"And she never pays vails to the servants," added Lady Horseley.

"She paid today," announced Lady Marchgate. "She lost three pins from that awful striped gown, but the retiring room maid refused to repair it until Lady Flint paid a full shilling, in advance."

Chuckles met this news. As the gossips moved on to other tales, Mary concentrated on her sketch, again letting the voices wash over her. "Blackthorn insulted . . . dancing master . . . Nortons leaving for . . . Grayson dying—"

Mary's pencil dug into the page. Lady Debenham had joined Lady Wharburton's group.

"You cannot be serious!" Lady Wilkins's voice squeaked.

"That's what Wigby claims," swore Lady Debenham. "Food poisoning. Grayson should have expected it the way his luck is running. Funston's cook is terrible, and the service grows worse every year. Debenham dropped his membership because of it."

Listeners cited other complaints. At least a dozen ladies had joined the conversation.

Lady Debenham continued. "Fifteen victims, but Grayson is the most serious. Wigby swears he is at death's door."

Mary covered her mouth, bumping the draperies in her agitation. He could not be dying! It was too much. A beating, a fire, food poisoning . . . It wasn't fair. What a waste of a good man.

Pain sliced her chest. No other man had set her so quickly at ease. Now she might never see him again. But at least she could stop fretting over Laura.

Laura!

The girl was bound to make a cake of herself when she heard. Having decided Grayson was her white knight, she would throw strong hysterics because he was dying. Catherine would need help.

Griffin had moved on, so Mary headed for her sisters.

Chapter Seven

Three mornings later, Mary rounded a shelf in Hatchard's and ran into Grayson. He caught her before she could fall.

"Good morning, my lord," she managed to croak. His hands burned through her pelisse.

Gossip had learned nothing beyond that initial report—a matter for much speculation, leading Lady Beatrice to gnash her teeth on at least two occasions. He had disappeared from Funston's before morning, but no one knew where.

"Miss Mary." He finally released her.

She stepped back. "I trust you are well," she began, then blushed. Even an imbecile could see that he was anything but well. His face was pale and pinched, his hand trembled as he pulled a book from a shelf, and he had lost enough weight to affect the fit of his jacket. Yet she had never been happier to see anyone.

"I am recov—" He sighed. "You are too astute to believe social lies. I am improving, to the disappointment of my detractors."

"Nonsense. No one wishes you dead. Not truly," she added, recalling Lady Horseley's satisfaction and the excited speculation that filled drawing rooms. That had been the titillation of the moment, for no one seriously expected him to succumb to food poisoning when the other victims had recovered within a day.

"But I would wager they discussed it quite avidly." His smile hid a wince.

Her heart went out to him. Despite his façade of insouciance, he felt every barb. "Of course they did. You know people spend hours discussing a stumble in the park or the pink cheeks on a girl returning from the garden. They would do no less for you. But the most animated discussions cover speculation of your whereabouts. Lady Beatrice is beside herself."

"Really?"

"She hasn't a clue where you are. I'm just glad that you will recover."

"No thanks to the fish."

"Was that what is was?"

"Has to be." He leaned against a shelf—casually, though Mary suspected he needed its support. "It was quite tasty—unusual for Funston's—so I ate several pieces. Which accounts for the severity of my illness. I should have been more prudent."

"I'd wager it won't happen again." Her hand touched his arm in a gesture of comfort.

"Never. Even the thought of fish turns me quite green."

Realizing that she was caressing him, she reclaimed her hand, then changed the subject. "How is that dog you rescued?"

Shock twisted his face. "How the devil did you learn of that? Is nothing I do private?"

"I doubt anyone else knows of the incident, but I was emerging from Mason's Book Emporium when you dashed across the street. Had those boys injured it badly?"

His face bloomed with color. Embarrassment? But he answered readily enough. "A few bruises, and he was underfed—hardly a surprise. He must have lived with a family at some point, for he is at home indoors and well mannered."

"Poor thing. Where is he now? You can hardly have taken him to your club. Or Albany, for that matter."

"Have people spoken of nothing but me lately?" He sounded disgruntled.

"Everything you do is grist for the gossips, so don't pretend shock. You'd probably feel neglected if they ignored you."

"They twist facts until I fail to recognize my own deeds." The pain was more evident this time.

"That is the nature of gossip." She again touched his arm. "So what did you do with the dog?"

"Sent him to my estate, where I've another house dog. My steward reports that Fred agreed to share the space, but he made it clear that he had precedence. When Bones tried to pass him on the stairs, Fred read him the riot act. Bones now follows meekly behind."

Mary chuckled. "You did not accompany him home, then?"

He raised his brows.

"I am not asking you to reveal secrets, but I admit to curiosity. I can't imagine how you kept Lady Beatrice ignorant. She was quite incoherent when the subject arose yesterday."

"Seriously?" He looked pleased.

She nodded.

"She must be slipping."

"Or otherwise occupied. Miss Norton is in disgrace and expected to leave town. Blackthorn's feud with At-water grows more ominous. Three betrothals, two births, and a carriage accident required attention yesterday. And we awakened this morning to news that Mr. Omney fled the country to escape his creditors."

He laughed, revealing a dimple that sent tingles clear to her toes. She would do much to draw another laugh.

"I am residing with a friend," he admitted, "though I would prefer to keep that quiet until I fully recover. I've no wish to receive callers."

His mistress. She reached for a book to cover a ridiculous spurt of pique. "Of course, but why then are you here? Remaining abed would hasten that recovery. You need rest after so many afflictions." She examined him closely. "Frankly, you look little better than when you staggered into Oxbridge's library. And even then you managed to hide some of your injuries, like that limp I saw the day of the fire."

"Damnation," he muttered. "Are you always there when I display my weaknesses?"

"So it would seem. But why not remain abed? Look what rising too soon accomplished the last time."

"I will lie down shortly, my dear Miss Mary. But I need something to read. Justin's library contains nothing of interest."

She shook her head. "You could have sent your valet."

"He is otherwise occupied."

"What you really mean is that you are bored."

This time the smile was rueful. "You know me too well. I wonder how. Even my closest friends can't read me so clearly."

"A guess, I assure you. I also find it hard to lie quiet for days, but you should know better." She returned the book to the shelf and pulled out another. The books themselves were of no interest—they described the mathematics of constructing buildings. But they kept her hands from smoothing his jacket or touching his pale cheek. "Rumor claims that a fireworks rocket started your fire. How did a boy find one?"

"That is the question of the hour." He paced two steps away, then returned. For a moment she thought he would turn the subject, but instead, he explained. "The rocket was the sort used by the army."

"A battlefield rocket?" Mary could not keep the astonishment from her voice. Her brother Andrew, who was a captain in the 95th foot, had mentioned such devices in his most recent letter from Spain.

"Precisely. Large and powerful. I know the inventor, so I recognized the remnants."

"Where would boys obtain one?"

"I'm not sure they did." He rumpled his hair. "A dozen people were in the street when the fire started. Each knows the tale, but none actually saw a boy or can name anyone who did."

Mary nodded as enlightenment broke. "Ahh. Deliberate falsehood. I've seen it done before."

"What do you mean?"

"I told you Rockhurst saved my sister from ruin. The culprit used the same technique. His lies suddenly appeared on every tongue, yet no one could name a single witness to her supposed crimes. Nor did they know who had started the tales. But who would wish to burn your rooms?"

"Wrong question. Those rockets produce chaos, but they are unstable and cannot be aimed with any precision. What I really want to know is how the culprit obtained one and whether he has more. The War Office insists that all of them were shipped to Spain."

"Curious."

"Exactly. I have a runner looking into the matter, but so far he has discovered nothing." He shrugged. "At least no one was injured. My valet noticed the blaze immediately, so the damage is confined to one room. Repairs should be complete in another week."

Mary returned the second volume to the shelf, then stepped past Grayson to a more interesting section.

"Are you looking for something in particular?" he asked.

"Anything on natural history. I would love to find that folio Lord Oxbridge has."

"You will have no luck there. They only printed a hundred copies, and all sold immediately. I have one myself," he added, then looked like he regretted admitting it. Did he deliberately foster a care-for-naught image?

But she dared not ask. "It would have been too expensive in that case. Can you recommend one of these?" She pointed to two books on the birds of southern England.

"Mr. Aubrey's writing is ponderous, but he covers the subject in great detail. Personally, I prefer Stewart's more amiable style, but he confines his comments to birds found between Hampshire and Kent."

"I will try Stewart, then. I've studied many of the west country birds myself."

Grayson stiffened as voices approached. "I must leave before someone sees us together." A raised hand forestalled her protest. "I know you do not expect a match this Season, but you must safeguard your reputation for the future."

Nodding a farewell, he grabbed a book and disappeared around a corner. Mary glanced through Stewart's book. Grayson was right. The style was quite readable and very informative. Only a dozen woodcuts were included, but the descriptions were precise.

She left Hatchard's a few minutes later. Her carriage would not return for half an hour, but she needed to visit the apothecary next door. Frannie would meet her there—she was running errands for Laura.

Grayson was standing at the curb, his head bowed as though in thought—or perhaps fighting dizziness. In the sunlight, his face was paper white.

She was opening her mouth to offer help when a cart driver whipped his horses into a gallop, careening past a carriage and around a flower cart. Then he aimed the team straight at Grayson.

Men shouted. Vehicles swerved to avoid collisions.

Grayson remained in a trance, seemingly oblivious to his danger.

In two frantic strides, Mary grabbed his arm and jerked him into the narrow passageway between Hatchard's and the apothecary. The cart thundered past, knocking an apple peddler into a horse, which bolted, dragging its teammate and a curricle with it. The tiger who'd been walking them raced behind, shouting.

Chaos filled the street. Horses whinnied. Curses vied with groans, wails, and hooves clattering over cobblestones. But the passageway remained an island of calm.

Grayson swayed, bumping the wall.

Mary stared at his white face. "Are you all right?"

"I'm bleeding."

His eyes remained on his wrist. Blood flowed from a gash, disappearing under his glove. The last vestige of color leeched from his face as his eyes rolled back.

Grabbing his chin, Mary forced his head up. He must be one of the unfortunates who could not handle the sight of blood. "Look at me, Grayson!"

He jumped.

"Keep your eyes on my face." Releasing him, she used

her handkerchief to wipe away as much blood as possible. "Where is your handkerchief?"

He fumbled in his pocket.

She tugged off his glove so she could bind his wrist, then replaced it, tucking the stained edge inside so the blood did not show. "Not quite the fashion, but it should do until your valet can look at it. I do not believe it will soak through. Now where is your carriage?"

"I walked from St. James's Square."

Gray stared at his wrist. No trace of blood remained. But relief quickly changed to chagrin. Having finally divulged his most hated weakness in public, he would never live down the ignominy.

"You must think me the veriest coward," he said, straightening so he no longer leaned against the wall. He glanced around, surprised to find himself in a narrow passageway.

"Not in the least. Blood affects many people adversely. Why blame you for something you cannot control?" She thrust her own handkerchief into her reticule. A package of books lay at her feet.

Should he explain? With most people, he would claim the lesser humiliation of dizziness from his illness. But Mary was different. When she'd touched his arm in the bookstore, her hands had sent ripples of pleasure to his groin. One reason he'd left so abruptly was his fear that she would note his reaction and start believing him a seducer of innocents.

Now he was again secluded with her. He ought to leave before they were spotted, but he had to make her understand. Something about Mary compelled confidences.

"My father—"

She looked up in surprise. "You cannot mean that he blames you."

He nodded. Discussing his father was hard, but he could not stop now. "His passions are hunting and shooting."

"Which you abhor."

He shrugged, as though the admission were easy. But even his friends did not understand his aversion to sport.

"So the tale that he kicked you out of the hunt was twisted."

"Very. I refused to ride with them, even as a youth. We argued often about it. In the end, I left." He didn't mention Rothmoor's determination to change his mind, his charges of cowardice, or his conclusion that Gray was less than a man. Rothmoor hadn't abandoned that suspicion until he heard exaggerated accounts of Gray's raking.

"Do you avoid hunting because the blood bothers you or because you hate killing other creatures?" asked Mary.

"Both."

"Which means you wouldn't hunt even without your blood problem. There is nothing wrong with that."

Gray stared, unable to believe his ears. He turned dizzy at the faintest hint of blood—had done so since childhood. He had disgraced his father by puking his guts out at his first kill, then fainting when presented with the fox tail. They'd carried him home on a litter like a swooning girl. Rothmoor had beaten him countless times, trying to turn him into a man. Yet no one had ever asked whether he would enjoy hunting if he could tolerate the kill.

"Do you wish to talk about it?" she asked softly, again laying that warm hand on his arm.

He led her to an alcove where they were out of sight of the street. The least he could do was protect her if anyone glanced this way, though it sounded like everyone was gawking at an accident. "What do you know about my father?"

"The Earl of Rothmoor never visits London. Supposedly he threw you out of the hunt for overriding the hounds. You responded by vowing to never set foot in the house again. But I cannot believe that is true."

"It is true that I vowed never to set foot in the house again," he admitted. "But my reasons had nothing to do with that particular argument. Rothmoor's passions are horses, hounds, and whor—hunting." He silently cursed himself for the stumble. "In his eyes, all gentlemen share those passions. My failure to join him in the field proves my cowardice. He blames my mother, of course. Her influence ruined me."

She turned you into a damned girl, Rothmoor had shouted during their final confrontation, his riding crop gashing the edge of a table. Gray had flinched, for it had too often gashed his flesh. *A mealy-mouthed, swooning girl. I'd hoped her influence would fade once she died, but it was too late. You will never be a man. My father would turn in his grave if he knew the earldom would end with a woman, as would every other Rothmoor. I never should have wed that lily-livered foreigner.*

Gray's hands tightened into fists.

"Fustian," she snorted indignantly, banishing his memories. "There is no shame in refusing to kill. Nor is there shame in hating bloodshed." She pulled his sleeve down to hide her makeshift bandage. "The fault rests with Rothmoor for ignoring your nature. The brute should be shot."

He nearly laughed. She understood. He wanted to pull her into his arms, but propriety forbade it.

"Have your valet check that when you return," she ordered. "Some salve would not be amiss. I doubt it needs stitching, but I may be wrong."

He wobbled, but shook his head clear. "Forgive me. I should not have forced my problems on you."

"You didn't. I was delighted to help. However, there are two things you need to know. The first is that you were so abstracted that you were nearly run down."

"What?"

"Run down, Lord Grayson. Smashed flat by a delivery cart. Fortunately, I hauled you out of the way." Her voice made light of the incident, but her cheeks had paled. "You should school yourself to ignore any potential injuries until it is safe to look."

"I owe you more than I thought," he managed through a new bout of dizziness. How fortunate that she was not prone to hysterics. But he found her competence puzzling. She had no trouble handling a crisis—she'd dragged a man twice her weight to safety without even dropping her parcel. So why did she consider herself inept and clumsy?

"You owe me nothing. Anyone would have done the same."

"I doubt it."

"We will not argue. More important than your near calamity is that it was no accident. The driver aimed his horses at you, and despite his claims to the contrary, they were under complete control."

"What?" He thrust his bandaged hand behind him, then stared at her. "What exactly happened? I recall little of the affair."

"Don't exaggerate." She glared.

"Very well. I remember nothing. Blood has that effect. Even if I remain conscious, my mind stops working."

"So I thought." She checked the passageway, but it remained empty. "When I left Hatchard's, you were standing on the curb, head bowed. I thought you were fighting another dizzy spell."

"It started with dizziness," he admitted. "I stumbled, fetching up against a carriage. When it lurched forward, something sliced my wrist. That is the last thing I remember until you forced my eyes up."

"You really should have stayed abed today, sir." Her tone scolded. "If you hope to survive, you must recover from one scrape before falling into the next."

"I will try," he said meekly. "Now continue your story."

"Before I could ask if you needed help, the cart driver whipped his team into a frenzy. Then he shouted that they were bolting. Vehicles scattered in all directions. He wove through the chaos, avoiding collisions, then aimed the team at you."

"But why?" Blood drained from his face. The situation had been more dangerous than he'd thought. Only her composure had saved him from yet another accident. Lady Luck had indeed abandoned him.

"No, she didn't," said Mary firmly. He must have spoken aloud. "Think, my lord. If not for Lady Luck, you would be dead by now. In the space of a week you have been set upon by a thief, nearly burned in your bed, poisoned, and attacked by a cart. Since this last was no accident, one must ask whether any of them were accidents. I suspect someone is trying to kill you."

"Impossible." He held his head in both hands. "While my reputation is tarnished, I am still received. I have no enemies." Yet he had felt those eyes more than once. And she didn't know he'd been drugged as well as beaten.

"Are you sure?" she demanded. "There must be someone who wishes you harm."

"Father would never abandon honor. Besides, he hates my cousin even more than he hates me." He bit off a curse. Where had that admission come from? No gentleman suspected his father of murder.

"What about your cousin?" asked Mary, relentless to the end. "I take it he is next in line for the title."

Gray shrugged. "He lives in Yorkshire and never comes to London. His estate is more prosperous than Rothmoor Park."

"Many men covet titles."

"Not Jamie."

"Is there trouble with your business? Rumor claims that you have amassed a fortune from it. Some might resent your success. Do any competitors take offense that someone of your expectations has bested them in their own field?"

"No." She was astute, though. She was asking the same questions Nick had posed. Perhaps he should examine the possibility more carefully. Peters had not enjoyed losing the contract to import Jamaican rum. Graves had recently lost two ships to a typhoon. Yet he could not imagine them blaming him. Nor could killing him help them recoup any losses. And his investors knew they made more with him in charge than with another.

"How about the girls who swear you ruined them? Lady Horseley claims nearly a dozen."

"She exaggerates. There were only the two I mentioned earlier. One is married. The other is dead. Granted, tempers led to threats at the time, but both matters were resolved long ago."

"Except for you," she murmured in defeat. She glanced around. "I must leave. My carriage will return shortly, and I still must visit the apothecary. Are you recovered enough to make it home?"

"Quite. Thank you for everything."

She nodded.

One thing was certain, he admitted as he bade her farewell. If she was correct—and he had no reason to doubt her word—then he had been a fool to ignore Nick's suspicions. Yet few men could accept that their life was in danger.

Mary's summary had been brutally honest, but he should have realized the truth days ago. He'd known the beating was deliberate. The eyes on his back had been enough to tip him off. The fire should have clinched it.

But he hadn't wanted to know. It hurt to be a target of so much hate. Now stubbornness had cost him nearly a week. There was no telling what the villain planned next. The incidents would not stop until he was dead.

Cursing, he headed for Justin's house in St. James's Square. This explained Bow Street's failure. He had hampered their efforts by employing different runners for each incident and not telling them about the other ones.

The rocket had probably been fired from a roof across the street—no one had looked up until the window broke. So the culprit must know how to aim the thing, at least over short distances. That boded ill if he had a second rocket. Thank God no one knew his current direction. He did not want attacks on Justin's town house.

But Mary had opened his eyes. If every attack was deliberate, then someone had poisoned the fish at Funston's—it had been stupid to stay there; the accommodations had deteriorated significantly in the last ten years. Perhaps the runner could find a witness among Funston's staff.

He turned into St. James's Square, walking faster than his weakened condition warranted. This would be a good night to remain in bed. A quick glance over his shoulder relieved one fear. No one had followed him. So presumably the culprit did not know where he was.

"Don't make assumptions," he murmured as he nipped past the door. How had the cart driver found him?

It was an uncomfortable thought. But with luck, he could avoid further attempts now that he knew the danger.

And he must thank Mary for today's rescue. Flowers would do, but definitely more than violets.

He frowned a moment, then nodded. His Daurian peonies would be blooming by now. He had several bushes in the hothouse at Shellcroft, along with dozens of other unusual plants his captains had collected from around the world. His groom could collect the best blossoms and be back by morning. It would give him time to decide how to sign the card.

Chapter Eight

The next day was Catherine's at-home day. Mary hated receiving calls, for there was no way to avoid notice, and the attention took its toll. Her most embarrassing mishaps had occurred in Catherine's drawing room—tactless replies, unintentional insults, dropping her cup in Lady Sefton's lap . . .

Fortunately Lady Sefton was the nicest of the Almack's patronesses, so her voucher remained safe. But each new incident increased her tension, making the next occasion even more difficult.

Laura did not help. After the teacup incident, she had demanded that Mary stay in her room so her clumsiness did not call censure on the entire family. Catherine had refused. Laura's tantrum had included scathing denunciations and prophesies of doom, but Catherine would not budge. So Mary was again seated on Catherine's left when Barhill announced the first caller.

Pasting a smile on her face, she kept a polite greeting on her lips and a few trite phrases in reserve with which to respond to questions. She hated gossip, but she'd discovered that an occasional encouraging response was all most ladies needed to keep talking. She was under no obligation to repeat anything they said.

Half an hour later, she finally relaxed. Conversation was dull today. No one had misbehaved last night. Blackthorn and Atwater had avoided each other. No fortunes had changed hands at the tables. And yesterday's accident on Piccadilly had caused little damage. So conversation centered on which matches were likely.

Mary's mind wandered to Laura's latest outburst.

They had been coming down to the drawing room when a late bouquet of flowers arrived. Not just flowers, but a dozen Daurian peonies, a variety so rare it took Mary a full minute to identify it. She'd only seen one watercolor of it—a very insipid watercolor, she now realized. Glossy dark green leaves were arranged to set off the blooms, whose fluted deep-rose petals surrounded a vibrant gold center. The variety had arrived in England only a dozen years earlier from somewhere deep in the Ottoman Empire.

Laura had squealed, grabbing the vase before the footman could object. But her face had twisted when she saw the card.

"It doesn't say who sent them," she said in bewilderment. The card was signed with a sketch of an owl.

"They aren't yours," said the footman, rescuing the vase before Laura could hurl it.

Laura turned the card over. "You!" She could not have been more shocked if the house had collapsed around her ears. "Who would send *you* flowers?"

"No one important," said Mary soothingly. "Merely a fellow bird-lover."

"But who? And why do I know nothing about him? I cannot believe anyone is so rude that he refuses to sign his name."

Mary heard the curiosity—and the anger. The idea that someone could enjoy Mary's company shocked her. "But he did sign," she countered, plucking Grayson's owl from Laura's hand. As the footman passed her the vase, she spotted the words *from my hothouse, with thanks* worked into the owl's feathers. Warmth blossomed in her chest.

"But who is he?" repeated Laura.

"No one you know. We chatted in the bookstore yesterday about birds found along the Kentish coast."

"But—"

"If you will excuse me, I must put these away before our callers arrive."

Now Mary admitted that Laura's reaction had hurt. Catherine or any of her brothers would have been pleased to learn that she had found a friend, and they

would have shared her enjoyment of the flowers. But
Laura had felt nothing but anger—furious anger. Perhaps
even a flash of jealousy.

Laura felt little loyalty to her siblings. The only person
she cared about was Laura. Not only did she expect all
the attention, all the adulation, and all the affection, but
she would have been just as disgruntled if Mary had
received a posy of weeds from her eighty-year-old friend
Mr. Fester. An exotic bouquet was too much.

But the drawing room was no place to brood. Mary
wrenched her attention back to Lady Marchgate's description of Atwater's attack on a beggar in Covent Garden. Society was shocked, for the incident did not fit
Atwater's saintly reputation. He was extremely popular
with the dowagers, yet Mary couldn't like the man. Thus
she was relieved when the subject changed.

"What is Lady Wharburton doing for her masquerade
this year?" asked Lady Cunningham.

"Nobody knows." Lady Marchgate shook her head.
"You know she never offers a hint."

"Remember the year she turned her ballroom into a
medieval castle?" asked Lady Horseley.

"And her Mount Olympus?"

"That Egyptian temple was shocking," claimed Miss
Evans.

"You didn't think so at the time," countered Lady
Cunningham.

Mary listened in astonishment as callers described fan-
tastic decorations from past Seasons. By the time the first
callers left, anticipation for the event was high. Then
Lady Wilkins arrived.

"Have you heard about Mr. Griffin?" she demanded
the moment Catherine handed her a cup.

"Only that he left the Sheffield ball in a rage because
Lord Bankhead declined to play cards."

"Does Bankhead suspect Griffin's play?" asked Lady
Marchgate, raising a brow.

"I doubt it." Lady Cunningham shook her head. "Bankhead rarely games—which Griffin certainly knows."

"You haven't heard." Lady Wilkins looked like a cat

who had been in the cream. "Griffin was arrested last night."

"Thank God," murmured Mary. The moment the words were out, she blushed furiously.

Lady Marchgate glared, then turned back to Lady Wilkins. The action was not quite a cut, but Mary felt like creeping into a corner. She'd been doing so well today.

"Why?" demanded Lady Cunningham.

"He tried to force himself on an innocent at Long's Hotel."

"Is that what the girl claims?" scoffed Mrs. Ware. "Everyone knows he enjoys the maids, and even a governess or two, but he never uses force. Doesn't need to."

"This wasn't a servant." Lady Wilkins slowly sipped her tea. "She is a doctor's daughter. Barely fifteen."

Likes country innocents of about fourteen . . . Mary shivered.

"But why an arrest?" demanded Lady Marchgate. "If she was innocent, he will do the honorable thing. If she isn't, then what is the fuss? And who would arrest him? The law never denounces a rake for following his urges. No matter what face he shows society, we all know Griffin is a rake."

Murmured agreement swept the room.

Lady Wilkins smiled. "The actual charges are destruction of hotel property, burglary, and assault on a Bow Street runner." Two ladies gasped. "The girl had accompanied her father to town—he is studying with Dr. McClarren. They were returning from the theater when a man in the taproom suffered an apoplexy. The doctor rushed to help, sending his daughter up to their rooms. Griffin followed, broke the lock on her door, then tried to force her. A Bow Street runner heard her screams and intervened."

A dozen voices spoke at once. Lady Wilkins's credit immediately soared.

Mary remained silent. None of her rehearsed responses was suitable for learning that an acquaintance—however unwanted—had been arrested. Her immediate reaction was relief, but she'd already fallen under censure for expressing it.

"Did you know his penchant for forcing young girls?" asked Lady Marchgate under the rising swell of voices.

"I had heard he preferred them, but no one mentioned force." Again she blushed. "I think his actions reprehensible."

"As do we all." A knowing eye pierced hers. "But you knew he was trouble."

"N-not exactly." She struggled for the right words. "He is a man who cares less for society's strictures than for his own d-desires. I didn't like him even before he tried to take me outside during Lady Debenham's b-ball. He was furious that I eluded him."

"You are relieved that he will no longer pursue you."

"Forgive me, my lady. I did not intend to say that aloud."

Lady Marchgate nodded. Lady Wilkins was repeating her tale for new arrivals.

When Catherine rose to escort Lady Westlake and Lady Cunningham out—they were anxious to spread the news—Laura leaned across her empty chair. "What a pity that the only man who tolerates your company turned out to be a cad." Her smile contained more than a little malice, probably because she was still seething over the peonies. "I wonder why you appeal to him. It couldn't be looks or conversation. Perhaps he likes following you into dark corners. Such a graceless habit invites liberties. Has he partaken often?"

Mary nearly choked, but pain was as strong as fury. How could Laura vent her pique in front of so many of society's leaders? Even if they could not hear the words, Laura's expressions radiated fury.

Catherine returned.

Mary tried to keep a social mask in place as a new thought occurred. Maybe it wasn't entirely the peonies that had overset Laura. Had she schemed with Griffin to seduce the unwanted sister, forcing her back to the country in disgrace? Laura had always blamed her for every setback—like the time Kevin Fields purchased colors and left without bidding Laura farewell. Laura had accused Mary of driving him away.

Perhaps this outburst resulted from Laura's growing disillusionment with London. It did not offer the excitement Laura had expected. Her court was large, but no one had made a formal offer. Mary not only remained in town, she'd acquired a secret admirer. The final straw had been learning that Griffin could no longer annoy her.

Or perhaps it was because Grayson was out of reach.

Mary bit back a sigh. Maybe she should abandon society and pursue her own interests. If her presence was driving Laura to unladylike outbursts, then she must ask Blake to let her attend the soirees she preferred. At the very least it would keep Laura from learning who had sent the flowers.

Ironically, Laura was responsible for her friendship with Grayson. If she hadn't encouraged Griffin, Mary would not have been behind that potted palm. Nor would she have been in Oxbridge's library.

Which means Grayson would be dead, her dreamer pointed out

Mary jerked her thoughts back to the drawing room, then groaned. Ladies Marchgate and Horseley were staring coldly at Laura. They must have overheard her remarks.

No matter how much she longed to wring Laura's neck, Mary could not allow her to shame the family. Striving to deflect their attention, she turned to Lady Marchgate. It was the first time she had initiated a drawing room conversation since arriving in London.

You can do it, she reminded herself. *Just relax. You saved Grayson from harm without tripping, and you never stammer with him.* The realization loosened her tension. Taking a deep breath, she spoke slowly. "Lord Hartford thinks I should wear green rather than white," she confided, naming Lady Marchgate's eldest son. "I know that he is renowned for his fashion sense, but I wanted to consult you before making changes. It is not my wish to play the peacock."

"You would rather appear demure." Lady Marchgate

nodded. "Quite a proper attitude, and a welcome relief from Very Forward Girls and their Selfish Plots." She cast a fulminating glance at Laura. "But too much modesty can seem dowdy. In your case, white turns your face sallow. Green would be a better choice, or perhaps blue." She raised her arm to bring her green shawl closer. "No, Hartford is right. Definitely green. It brings out a touch of green in your eyes that is quite intriguing."

"Thank you, my lady. Your confirmation is most welcome." She stifled a sigh. She must now acquire a green gown. But there was little she could do about it. Hartford was even more revered than Brummell when it came to ladies' clothing. That he had sought her out with his gentle suggestion was an honor.

Laura's smile was forced. Too late Mary remembered that Hartford had ignored Laura's attempts to attract him. Not that Laura wanted him. She thought his lisp ridiculous, his manners effeminate, and his interest in decorating and women's fashion suspect.

Now Laura gave in and glared. "Again you've shamed the family," she snapped. "Your taste is so bad that even the gentlemen are goaded to fix it."

"What an odd complaint," said Lady Marchgate coldly. "Hartford's advice is sought by the highest in the land, but he bestows it only on those he deems worthy."

"As it happens, I heard his comments last evening," added Lady Horseley. "He commended Miss Mary for knowing that simple lines suit her better than ruffles, flounces, and excessive ornamentation." She cast a disparaging look at Laura's gown. "His only suggestion concerned color."

Even Laura understood the message. She blanched. Two of society's most powerful matrons were now implacable enemies.

The ladies left, making room for more callers. The rest of the day passed smoothly with Laura as a pattern card of propriety. But Catherine had noted Lady Horseley's set-down. The moment the last guest left, she exploded.

"That was a despicable scene, Laura. Malicious, childish, and unworthy of a lady. I won't tolerate spite." Mary tried to leave, but Catherine motioned her to stay. "You've no cause for jealousy."

"Jealousy?" Laura's face purpled. "Why would I be jealous of her?"

"Do you need a reason for your megrims?" demanded Catherine. "You may think me unaware of your tantrums, but you are wrong. It was a mistake to treat you like a adult capable of conducting your own business. I should have stayed close at hand every minute to prevent trouble. You have a wonderful advantage, Laura. Your face draws immediate attention. With adherence to manners, you could become the darling of society. Instead, you scheme to ruin those around you. I've had enough of your selfish arrogance, as have others. Lady Marchgate was displeased, and Lady Horseley would gladly flay you after today's demonstration. Either can ruin you."

"Absurd," said Laura with a snort. "No one will blame me for telling the truth. My court grows larger every day."

"Enough," snapped Catherine. "Most of your court are preening puppies who won't think about marriage for many years. The ones ready to set up their nurseries demand more than a pretty face. They want a wife they can trust, who will cause them no distress. I don't know how you reached the advanced age of two-and-twenty without learning that a lady never reveals irritation in the drawing room, and that the world rarely arranges itself to suit her desires. Reputations can change in an instant, and often do. Where was your vaunted credit when Mr. Rankin turned against us last year?"

"That had nothing to do with me."

"Of course not. You were entirely blameless. Yet for nearly a fortnight, everyone in Exeter considered you a whore."

Laura gasped.

"Yes, a whore. Never mind that they'd doted on you for years. One sordid rumor, and they turned their backs. If not for Blake, you would still be an outcast. So do not underestimate the power of rumor. And do not prattle to me of truth. The only truth that matters is what people choose to believe. And right now what they choose to believe is that you are a vindictive harpy seeking to destroy your own sister out of misguided spite."

Laura sputtered, but Catherine had not finished. "How long do you think your credit would last if someone repeats those old lies in town? Do not think it impossible. Many people heard echoes of the tales at the time. They could be revived in an instant if anyone felt irritated enough to do so. And Lady Horseley was certainly irritated when she left. I believe her next call was on Lady Beatrice." Lady Beatrice lived only two doors away.

Laura burst into tears. "I am sorry, Catherine. I don't know what came over me. But it won't happen again."

Mary didn't believe her, escaping to the window during the subsequent exchange of apologies. She wished she could leave, but she dared not try. Catherine would chastise her as soon as she finished with Laura. And rightly so. She had goaded Laura into making those cutting remarks by allowing Lady Marchgate to see her own disgust with Mr. Griffin.

But she was wrong. Once Catherine had soothed Laura's distress and dismissed her, she demanded that Mary visit the modiste in the morning and order at least three new gowns. Blake would cover the expense. But Mary could not insult Hartford by ignoring his advice.

Mary finally reached her room, torn between embarrassment and fury. She dreaded the Cunningham ball this evening. Not only would she have to face Lady Marchgate again, but she had no idea what Laura would do. Had those tears been genuine, or would she plot some new revenge?

Two hours later, a footman pounded on Laura's door. When she tried to dismiss him, he ordered her to Blake's study.

Mary cursed. Catherine must have told him about the at-home. But his criticism atop everything else would make Laura worse. Heaven only knew what she would do.

The study shared a wall with Mary's bedchamber. At one time, the two rooms must have been one, for the wall was the thinnest in the house. Normally that did not matter—Blake rarely conducted business there—but today was different.

"I have never been so embarrassed in my life," he snarled the moment the door closed. Perhaps he did not realize how thin the wall was. "Lady Marchgate was so incensed by what she calls your malicious attack on Mary that she dispatched a letter to me at my club."

"She exaggerates. I merely expressed sympathy because her only beau was arrested last night."

"Do not twist the truth with me," he snapped. "Catherine heard every word you said—and the tone, as well. I am through with your arrogance. You care nothing—"

Mary tried to ignore him, moving to the far window and concentrating on a book. But Laura shouted that the tale was a lie. Blake questioned her sanity, swearing that she was incapable of behaving like a lady. Something crashed against the wall. He threatened to send her back to Seabrook Manor. Laura screamed that it was Mary's fault. Everything was Mary's fault. Mary was scheming to ruin Laura's Season because she hated Laura's beauty. Hated the competition. Hated—

Mary pulled a pillow over her head, covered her ears, and tried humming loudly. But the voices still buzzed in her ears.

A quarter hour later Laura fled the study, slamming the door behind her.

"Dear Lord," Mary whispered. They had to leave in an hour. Laura would never calm down in time, and she had a long history of outrageous behavior when furious.

She wished she could stay home. Eighteen months ago public scorn had pushed Laura into compromising Blake. Tonight was sure to be embarrassing, though at least Grayson was out of reach.

Her eyes drifted to his peonies.

Mary slipped unnoticed into an empty antechamber, glad to escape for a few minutes. The ball was every bit as nerve-wracking as she had feared. Laura was flirting with every man in the room, from the greenest cub to

old Lord Delwyn. She had demanded that Mr. Fitzhugh
dance with her, despite knowing he was a scoundrel.

Blake's scold had only been the beginning. Lady
Marchgate had cut Laura the moment she arrived. Then
Lady Horseley had accosted two of her admirers and
sent them away. And they weren't the only defectors.
Two others now hovered near Miss Harfield. Several
were spending the night elsewhere, probably waiting
until they knew the outcome of this contretemps.

The final outrage occurred when Mr. Larkin and Sir
William Burney asked Mary to dance. It didn't matter
that Laura had already awarded those sets. Nor did it
matter that Mary had danced with both of them previously. Laura considered the offers personal insults.

Mary had cried craven and left the ballroom.

Now she settled near the window and pulled out her
sketchpad. Two lamps burned softly on the mantel, and
the draperies stood open to the terrace, providing just
enough light for drawing. The seductive dimness soothed
her nerves.

She had yet to manage a satisfactory sketch of Grayson. The latest attempt depicted him as a mouse at the
mercy of a cat resembling Lady Horseley. Yet he was
not just a victim of unkind tongues. Another sketch
showed him as a border collie protecting lambs from a
shadowy wolf. A panther. An eagle. A wise old owl.

Nothing.

Again she reviewed what she knew of him, searching
for inspiration.

At age eighteen, he had been one of London's wilder
rakes—and one of the least discreet, or so gossip claimed.
Mary suspected the fight with his father had prompted
that wildness. Rothmoor had probably questioned his
masculinity. What better way to prove him wrong than
to flaunt an endless parade of bed partners? But Grayson
had soon settled into the accepted youthful indiscretions,
abandoning opera dancers for a succession of increasingly expensive mistresses as his finances improved. No
matrons were linked with him, and no one claimed he
had seduced maidens until Miss Irwin.

Lady Debenham swore that Lady Rothmoor had exerted considerable influence on Grayson. She'd been French, the daughter of a duke. The horrors that followed the revolution in her homeland had spawned a deep-seated aversion to killing that she passed on to her son. At least her own death had been bloodless—a fall on the stairs. But Grayson had discovered the body. He'd been twelve.

Mary shook her head as her pencil sketched his hand. Binding his wound had imprinted it on her mind. Warm. Powerful. Yet gentle as it had stroked a terrified dog. Many times it had returned in imagination, sifting her hair, caressing her body, teasing her until she yearned for more. Tonight was no different. She shifted in the chair, uncomfortably aware of heat growing between her legs and of throbbing in her breasts. Knowing she should not encourage such thoughts, she forced her mind back to Grayson. He was a daily topic of conversation.

The first Lord Rothmoor, who had acquired the title from Charles II, had been a cosmopolitan man equally at home in court, with scholars, and on his estate. Lady Beatrice's grandmother had known him well, so Lady Beatrice had heard many tales about his love of the arts, his patronage of artists and musicians, his role as a privy counselor, and his curiosity about anything mechanical. Grayson seemed much like that forebear.

The third earl had left court after a falling-out with George I, returning to his Yorkshire estate. The fourth and fifth earls stayed there, venturing away only to make a truncated grand tour to relatives in France. Both had married French cousins before returning home. Thus the current earl didn't understand Grayson's interest in London.

Picking up the pencil, she sketched a dozen trees looming over a sleeping kitten, branches stretched out to gouge it in the eye.

Still not good enough.

Gray skirted the edges of Lady Cunningham's ballroom, exchanging pleasantries with friends and accepting congratulations on his recovery. Some sounded insincere, but none were overly hostile—not that he expected to find his enemy here. He'd never felt the eyes indoors, so he'd concluded that the man was either an unscrupulous competitor hoping to take over his company, or a mad scientist seeking revenge because Gray had refused to fund him. Unfortunately, he could not name a likely candidate for either role.

He avoided prolonged conversation, for his immediate goal was the door, which seemed as distant as China. Attending this ball had been a bad idea. Nick was not here, nor was Justin. Unfortunately, Miss Seabrook was.

"Damnation," he mumbled, smiling at Lady Debenham.

The chit had accosted him the moment he'd entered the ballroom. "I am delighted that you are over your ordeal, Lord Grayson," she'd cooed, fluttering her eyes as she pressed against his side. "It must have been terribly painful."

"Who the devil are you?" he'd blurted, shocked at her behavior. Even Mary's warning had not prepared him for this. Nobody was this forward.

"You are so droll." Her smile made his skin crawl. "Dance with me. I've this set free."

"I never dance without a proper introduction," he said firmly. "Now run along and find your governess. You shouldn't leave the schoolroom until you master basic manners."

She'd blanched but ignored his irritation. Grabbing his arm, she'd moved closer than ever. "Then walk with me, my lord. Were you quite deathly ill?"

"No," he had said dampeningly, pushing her far enough away that their bodies no longer touched. "I have been at my office."

Again she flashed a brilliant smile. "You must describe your business, sir. Shipping, isn't it? It sounds fascinating. We can talk more easily in the garden where it isn't so noisy."

He'd stopped so abruptly she stumbled. "I will not be responsible for ruining you," he swore, "though your own bad manners are likely to accomplish that without my help. Nor will I allow you to ignore the gentleman to whom you promised this set."

"But *you* are that gentleman, my lord." Again her lashes fluttered.

"I am not." Jerking free of her grip, he cut her dead, then stalked away.

Amazingly, Lady Marchgate smiled, nodding civilly as he passed. It was the first sign of approval she'd offered in three years. Something must have happened since he'd seen Mary in Hatchard's yesterday. She would have warned him if his danger had increased.

Now his mind remained on the Seabrook sisters even as he greeted Lord Wigby. Mary had seen enough scandal. She didn't deserve more, which stopped him from denouncing Laura to the world. But would denunciation cause a scandal? No one seemed to care that he'd just cut her dead.

"The chit is far too arrogant," announced Wigby, nodding toward Miss Seabrook. "Treats her family like servants, especially her sister."

Gray winced.

"And she spreads exaggerated tales about anyone she considers a rival," added Lord Edward Broadburn, joining them. "She swore Lady Eleanor Mannering used to sneak away from school—which we all know is untrue. Lady Marchgate is furious with her."

That explained the lady's smile, but Lord Edward hadn't heard the actual exchange, and Gray's own experiences made him wary of accepting gossip.

The moment Miss Seabrook stepped into a set with young Ingram, Gray headed for the door.

Griffin's arrest was the other topic on everyone's lips. The situation was not as tidy as Gray would have liked, but it would do. The runner had reached the room just as Griffin tore the girl's gown, breaking her necklace in the process. Since the jewelry was still in his hand, they were charging him with theft. And since the doctor was distantly connected to a duke, Griffin would pay. Those pearls would send him to Botany Bay for twenty years.

So far no one had thought to ask what a runner had

been doing in that hotel corridor. He hoped no one ever did. But Mary need no longer fear being trapped alone by a scoundrel. He wanted to tell her the story, but she wasn't in the ballroom—he'd already looked behind palms and pillars. She was probably in the retiring room again. Laura was attracting censure tonight. Mary would have fled the embarrassment.

He was beginning to understand her. Mary was intelligent, sensible, and highly competent, but she undervalued herself badly, particularly in social situations. Her sister had made sure of that, calling her plain, clumsy, and inept so often that Mary now believed it. Thus she couldn't see how her eyes sparkled, how the freckles across her shoulders drew the eye unerringly to the swell of her bosom, how animation turned her face beautiful. Somehow he must convince her of that truth. She deserved the happiness her sister had denied her.

White's would be his safest retreat this evening. He cast one last glance over his shoulder as he reached the stairs, then cursed. Though the set was still in progress, Laura had abandoned Ingram, probably claiming a torn hem. She was closing on him fast.

Gray bolted toward the street, but ducked behind a statue of Zeus the moment he cleared the ballroom doorway. Leaving by the front door would be too slow—waiting while a footman fetched his greatcoat, then waiting again while a groom summoned his carriage. She would arrive long before his coachman. He could cause a scene that would insult her unforgivably, but for Mary's sake, he would rather not.

Several antechambers lay in the other direction. When three gentlemen momentarily screened him from view, he slipped into the first and headed for the window overlooking the terrace. He could walk to White's, then send a servant for his greatcoat and carriage.

But he'd crossed only half the room when the door burst open behind him.

Furious, he turned to face her. "What the devil do you think you are doing?" he demanded.

"Talking to you. I know you have hesitated to greet

me because you feared your reputation would tarnish mine, but that is silly. My credit is high enough to improve yours."

"You belong in Bedlam," he began, then cursed himself for arguing with a madwoman. "Leave this room at once."

But footsteps approached in the hallway. She must have been expecting them, for before he could react, she threw herself against him, shouting, "We are discovered, my love."

Chapter Nine

Gray shoved Laura into a chair, so angry he could barely see. "You are the most vulgar hoyden I have ever met," he hissed. "And I've met plenty."

She ignored him. "Why didn't you close the door?" she wailed as Lady Debenham and Lady Horseley glared through the opening. "You should know better than to kiss me where we might be seen."

"Don't play the injured innocent with me, trollop," demanded Gray. "Even that scheming Miss Turner had better manners than you. I would welcome ostracism rather than touch you."

"My lord—" began Laura, but another voice interrupted.

"For shame, Laura," snapped Mary, stepping from the shadows. "Rockhurst will be appalled that you insisted on attending tonight. You know you must stay in bed on days you suffer megrims. They cause delusions that distort your judgment."

Laura leaped up, anger stripping her face of beauty. "Get out! How dare you interfere in my affairs? Do you seriously believe you can steal Grayson for yourself?"

Gray shook off his paralysis and stepped between the sisters. A crowd was gathering in the hallway, craning to see past the blockade formed by Ladies Horseley and Debenham. But he no longer cared what they thought. If Laura wanted a scene, he would provide it.

"Your affairs don't include me. We have never even been introduced, for which I am eternally grateful. I despise spoiled children."

"How dare you deny—"

"Silence! I know all about your absurd fantasies and

selfish plots. And I know this is not the first time you have stooped to dishonor. You like to pretend that every man loves you, and you actually believe your imaginary courtships. That is the mark of a madwoman."

"Ma—"

"Quite mad. You know even less about me than about your previous victims, for the rumors attached to my name are false. But even if every word were true, we would not suit. I would leave the country rather than tie myself to a harpy, so take your lies and vulgarities somewhere else."

"And let you force yourself on my sister? Never!" But her voice held panic. Having guaranteed an audience, she had no place to hide.

"You need rest, Laura," said Mary quietly.

"So I should just walk out and leave you together. Do you think I am that foolish?"

"You are overset." Mary tried to lead her to the door. "We must put you to bed and call a physician at once. He will give you a tonic to quiet your nerves. By morning this will all be a bad dream."

But Laura was past caring. She knocked Mary down, cracking her head against a table. "You were waiting for him, weren't you? An assignation. A filthy, despicable assignation. Yet you dare criticize me."

"We all dare," snapped Lady Horseley, her hands planted firmly on her hips as she surged into the room. "I watched that appalling exhibition in the ballroom. Grayson is right, for once in his misbegotten life. Only a madwoman would chase a man who cuts her dead. Not that you don't deserve each other. That murdering beast should have been hanged three years ago."

"So should you!" snapped Laura, abandoning all semblance of control. "I've never met such a poisoned-tongued nosy Parker in my life. Why anyone tolerates you is beyond comprehension."

Mary moaned in mortification.

"Keep your filthy tongue between your teeth," snarled Gray, fisting both hands to keep them off her neck. "If you don't want to spend your life locked in an attic, you'd best be quiet. You know nothing about me, or Lady Horseley, or even your sister. She is more a lady than you can ever be. Now take your jealousy and bad temper somewhere else."

Laura opened her mouth, but shut it without a word when she saw Rockhurst fighting his way through the growing crowd in the hallway.

Gray helped Mary to her feet, drawing her against his side in protection. "Yes, Mary and I had an assignation—arranged by Lord Rockhurst when I offered for her this afternoon." He caught the earl's eye, praying the man would cover the lie. Between gentlemen, his words constituted a vow to do right by Mary, who had sacrificed her reputation to save him from her sister's scheming. But he had no idea whether Rockhurst considered him a gentleman.

Rockhurst nodded as Lady Debenham stepped aside to let him in. Motioning Lady Horseley back into the hallway, he glared at Laura. "I warned you I would no longer tolerate your antics. If you haven't received an offer, it is because few gentlemen wish to wed a spiteful child. Now enough of your tantrums. It is time you retired."

"But why would you allow a man of his reputation to address her?" Laura demanded.

"Why did you throw yourself at me?" growled Gray, low enough that the watchers could not hear. "Have you run out of bed partners?"

Laura blanched.

Rockhurst gripped Laura by the arm. "You of all people should know that gossip often lies." His eyes held Lady Horseley's before he turned to Gray. "My apologies for not controlling her, Grayson. I was across the room when she left, but I should have expected her to turn this into a farce. She has never accepted other people's fortune gracefully, particularly Mary's." Without waiting for a reply, he twisted Laura's arm behind her and propelled her toward the door. "You successfully hid your other compromise attempts, Laura, and few suspect your penchant for starting scurrilous stories about your rivals. But this escapade will be impossible to hide. You are ruined, and entirely through your own efforts."

The door closed firmly behind them.

Gray stared, trying to understand what had just happened. "Did he just declare me innocent?" he asked aloud. Rockhurst knew him only by sight, being several years older and from a different school.

"He had to do something to atone for Laura's disgrace. But he has long decried injustice and worked to right old wrongs, so you need only explain matters to win his support." She pulled out of his grasp and walked to the fireplace.

"Are you cold?" he asked, shaken. Her face was stark white.

"A little. Laura's tantrums usually have that effect. Why did I not stay in the ballroom?"

He flinched to see tears on her lashes. "I am very glad you were here, my dear, though I should apologize for bursting in without warning. I did not know the room was occupied."

"You don't understand." She moved restlessly to draw the drapes, then shove her sketchpad into her reticule. "I knew she was in a fey humor tonight. I seemed to be making her worse, so I left. But had I been there, I could have kept her from following you."

"I doubt it. She abandoned Ingram in the middle of a set. What put her in a fey humor?"

Mary returned to the fire. "Your flowers, to start with. I love them, by the way. Thank you. But Laura has never received anything half so exotic."

"So she turned on you?"

She shrugged.

"Is that why she accosted me tonight?"

"No. She doesn't know who sent them." Her gaze settled on her hands. "But because they put her in a temper, she spoke without thinking and infuriated Lady Marchgate, who then complained to Blake. He read her the riot act and threatened to send her home—a mistake he doesn't usually make, but he was also in a temper because Lady Marchgate's complaint reached him at his club. So Laura's composure was ruffled even before half her court abandoned her."

"Rumors claim she abused you in public." His fists again clenched.

"It wasn't quite that bad. Merely a few unkind words, but the drawing room was crowded, and Lady Marchgate did not hide her disgust. Nor did Lady Horseley." She hugged herself. "Drat her! I warned her that diamonds fall farther and faster than the rest of us, but she thinks herself invulnerable. So she never watches her tongue. Several people alluded to the incident this evening, and not kindly, so I suspect it has already been exaggerated. Two of her former admirers asked me to dance. That's when I left. I'll not be used to punish her. Since she refuses to believe that most men flirt because it is fashionable, she always blames me for any defections."

"Hence her tantrum when she realized you were here before we arrived. Thank God you were. I would much rather wed you than accept blame for ruining another hoyden."

He would do his best to make her happy. It was his fault she was in this pickle. If he'd paid attention, he'd have known the room was in use. Laura's reputation had been suspect even before this incident, so he could probably have repudiated her without hurting himself, even with Lady Horseley in the audience. But Mary was another matter. He could not embroil her in another scandal. All he could do was fulfill enough of her dreams that she might someday forgive him for tying her to a man she did not love.

Mary silently paced the room as his words echoed hollowly in her head. It was clear she was the lesser of two very great evils. Grayson was honorable enough to protect her and make the best of the bargain. And she had no choice but to agree.

Guilt engulfed her when she identified her light-headedness as joy. He was a wonderful man—kind, sensitive, and eminently capable. But marrying her would be a disaster, not a blessing. He deserved so much better. If she really cared, she would find a way to free him.

But she couldn't think. Everything had happened too fast. Her attempt to smooth over the situation had failed.

In retrospect, it had been too late to blame this on a fit of megrims. Too many people had witnessed Laura's dishonor, and it seemed she had already made a cake of herself in the ballroom. How could the girl have been so stupid?

But she could address that later. Now she must help Grayson. She was the worst possible wife for him. Besides being a laughingstock on her own account, he could never look at her without recalling Laura's perfidy. And marrying her would make Laura a permanent part of his life. Having destroyed herself so thoroughly, Laura would always be around, if not at Rockburn, then at Seabrook.

"Is there no choice?" she asked, then cursed her trembling voice.

"No, my dear. These are not the circumstances you deserve, but we should deal quite well together."

"But you c-cannot want a wife who draws scowls wherever she goes," she stammered. "I have no g-graces and am not an accomplished hostess."

"Enough, Mary." He caught her hands in his. "That is your sister speaking. She has criticized you from the moment she first looked into a mirror. No, don't contradict me," he added, covering her mouth with a gentle finger. "She probably knew from childhood that you embodied all the virtues she lacked. I've yet to meet a beauty who could tolerate competition, and she is too selfish to have hidden her anger. Her criticism prevented you from trying, forcing you to hover on the fringes of life instead of embracing it. But you can manage anything you choose. If you wish to be a hostess, then learn. Or ignore society completely if you prefer. What matters to me is your kindness, your sense, your intelligence, and the way you've believed in me from the moment we met. We are already friends, are we not?"

She nodded. And she knew he was right—there came that spurt of joy again. If he and Laura had entered the room together, things might have been different. But at least two ladies knew Laura had found them alone. And one of those was Lady Horseley, who had pilloried Grayson for years. Refusing his offer would convince society that she thought him venal. Or perhaps they would assume he had made no offer. Either way, his reputation would be sunk without a trace. He would never again be welcomed in polite circles.

"Very well, my lord. I will endeavor to make you an acceptable wife, though God knows how. I have never been comfortable in society and don't see that changing. Particularly after this."

"Forgive me, Mary—I may call you that?"

She nodded.

"And you must call me Gray. I know you hoped to wed for love and that taking on a tarnished viscount is far from what you had in mind, but I will try to make you happy."

"I understand. And at least we begin as friends. That is more than many couples have." She shivered.

He pulled her against him, but gently, soothing her as he had soothed that frightened dog. His hand stroked slowly down her spine, cradling her against him.

She stood quietly, allowing only one arm to creep around his waist, though she longed to squeeze closer. She was so cold. But embracing him would remind him of Laura and of how helplessly trapped he was. It would also recall memories of Miss Irwin and Miss Turner, whose pursuit had hurt him so badly. He might even think she had somehow forced him into this betrothal.

But restraining herself was difficult. His warmth beckoned, as did his hard body. Too many nights she had awakened from dreams of him, tingling from head to toe. Now her heart soared, forcing an admission that she had wanted him from the beginning—another secret she could never reveal. Gray had suffered too much. She could not become another hoyden expecting him to make her dreams come true.

"I will see that you are happy," he repeated, tilting her head so he could see her eyes.

She smiled. "And I will do likewise."

"We are agreed, then." He lowered his head to seal their bargain.

Mary had never been kissed, not even by a relative.

The electricity sizzling from his lips surprised her so much that she gasped, opening her mouth. He deepened the assault, tasting her thoroughly.

Heat exploded, melting her knees until she had to cling to keep from falling. If she had known what kisses were like, she might have sympathized more with Laura. Or was this reaction unusual? Perhaps Gray's rakish experiences had taught him how to produce effects unknown to others. Certainly the conversations she had overheard about marriage duties had never mentioned this.

She moaned as he pulled her against him, scrambling her wits until she could barely think. His hands cupped her bottom to lift her closer yet. She hardly realized that he'd moved until he collapsed on a couch with her in his lap.

"Your skin is so soft," he murmured huskily, trailing kisses along her jaw until he reached her ear. Drawing the lobe into his mouth, he nipped it.

"Mmmm." She touched his cheek, surprised to find rough nubs sprinkled along the jawline. Hairs. Yet the hair on his head was as soft as hers, so why did this feel coarse? She slid her hand back and forth to test the different textures, but was distracted when the tip of her breast brushed his arm, exploding into more new sensations. She moaned again, then froze.

Dear Lord! She was no better than Laura, flinging herself at a near stranger as wantonly as if she yearned to consummate their union here and now. How could he feel anything but disgust for her after this?

This was not the time or place for lovemaking. There had been enough scandal for one night. Courting more could ruin them both.

"We had best return to the ballroom, Gray," she said, surprised that her voice was husky. "Not that I object to your kisses—they are quite remarkable. But people will be watching for us."

He sighed. "You are right, as usual. Very well, my dear. We must do our duty." He frowned. "Is your sister likely to be there?"

"No. Blake will send her home. He was furious enough

that he might send her back to Seabrook. That was one of his threats this afternoon."

"He would be better off keeping her here where she can suffer the consequences of her actions. She might learn more."

"And embarrass us all."

"She can no longer harm us, Mary. Any attempt to retaliate will redound on her. By morning, there won't be a soul in London who believes a word she says. Rockhurst's support will prevent anyone from blaming us. But we can discuss that later. There is one more piece of business before we face the world." His arm tightened.

"What is that?" Her hand slid beneath his coat, stroking his shoulder. As his manhood twitched, she stilled.

"No need to stop," he said, kissing her lightly on the nose. "I enjoy your touch. But we must set a wedding date."

"That is hardly usual this early in a betrothal."

"Rockhurst cloaked us in propriety, but there is no denying this situation is irregular. We needn't wed instantly, but I would like to do so before the Season ends. Unfortunately, I have no town house. Albany does not permit ladies, and I have no wish to share a roof with your sister, even for a week, so we will have to live at Shellcroft in the beginning. But I've business matters to conclude first, and we need time to quell any gossip. Three weeks should suffice."

"That sounds perfect." She had feared he would suggest waiting until summer. She didn't want to share a roof with Laura, either. After tonight's fiasco, she never wanted to see Laura again. But she could tolerate three more weeks. And an early wedding should prevent speculation that he meant to cry off once the Season ended.

"To the future," he murmured, kissing her again.

Only snatches of the ball remained in Mary's mind afterward. The moment she and Gray appeared at the top of the stairs, the music ceased, drawing every eye to the door. A hush settled over the room, broken only by Lord Harding's querulous voice demanding to know what was happening.

Blake was waiting in the doorway, having sent Laura home with a footman. When Gray nodded, he made the announcement. Catherine rushed to Mary's side, the concern in her eyes belying her smile.

"Wonderful news, Mary. I am so happy for you. And you are perfect for each other, as I noted the first time I saw you together." Leaning close to kiss her cheek, she murmured, "Are you all right?"

"Perfectly," Mary answered. Aloud she said, "I could not be happier. Lord Grayson shares so many of my interests. It was a dream come true to learn he returned my affections." It seemed best to claim a love match. Nothing else would explain their story.

Half an hour later, she was ready to collapse. People she barely knew crowded around to offer felicitations. Some seemed sincere, but too many voices held pity or disbelief. Gray would need more than Blake's support to overcome so many years of distrust. She longed to escape, yet when relief arrived, it made her even more nervous.

"You make a lovely couple," said Lady Jersey, smiling. "And as long as she avoids cream cakes, she will do you proud, Grayson. Partner her. This set is perfect for a betrothal dance."

"Thank you, my lady," murmured Mary as the musicians began a waltz. But inside she cringed. This would be the last straw for Laura's temper. She would never be granted permission to waltz now.

"I've had very little practice on this step," she warned Gray as he swung her into the first turn.

"Relax. You will be fine." He held her eyes, pulling her an inch closer than propriety allowed.

"What about you? Only yesterday you were weak as a kitten. And that limp is not completely gone." She'd noticed it as he dashed into the antechamber.

"Ankle sprain, but I'll manage." He twirled her through a complicated turn that she hadn't known she could do, then grinned, flashing his dimple. "What did she mean about cream cakes?"

"One of my less stellar moments." It was hard to keep a smile on her face while revealing what a bad bargain she really was. "I tripped on the edge of a carpet and crashed into a footman, who dropped a plate of cream cakes on Lady Jersey's head. I was sure she would cancel my voucher on the spot, but she merely glared at me, then turned her ire on two girls who giggled."

"I would love to have seen it. But since you have a voucher, I will accompany you to Almack's tomorrow."

"Will they let you in?"

"Certainly. Lady Jersey just confirmed my standing by presenting me as a suitable partner for the waltz. They never actually revoked my voucher, though they would have done so had I attempted to use it. I wonder why she decided to accept me now."

"To punish Laura. Since she granted our vouchers, she cannot like such public evidence of poor judgment."

"Perhaps." He pulled her another inch closer. "I won't object."

Mary's knees again melted, though she knew he sought only to convince society that they were in love. To deflect her mind so she wouldn't disgust him by revealing feelings he didn't want, she concentrated on the crowd. Faces spun past, frozen as if in a painting.

Lady Marchgate, smiling indulgently. Even that rigidly proper matron enjoyed a betrothal waltz, particularly when it provided a slap in the face to a girl she disliked.

Lady Beatrice, delivering some pronouncement to Lady Debenham.

Lord Whitehaven, nodding approval. That boded well.

A young sprig in the towering cravat of the fop, glaring. Mary shivered at the hatred in those eyes.

"Who is the dandy next to Lady Wilkins? Green jacket, flowered waistcoat, chin shoved upward by his cravat."

On the next turn, Gray spotted him. "I don't know," he admitted. "Just down from school, I expect. He can't be above eighteen."

"He has the oddest look on his face, as if our betrothal were the final insult to a life already made intolerable."

"I doubt it." He squeezed her hand. "He's probably bilious from too much punch. Not everyone is concerned about us, my dear. Most of society has resumed its dissection of Griffin's arrest, Blackthorn's latest attack on Atwater, or Mannering's new bride."

Or Laura, but neither of them mentioned her.

Once the dance ended, Gray escorted her to supper. News of their sudden betrothal was already on the wing, bringing the curious from other gatherings and producing the heaviest crush of the Season. Lady Cunningham's ball would be remembered for a long time.

But Mary couldn't forget that malevolent face. She had seen hatred in its purest form before, so the dandy's thoughts were clear. As were his intentions. As soon as the crowd of well-wishers thinned, she turned to Gray. "Can you take me home?"

"Of course. You must be exhausted."

She nodded numbly.

"Everything will be fine," he promised, seating her in his carriage. Rockhurst House was only two streets away.

"I hope so, but I'm too tired to think. How about you? Do your injuries still bother you?"

"Only a trifle." He dropped into the seat across from her and crossed his arms. "Now suppose you tell me why we are courting new scandal by disappearing alone."

She dropped her voice so the coachman would not hear. "Miss Ormsby identified that young man—the one I spotted when we were dancing."

"The cub who drank too much?"

"That's the one. But he wasn't foxed. I know hatred when I see it. If looks could kill—"

"But they can't."

"Not by themselves. But hatred too often leads to trouble. He is Leonard Turner, Miss Turner's younger brother. According to Miss Ormsby, his friend had to constrain him from attacking when Blake announced our betrothal. He is enraged that you are happy—which raises the question of whether he is responsible for your accidents."

Chapter Ten

Mary invited Gray inside, but he declined. She understood. Their sudden betrothal left him in a daze, and her news about Mr. Turner was the final straw. She'd seen his brain shutting down from the shock.

Her own was little better. Never again could she slip away to hide from society. No matter how crowded she felt or how many mistakes she made, she must stay in the public eye. Everyone would be watching her closely. Laura had already brought disgrace on the family. She could only pray she wouldn't make it worse.

But upholding the Seabrook name was not her biggest problem. She also must protect Gray's. He would one day be an earl. Would her country ways and nervous faux pas shame him? He deserved better than a bluestocking bird lover. Why hadn't she applied herself more firmly to Miss Mott's lessons in manners, music, and entertaining?

It would reflect poorly on Gray if people thought he had chosen a poor-spirited wife. And hiding would cast doubts on their claim of a love match. Somehow she must convince people that she was worthy of him. He deserved no less.

Sighing, she climbed slowly upstairs. Catherine and Blake would demand a complete explanation in the morning. At least Gray's flowers would support their claim of a courtship and explain Laura's supposed jealousy.

She must also write her brothers. William would be furious with Laura, and he would never approve of Gray. William was a prude—there was no other way to describe him. His primary interest was his estate, his voice growing animated only when discussing crop rotation or the benefits of manure. It had taken Catherine a month to persuade him to let Laura and Mary live at Rockburn Abbey, for he had heard that some of Blake's friends were rakes.

Andrew would accept anything that made her happy, though he, too, would be furious with Laura. His closest friend had been one of her early victims. If only he were here. He had long been her favorite brother. Only he could advise her how to turn this debacle into a workable relationship. Catherine couldn't help, for her own marriages had been love matches.

Her youngest brother Thomas was still in school, but he would welcome Gray the moment he learned about Gray's ships. He had recently evinced an interest in sailing, though at sixteen he was a little old for the navy. They preferred to start potential officers as cabin boys.

She also needed to learn more about Gray, starting with his name. Details like that could put the lie to their supposed courtship, and she could not trust gossip to have the facts right.

On the thought, she stopped in Blake's study to check Debrett's *Peerage*. It took only moments to find the entry. Viscount Grayson, heir to the fifth Earl of Rothmoor, christened Oliver Leslie Dubonne after his father—that explained why he never used the name. The entry was brief, listing only his date of birth and his London direction. The book had been compiled before he acquired his Sussex estate.

Replacing Debrett's, she pushed open her bedroom door, then cursed. She should have expected another confrontation.

"I hope you're satisfied," hissed Laura from the chair by the fireplace. "You ruined everything."

"I see you are clinging to your fantasies," Mary said wearily. "Go to bed, Laura. You brought this on yourself."

"Me?" Laura surged to her feet, whirling to confront her sister. "You stole the man I wanted. How dare you?"

"I stole nothing!" Mary tossed her reticule on her dressing table, relieved that Laura had not shredded the peonies in her fury.

There was no way to avoid an argument, and that was probably good. It was time to step out of the shadows and stand up for herself. Gray had forced her to recognize how cowed she had become.

"Just because you want someone does not mean he returns your regard. Only an idiot would try to force a stranger into marriage. Yes, a stranger," she snapped, ignoring Laura's protest. "You know nothing about him beyond malicious rumor, most of which is false. Didn't that fiasco with Blake teach you anything?"

"I learn from every encounter." Laura's eyes blazed blue in the candlelight. "Blake taught me to be bold. Too much preparation gives others a chance to interfere. Just as Kevin taught me the need for an audience."

"You will rot in hell for what you did to Kevin. He would never have bought colors if you hadn't hounded him. I've never met a man so unsuited for war. I hope his ghost haunts you forever."

"Why should it? Sneaking away to the army was his choice. We could have shared a glorious life, following adventure around the world. But no matter. He proved himself unworthy. As did Blake. Imagine preferring an insipid widow burdened with a sniveling brat."

Mary's jaw dropped to hear Catherine and Sarah described thusly.

"But this time would have been perfect if not for you," continued Laura. "I would be married at last."

"Hardly. What self-respecting gentleman wants a scheming wife? Hasn't it sunk into your head yet that a man can lock his wife away if he chooses?"

"No one would do that to me. Everyone loves me."

Mary shook her head. Laura had abandoned reality. Maybe there was a streak of madness in the family after all. God knew logic could not explain her delusions. "Gray hates you. He would flee the country rather than tolerate your antics. He called you a vulgar trollop, a madwoman, and a spoiled child."

"I don't believe you."

"Why? You were standing right there. Everyone in the hallway heard him. But you never listen when you are scheming. He was fleeing your plots when you cornered him in that antechamber."

"The only plotter was you, seeking to destroy my happiness."

Mary shook her head. "You can't duck this one by claiming innocence, Laura. Three hundred people watched you throw yourself at him. And hundreds more have heard the tale by now. You were the main topic of conversation in the ballroom. Most consider Lady Caroline Lamb a pattern card of propriety compared to you. They were already tired of your airs and graces, so don't expect forgiveness."

"Of course they'll forgive me. They will see how you stole my beau."

Mary's temper snapped. "For God's sake, Laura. He was never your beau! This is not one of your gothic novels where you can rewrite the ending to match your fantasies. You are ruined, and I'm betrothed. And there is nothing either of us can do about it."

"There has to be. It isn't fair that you will have the life of excitement and travel I want."

"What excitement? What travel?" demanded Mary. "Gray stays on his estate except when business draws him to his shipping office. He left England only once in his life—for one week in Brussels to negotiate a contract. Hardly the high adventure you seek."

"That's a lie. His ships travel all over the world."

"But he doesn't go with them," explained Mary patiently. "He employs captains to sail his ships and agents to arrange his cargoes. He prefers a quiet life at home." She tried to imagine a sensitive bird lover who fainted at the sight of blood craving adventure, but the image would not form.

"I don't believe you." Laura surged to her feet, dashing her cup into the fireplace. "You are lying to spite me. You've always hated me because I am beautiful and you aren't. But you'll be sorry you interfered. Grayson may play your game tonight, but you'll soon bore him. Within the week he will jilt you as publicly as he jilted Miss Irwin."

"Another of your fantasies. Miss Irwin was just like you, trying to force an offer from a man she didn't know. He refused."

"Lies!"

"No. You've also ignored the fact that he's been courting me since arriving in London. Who do you think sent me the peonies? They aren't the first, either, as Barhill can attest."

"I don't believe you. You probably sent them yourself in a pathetic attempt to seem interesting—as if anyone would believe so dull and ugly a girl could attract a suitor. That stupid bird proves it. You draw weird little pictures like that all the time. But you won't take him away. You won't! He loves me and must despise the very thought of touching you."

"Laura!" Blake stood in the doorway.

Laura's bravado collapsed. Fear flashed through her eyes.

"In my study. Now!"

Laura stormed out. The moment the door closed, Mary sank into a chair with her head in her hands.

Had she ever known Laura? Gray's voice echoed in her head. *She has criticized you from the moment she first looked into a mirror.*

Tonight had torn the scales from her eyes in more ways than one. The family had accepted Laura's bouts of kindness and occasional benevolence as the real person, excusing her fits as childish whims she would eventually outgrow. But they'd had it backwards. Laura had manipulated them from the first, using smiles and a helping hand to screen her selfish determination.

But those fits defined the real Laura, the venal Laura, she craved excitement the way most people craved food. And she would do anything to find it, causing fusses and even scandal whenever she was bored. She wanted to be a goddess, waited on by an army of servants, worshiped by thousands of men, envied by every woman. She wanted to see the world, which she imagined to be an exotic place offering limitless adventure, though never discomfort. Some of her dreams grew from books, but most were the product of imagination—if only their mother had lived; if only their father had been a wealthy pirate or pasha or king; if only she had taken London by storm at seventeen instead of wasting precious years buried in the country. She used her belief that fate had abused her to justify any dishonor.

And she was growing worse. Gone was the girl who had helped Catherine distribute food and clothing to the parish poor, had run the household after Catherine's first marriage, and had helped care for the Seabrook tenants. Gone was—

Voices interrupted. Mary wished she'd told Blake how thin the wall was. The last thing she needed tonight was another argument.

"Your reputation will never recover," said Blake coldly.

"You exaggerate." But fear trembled in Laura's voice.

"Not at all."

"Then why not blame Mary? It's all her fault!"

"No! I am through with your spite," he snapped. Something thudded—perhaps a fist on his desk. "Mary is blameless, as everyone in that ballroom knows. So far, they impute your tantrum to jealousy."

"*Me* jealous of *her*? That mealy-mouthed ingrate. That—"

"Enough! I will not tolerate another word. There isn't a soul in society who will support you now."

Laura burst into noisy sobs.

Mary flinched. Laura often used tears to elicit sympathy, weeping inconsolably until her listeners were willing to forgive anything if only it would comfort her.

Donning a nightrail, Mary climbed into bed and clamped a pillow over her ears, but it did no good. The pillow was as thin as the wall.

"Tears do not affect me," said Blake coldly, having let Laura wail for several minutes. "I've seen you produce them too often."

"If you think to send me back—"

"No," Blake interrupted. "I won't choose the easy way this time. There will be no retreat to the country. You would shame the family by causing new scandal the moment you arrived. Thus you will stay under my eye."

"You mean you will ignore this misunderstanding and do nothing to punish Mary for her interference?" Laura's tears were gone in a flash, buried under fury.

"Mary is innocent, and if I hear another word to the contrary, I will lock you in your room for the remainder of the Season. From now on, you will behave like the proper miss you are not. At Catherine's urging, I covered your perfidy once—something I would not have done had I known about your earlier crimes. I should have turned you over to Squire Baker when he offered for you last summer. Instead, I let you wheedle a Season from me—and look at how you've repaid me. No more cooperation, Laura. This time you will face the consequences. If any invitation includes you, you will accept it. You will maintain an even temper no matter what people say or how often they cut you. And you will not utter a word, even by innuendo, against Mary or Grayson. Is that clear?"

Laura agreed with alacrity, clearly believing that everything would be back to normal by morning.

Mary sighed. They could expect hysterics the moment the morning post arrived. It would bristle with cancellations.

Gray found Nick in the reading room at White's. The club would not be crowded for another hour, so they would have privacy for a time. He needed it. Too much had happened this evening—Laura, Mary, Turner.

His head was ready to explode.

"You are early," remarked Nick once the steward delivered wine.

"I am betrothed."

Nick bolted to attention. "What?"

"I have been courting a most charming girl for some time," said Gray lightly. "She is delighted with my gifts, especially the Daurian peonies I sent round this morning."

"Not that rose and gold variety!" exclaimed Nick. "They cost a fortune."

"And worth every shilling, though these particular ones came from my hothouse. I spoke to her sponsor this afternoon and paid my addresses this evening. She accepted."

Nick pursed his lips, eyes riveted to Gray's face. "Whom are we discussing?"

"Miss Mary Seabrook." He chuckled. "She is quite out of the ordinary and will make me a perfect wife. We share many interests."

"Whoa." Nick drained his glass and poured another. "Let's try this again. Now that I know the public tale, how much of it is true?"

"You have always been a student of human nature, Nick." Gray shook his head. "No one can take you in for long. It is true that I am betrothed. It is true that Mary and I are friends and that I've sent her flowers on two occasions, most recently the peonies. It is also true that I had considered offering, but was put off by her unscrupulous sister." A slight stretch, but not much.

"I know you dodged the sister at the Oxbridge ball. I covered for you."

"I should not have gone out that evening. It was too soon after meeting that footpad. Mary read me quite a scold for it." He sipped wine. "As for the rest of the tale, Rockhurst will claim we spoke this afternoon."

"Why would he lie to help a man of your reputation?" asked Nick idly.

"For Mary's sake. And to make the sister appear jealous rather than mad. That way he can keep her in town. He has his own reasons for forcing her to face censure."

"She must have tried to compromise you." Nick shook his head. "Nothing else would explain that note of satisfaction you can't quite hide. How did you befriend her sister, anyway? And when? You returned to London barely a week ago."

Gray laughed. "Fate. As Mary pointed out yesterday,

Lady Luck has not deserted me after all. She has been busy protecting my back. When I dodged behind a potted palm to escape Miss Derrick last week, I found Mary already there. Ever since, fate has placed her near at hand whenever I needed help. She saved me from colliding with a cart yesterday—hence the peonies."

"What tale is this?" Nick shook his head.

"Later. Tonight when I sought refuge in an antechamber, she was already there."

"Are you sure she did not plan this?"

"Positive. Mary would never scheme." And Laura would die before sacrificing her reputation for a sister. But the details would make the rounds without his help. "On another note, Mary convinced me that my accidents are not so accidental."

"I believe I raised that possibility last week."

"You did. But there had been only one incident then. My hard head is now more receptive, particularly since Mary identified a suspect."

"Why did you say nothing this afternoon?" He shook his head. "Or did you actually argue the nature of your accidents while arranging a questionable betrothal?"

"There is nothing questionable about my betrothal." Gray glared.

"I beg your pardon."

Relaxing, he continued. "I will admit to haste, but that is unavoidable. Yesterday she convinced me my mishaps weren't accidents, but I did not wish to discuss it until I knew who was behind them. Mary revealed her suspect when I took her home just now."

Nick was staring at him, laughter lighting his eyes. "How often have you actually met? I've not heard a word even from Lady Beatrice."

"Let's see." Gray sipped in contemplation. "There was the potted palm at Lady Debenham's; Lord Oxbridge's library—I swooned at her feet that time; Coventry Street and the Albany fire, though we did not actually speak that day; Hatchard's; Piccadilly, where she saved my life; and tonight, of course."

"Quite a courtship." Nick chuckled.

"Very. But enough teasing. In less than a week, I have been drugged, beaten, seen my rooms burn, suffered food poisoning, and been run down. Far too much for coincidence."

"You say Miss Seabrook knows the culprit?"

"Miss *Mary* Seabrook. The dragon is the elder. Call her Mary. I don't wish reminders of the sister."

Nick nodded. "Between us."

"Good. While we were waltzing, she spotted a young man consumed by hatred and furious that I had contracted a love match." He managed the claim without a stumble, surprising himself. "Neither of us recognized him. I paid little attention, as I was intent on convincing society that our tale was true. But Mary discovered that he is Constance Turner's brother, just up from Eton."

"Leonard?" Nick frowned. "He does not seem old enough to manage such a variety of incidents. He can't be above seventeen."

"You know him?"

"We met at Watier's a week ago."

"Mary swears he hates me, and she is nearly as astute as you. In fact, she can read my mind even better than you can."

"You haven't been yourself lately." Nick refilled their glasses. "If Turner is guilty, then he must have been planning this for three years. He is rather slow in his thinking, you must understand. Someone mentioned at the time that Constance's younger brother would be devastated by her death, so I gather they were close. Perhaps he merely wishes to injure you."

"If they were truly close, he should know that I had nothing to do with her death."

"Hardly. She described your fictitious courtship to everyone she met. Why would she tell her brother any different?"

"Do you know anything of the family?" asked Gray.

"Only what I heard at the time." Nick frowned in thought. "Constance was unstable—as was her mother apparently. The mother died when Leonard was a babe, so neither of them remember her. Their elder brother,

Harold, was fifteen years Constance's senior, a product of a first marriage to a dullard, whom he closely resembles. His difference in age and temperament explains why Constance and Leonard were so close. After the father died, Harold did his duty, but he cared little for either of them. Her chaperon that Season was incompetent."

"Miss Pettigrew. We discussed her shortcomings at the time."

"What I can't recall are any details of the instability. If it was a weakness of spirit, it may only have affected Constance, but insanity could surface in both."

Gray groaned. "If he is guilty, then he has been nursing his grievance for three years already. I do not believe such a man would be satisfied with inflicting a few injuries. I never saw the suicide note that blamed me for her condition, but it reportedly contained a plea that she be avenged."

"Dangerous." Nick drained his glass. "I had forgotten that as well."

"Or never knew it. The family tried to cover the manner of her death by claiming a fall. It was her maid who spread the tale. But I cannot accuse young Turner without evidence. Rockhurst announced that he considers me innocent of scandal. I won't do anything to cast doubt on that judgment. Mary deserves better than a tainted name." Gray dropped his voice as a noisy trio entered the room. "Will you accompany me in the morning? I wish to interview the cart driver who nearly ran me down. He should know who paid him. He cannot have conceived the plot by himself."

"Have him charged with attempted murder."

Gray shook his head. "We will talk with him first. I need facts before I decide the next step."

"Where will we find him?"

"Near the docks. He works for one of my competitors."

Chapter Eleven

When Gray collected Nick at seven, he had yet to find sleep. After leaving White's, he had sketched the design he'd been mentally refining for the last year. Then he'd dispatched a footman to see that Rundell and Bridge opened by six. A hefty bonus soothed the jeweler's dignity and guaranteed that the work would be done by noon.

"I have been thinking," said Nick once he was settled in the carriage. "The fact that the cart driver works for another import company is suspicious. Perhaps Turner is guilty only of hatred. If you recall, I suggested a business rival from the first."

"But not Medford. He is more friend than rival. We often purchase shares in each other's ventures as a hedge against losing one of our own ships." He owed Medford a great deal. Shares he'd purchased while still in school had earned enough to pay his expenses that first year in London and allow him to live at Albany. Shares in a second voyage had won the stake to start his own company. And Medford's advice had made that company profitable. He'd stake his life that Medford had nothing to do with his accidents. "Besides, he would never send an employee to attack me," he continued. "How could he hope to keep his involvement secret?"

"Good point," conceded Nick.

"I suppose a less friendly competitor might have hired Browning—which is why I must see him. I'll not accuse Turner without evidence. And though I respect Mary's acuity, she knows nothing about my business. So we will proceed methodically." He had suffered from too many baseless charges himself to risk making them against others.

Gray withdrew into silence as his coachman threaded the crush of commercial traffic. Night dirt wagons carried reeking loads toward the Thames to be dumped. Water carts and milkmaids were making their morning deliveries. A laggard herd of cattle straggled toward a slaughterhouse. Farm carts trundled produce to market, along with flowers, hay, sacks of grain, and a hundred other products.

Delivery wagons already fanned across the city, carrying silks, spices, china, furniture, sugar, and other imports from the four corners of the globe. Hoping he would not have to chase Browning all over town, Gray jumped down the moment the carriage rocked to a halt before Medford's warehouse.

"Is Thomas Browning still here?" he asked the harried manager.

The man frowned. "What might you be wanting with Tom, my lord? We've orders to deliver."

"Some questions arose about that accident on Piccadilly the other day. We hoped he could answer them."

"What's this about an accident?" He seemed honestly puzzled—evidence that Browning had not been in Piccadilly on Medford's business.

Gray shrugged. "A curricle bolted, causing considerable damage. Browning was one of the witnesses. I won't detain him long."

"If you say so. But he has a full schedule today." The manager pointed to a partially filled cart attended by a burly man wearing a patched shirt and thinning trousers. As he heaved a heavy crate inside and shifted another to balance the load, the adjacent cart pulled out, leaving his isolated.

"It should only take a minute." Gray headed for Browning's cart, signaling Nick to join him.

As they approached, he called, "Mr. Thomas Browning?"

Browning turned, then paled.

"I thought so," said Gray, sighing. "Who paid you to run me down the other day?"

"Ye're barmy." Browning's fists clenched.

Nick stiffened. "Witnesses saw you whip your horses into a gallop, then aim them directly at Lord Grayson."

"T'were an accident."

"Easy, Nick," murmured Gray. He kept his eyes on Browning, letting the silence drag out. Finally he nodded. "You look like an intelligent man—and an honest one. I suspect this was the first commission you've accepted."

Browning again protested, but Gray kept talking. "There is no point claiming accident. Witnesses recognized the skill required to traverse the chaos of Piccadilly without a scratch. But beyond that, I know it was deliberate. In the past week I've escaped four brushes with death. If that happened to you, would you think it coincidence?"

Browning gasped. "What do ye mean four? Ye can't blame me for yer own bad luck."

"I know. Just as I know you had nothing to do with the first three. But someone arranged every one. You know who he is. So talk. Who paid you to run me down?"

Browning said nothing.

Nick started forward.

"Let me make myself clear." Gray restrained Nick with a gesture. "You have two choices, Browning. You can tell the truth, in which case we will let the incident remain an accident—but I warn you, if you ever attack anyone again, you will pay. Or I can turn you over to a magistrate, produce my witnesses, and watch you be transported."

"Ye can't! My wife and sons would starve. The boys ain't big enough to be aught but sweeps."

"You should have considered their welfare earlier," snapped Nick.

Browning sagged against the cart. His eyes pleaded with Gray. "I *was*, my lord. Billy's been ailing ever so long. 'E needs a doctor bad." He shook his head. "Ten guineas the cove offered. More'n I make in a month. But

I was only s'posed to knock ye down. I wouldn'ta done
it if 'e wanted ye dead. Not even for Billy."

"How did you know where to find me?" asked Gray.

"I followed ye. I knew ye on account of ye meetin'
with Mr. Medford so often. The man said ye was stayin'
in St. James's Square, though 'e wasn't sure which 'ouse.
Piccadilly was the first time I 'ad a good shot at ye." He
shuddered. "Course when that lady pulled ye away, I
missed. So he paid nothin'."

Ice pooled in Gray's stomach at this confirmation. No
matter what Browning claimed, there was no guarantee
he would have survived an impact. And his enemy
knew it.

But this was not the time or place to think about it.
He focused on Browning's last statement. "He did not
even pay part of the sum in advance?"

Browning shook his head.

"Who was he?"

" 'E never told me 'is name."

"Yet you believed him honorable enough to reward
you when the deed was done. He must know you would
have small chance of finding him and less of convincing
the authorities that he hired you."

Browning paled. "I was a fool."

"Yes, you were, though it proves that you are new to
this business." He wondered if the footpad had received
any pay. Or had the man agreed to assault him in exchange for his purse and watch. Perhaps drugging him
to make the job easy was enough reward. "Had you injured me, you would now be on your way to Botany
Bay."

Browning straightened and met his eye. "I know."

"Tell me everything. What did the man look like."

" 'E were a Swell, though young. About your height,
but not filled out." His eyes measured Gray's chest and
shoulders. "Pale face, collar to 'ere." He touched his
cheekbone. " 'Is voice cracked like 'e was nervous. Or
maybe excited."

"Did he give any reason for wishing to hurt me?"

Browning shook his head. "I didn't ask. The money

seemed a answer to prayer, so I kept quiet. 'E acted like 'e'd take 'is business to another if I balked."

"Nervous, you said. As if he had second thoughts?" asked Nick.

"No. 'E weren't scared at all. But strung tight like a bow 'eld at the ready. 'E'd been plannin' this awhile, or so it seemed. 'Ad all the details worked out in 'is 'ead. Muttered 'bout revenge, though. Don't see that much with the nobs. Most of 'em are either drunk or bored."

"Hair color?"

"Brown. Nothing special. But 'is eyes were a queer blue. Piercing. And 'is nose bent to one side." He pushed his own to the left.

"Turner to the life," murmured Nick.

"Good." Gray concentrated on Browning. "You will never accept such a commission again, will you?"

Browning shook his head. "No, sir. I ain't slept good since, thinkin' 'bout 'ow many mighta been 'urt that day. I shoulda thought 'bout the other traffic."

"You are lucky no one died. How is Billy?"

"Poor." Anguish twisted his face.

Gray was moved that a man would risk his neck to help his son. His own father hadn't even realized six-year-old Gray had broken an arm until four weeks after the incident—nor would he care overmuch if Gray died, even today. Gray had never fit into Rothmoor's world. "Take the boy to Dr. McClarren in Berkley Square. He is Scots trained and the best physician I know. If anyone can help, he can. Tell him to let me know if he has any questions." He handed Browning his card, wrapped in a ten-guinea note.

"I can't—"

"You can." He held Browning's eyes. "You owe me for the distress you caused. You can repay that debt by seeking help for your son and by never engaging in such dealings again."

"Thank ye, my lord." Browning's eyes glittered. "Ye'll never regret this."

"Make sure I don't." Nodding farewell, he and Nick strode back to his carriage.

Nick shook his head. "You surprise me, Gray. The man tries to kill you, so you pay him?"

"Unlike that footpad, Browning is not a criminal. And how can so devoted a father fail to touch a chord? Besides, he confirmed that Turner is behind this. Such information is worth a reward."

"Where to now?"

"Turner's rooms. It's time to have a serious talk with that boy. Did you learn anything new about him?" Gray recalled little of the family, though the Turners lived near Rothmoor. Neither the old nor new Lord Turner shared Rothmoor's interests.

"Not as much as I would like. After you left White's, your betrothal and Miss Seabrook's fall from grace dominated conversation, but I did manage a few questions. The subject of Miss Turner arose when Atkins mentioned Rockhurst's defense of you."

"I would hardly call it a defense," protested Gray.

"Apparently he was more forthcoming after you left. He claims that your determination to avoid Miss Turner had made him doubt her tale at the time."

"Good of him."

Nick nodded. "I asked Atkins about the Turner family. He knew little, but Wainscott attended school with the current lord."

"Constance's half brother?"

"Harold," confirmed Nick. "Odd family. His father's passion was racing pigeons. He ignored Harold from birth and hardly noticed when his wife died two years later. Harold was a devoted son despite the neglect, even evincing an interest in pigeons as a way to spend time with his father. Turner shocked everyone by taking a second wife when Harold was fourteen. He doted on his bride, paying her more heed than his birds."

"No wonder Harold hates his half siblings."

"Hate is too strong. But he resented them, even though Turner ignored them, too. Turner and his wife died in a carriage accident after six years of marriage, naming Harold guardian for Constance and Leonard. Harold followed his father's example by ignoring them.

He didn't even hire a governess until Constance was eight."

"So they truly had only each other. That does not bode well."

It was after ten by the time Gray's carriage returned to Mayfair. Dozing for much of the trip left him groggy and slow, but he could not afford to put off this confrontation.

Turner's valet blocked the door. "Mr. Turner is not at home to callers."

Gray had expected no less. "Meaning he is sleeping off last night's debauchery. We will wait," he declared, boldly shouldering past the valet. Nick followed. They took chairs in a small sitting room. Harold obviously kept his brother on a tight rein. The rooms were cramped and located on an upper floor of one of the cheaper rooming houses along Jermyn Street—cheap because the gaming hell in the cellar supplied the owner with a nice profit.

"What are you waiting for?" Nick demanded of the slack-jawed valet. "Wake your master and tell him that we have urgent business with him."

The valet fled.

Protests arose in the adjacent room.

"Surly in the morning, isn't he?" remarked Nick.

"Also hotheaded. Don't antagonize him."

They fell silent. Within minutes, Turner burst into the room. He had dressed in haste, leaving off his cravat.

"You have nerve," he snapped, stalking to the fireplace, where he assumed a dramatic pose. "Are you planning to kill me like you killed my sister?"

"I had nothing to do with her death," Gray said calmly, determined to hold his temper, no matter what. "I was not even in town at the time, as everyone knows."

"What difference does that make?" snarled Turner. "You drove her to it. She was carrying your child!"

"Not mine."

"Liar!"

"Never." Gray paused to unclench his fists. "It is time

you accepted the truth, Turner. These childish attempts on my life must stop."

"I'll not listen to your insults." Turner assumed a fighting stance.

Nick tensed.

Gray continued. "Denying your intent is even more cowardly than hiring ruffians so you needn't dirty your hands."

"How dare— You deserve to die."

"I disagree."

"As would anyone who knows him," added Nick. "If you were truly a gentleman, you would discover the facts of the case. Then, if you had a grievance, you would deal with it in person."

"Only if my opponent were a gentleman." Turner glared down his crooked nose. "A cad deserves no respect."

"Misguided youth," murmured Gray with a sigh. "Always jumping to conclusions, then refusing to admit they were wrong."

"How dare you, Grayson?" Turner's temper snapped. "And how dare your dastardly friend imply I have no facts?" He tugged open a drawer and pulled out a tattered stack of letters. "Who knows more about your dishonor than Constance? You may be heir to a title, but I'll see you dead for what you did to her. So sweet and kind and loving. Yet you callously destroyed her. But it won't happen again. I've already sent your latest victim a warning."

"Leave Mary out of this, Turner." Gray's temper flashed so fast he was on his feet before he restrained it. "I'll not have you annoying her with your lies."

"Bastard!" The letters narrowly missed the fireplace as Turner attacked. Gray ducked to avoid a fist in his bruised eye, knocking his arm on a table. Then he barely sidestepped a kick. Memories of that footpad made his hands tremble. He hated situations in which he ought to exchange blows. Fear of exposing his weaknesses kept him helpless.

Nick grabbed Turner from behind and slammed him

into a chair. "Sit down!" he roared. "I'll turn you over to a magistrate right now if you don't behave."

"Relax, Nick." Gray resumed his chair, donning a calm expression to hide his lingering fear—and sliding his wrist behind his back; it stung, as if he'd reopened that wound. If Turner discovered his problem, society would have a new weapon against him. "We are making progress. I was wrong to think him mad. He is merely loyal to his family. Commendable, though undeserved in this case. Don't threaten him until we discover her lies."

"Don't impugn my sister!" Turner struggled against Nick's hold. "She was the most loving girl in the world until you killed her." His voice broke.

Gray sighed. "Only three people know what transpired, Turner. You are not one of them. Constance lied from the moment we met, pretending a courtship that did not exist. In truth, I spoke with her only once, at Lady Debenham's ball. I had never seen her before that night and never sought her out afterward."

"Why? Wasn't she good enough for you?" sneered Turner.

"Her worth is irrelevant. I did not dance more than once with anyone that year."

"So arrogant," snapped Turner. "You think your title allows you to dally wherever you choose, then deny blame when you are found out."

"You aren't listening." Rising, Gray leaned over Turner's chair, trusting Nick to control Turner's fists. "Your sister lied. There was no dalliance. No friendship. No seduction. The entire affair was a fantasy that existed solely in her mind." He toyed briefly with locking Turner and Miss Seabrook in a padded room where they could entertain each other with their fantasies, but this was no time for woolgathering.

"You cannot deny her condition."

Gray paced to the fireplace. "No, but I did not cause it. I suspect she grew desperate when her lover disappeared, so she threw herself at me. Maybe she thought I would do anything to avoid scandal. But she was wrong. When her stalking became too annoying, I left."

"Fancy words, Grayson. But I don't believe them." Only Nick's grip on his jacket kept Turner in his chair. "Constance was painfully honest, especially with me. She wrote almost daily, you know, describing every detail of her life. I know about the night she met you, the events you attended, the secret strolls through gardens, how you seduced her in the dark walk at Vauxhall. She also repeated your promises of love, marriage, and wealth uncounted."

"Fantasies, every one. Lady Beatrice would have known if she had been conducting trysts in various gardens. And I haven't been to Vauxhall in ten years. I despise the place. Perhaps she substituted my name for her escort's, but it is more likely she lied from start to finish." Gray was losing patience. "I did not court your sister. I did not seduce her. I did not seek her out in any way."

Turner ignored him, seeming lost in his own memories. "She wrote me the last day, her tears staining the page. You'd spurned her, you bastard. Cast her off without thought. She had no choice but to end it." Hatred flared as he met Gray's gaze. "I must avenge her if I am to live with myself. But first you must suffer as she did."

"Enough of this farce," said Nick, his disgust penetrating Turner's trance as Gray's anger had not. "Haul him to the magistrate and be done with him. You've witnesses enough to convict him. He'll leave for Botany Bay on the next ship."

"Not just yet." Gray frowned, searching for a way to convince the boy. Turner had lost the only family who cared about him, then been mired in hatred for three years as he plotted revenge. It was time to move on.

His motives were not altruistic, Gray admitted, pacing. Unless he convinced Turner he was innocent, he would spend his life dodging plots. There was little chance of convicting him without additional evidence. Today's admissions were useless—his own word carried no weight, and even Nick's would be suspect in this situation. Asking Browning to testify would condemn the man to transportation. Besides, involving the authorities would focus attention on Constance's death, forcing society to judge him. Unless he won, they would ostracize him. There would be no more careful dance that allowed him to mingle as long as he behaved with more propriety than anyone else.

"No matter what Constance claimed, there were only three people who knew what happened," he repeated. "Constance can no longer confess. The others are myself and the man who seduced her. Think about it, Turner. I could not have been responsible for her pregnancy. I reached London only a month before her death."

"I am aware of that," said Turner. "But Rothmoor Park is only ten miles from Turner Hall. Constance wrote often about the gatherings there."

"If she valued her reputation, she never set foot in the place and avoided anyone who did. But you must know that it has been ten years since I last visited my father's house. Our differences have entertained the neighborhood most of my life."

For the first time Turner frowned.

"Think about it. You say she wrote daily, yet not once did she mention my name before arriving in town. She couldn't have. I had never met either of you. My father sent me to school before you were born, and I returned as rarely as possible. If she mentioned no men at the time she must have conceived that child, then she could not have told you everything. And if she actually did attend Rothmoor's parties, that would explain her pregnancy. They are fit only for the most debauched lechers. Every woman invited is a whore."

Turner said nothing, but his eyes seemed puzzled.

"You knew your sister better than anyone," continued Gray relentlessly. "What would she have done if she found herself with child by a scoundrel? Would she admit her mistake, or would she have covered it up?"

"Harold had no patience with either of us," he admitted. "So she might well have lied to him. But never to me. We had no secrets."

"Yet you were a schoolboy. Fourteen years old and under the thumb of harsh tutors. What could you have done? Why would a loving sister burden you with such knowledge, knowing that you could do nothing?"

"That did not matter. We had no secrets."

Gray's frustration spilled over. "Stubborn pup! I will produce proof that she lied," he snapped. "Since she left you a detailed account of her activities, draw up a list. I will disprove it. Just as I can prove that I was nowhere near Rothmoor. I've not been within a hundred miles of the place since my eighteenth year. In the meantime, there will be no more attacks. Your obsession has already sickened a dozen innocents, injured four others, and damaged property that does not belong to me. One more incident, no matter how trivial, and you will face the magistrates on a charge of attempted murder."

"Vengeance is not murder!"

"No one will believe that. Nor will they condone your methods. That fire could have harmed dozens of innocent bystanders, just as that stunt in Piccadilly did."

"Prove it."

"I can. I have already found several witnesses. Runners will easily find others once they learn your identity. You have no hope that the outpourings of a distraught female will convince a court of my guilt. Rumor and innuendo might carry the day in a drawing room, but courtroom standards are more rigorous."

Collecting his hat and cane, he left.

Nick followed. "You are in a strange mood today, Gray. You've had two miscreants in your hands, both of whom admitted their guilt, yet you allowed both to remain free. What is wrong with you?"

"I feel sorry for him. He was ignored by his parents, ill-used by his brother, abused by the sister he trusted, then left to nurse his grievances in solitude." In truth, Turner's upbringing was too much like his own. "Since I doubt his constitution is sturdy enough to reach Botany Bay alive, I do not want his death on my conscience. So I will force him to face the truth. But I am not completely lacking in sense. Until this is over, I'll have men watching him so he can do me no further mischief."

He must also protect Mary. Turner had already sent

her a letter. If he believed it was a love match, he might use her to hurt Gray.

"He will never believe you innocent. His hatred has festered too long."

"He will. And once he does, society will follow. Rockhurst has already raised doubts." He should have fought for his honor three years ago, but he'd been too shocked to think clearly.

"Clever. I should have seen that for myself."

"You would have if you weren't so bloodthirsty this morning. But I will need help to convince him. His belief in Constance's veracity is so strong that producing her lover might be the only way to overturn it. I am convinced the man is a gentleman, for she was not the sort to risk her future for a romp in the hay. She came after me only out of desperation. People noticed a change in her conduct when we met. So ask questions. Few discuss it now, but they will remember. Gossip never really dies."

Chapter Twelve

Mary stared at Frannie. "Lord Grayson is here?" she repeated.

"He insists on seeing you, even though Lord Rockhurst is out, as are Lady Rockhurst and Miss Laura." Her tone implied that his request was not respectable.

"We are betrothed," said Mary, then cursed herself for explaining to a servant. Frannie too often mimicked Laura's airs, especially toward the unworthy and unwanted baby sister.

"Miss Laura says he'll jilt you before the week is out," sneered Frannie. "He can't want a clumsy oaf with no conversation. You should run home before he locks you in an attic."

"Enough, Frannie. It is not your place to judge your betters. Nor does a proper maid repeat her mistress's tirades. Not if she wishes to retain her position." She ignored Frannie's sudden frown. Never again would a servant intimidate her. It was time to find her own maid. "Tell Lord Grayson I will join him in the drawing room. And ask Barhill to order a tea tray."

Barhill would have already done so, but she wished to be alone for a few minutes. What could Gray want? He had said nothing about calling today. Had he hoped to speak with Blake, asking for her only when he found Blake gone?

She caressed a peony, reminding herself that they had been friends before last night. She needn't fear this meeting. All she had to do was remain the proper miss he deserved.

A formidable task.

Gray was standing by the fireplace when she reached the drawing room. Shadows under his eyes spoke of a sleepless night, which did not bode well for their marriage. He might claim acceptance, but no man accepted coercion lightly, especially a lord.

He was dressed in somber black this morning, even his pantaloons, which gave him a puritanical look. And his frown made her wish she'd changed into one of her new gowns. Laura had discarded this one three years ago. But changing would have required Frannie's help.

"You wished to see me, my lord?" she asked, perching near the tea tray and gesturing him to a settee.

"I thought we settled on Gray." He lifted her hand to his lips, then smiled, reviving the friend she knew. "Is something amiss, my dear?"

"I remain overwhelmed." And terrified that he would come to hate her, though she couldn't admit it. "I just realized that I must find a new maid. Begging help from Laura's is no longer feasible."

His face darkened. "Is a servant giving you trouble?"

"No more than usual. Would you care for wine, Gray? You look exhausted—again."

"Thank you. I've not had time for sleep." He sat. "What do you mean by *no more than usual*?"

"Frannie has always prided her position as dresser to a diamond."

"I see. I've heard that Brummell's valet is insufferable. But what has that to do with you?"

"Frannie has served Laura and me for ten years. But her pride rests in Laura. She resents wasting time and talent on someone who doesn't improve no matter what she does."

"Surely Rockhurst supplied you with your own maid for the Season." He sounded shocked.

She shrugged. "No one expected me to make a match." Taking refuge in her cup, she chided herself for whining. It wasn't like her to complain, and she never shared personal problems with others. This wasn't the time to start.

"But you did." Setting his glass aside, he reached into

a pocket. "And we are well suited, Mary, no matter what you may fear at the moment. I will do everything in my power to see that you are satisfied with our bargain. As a token of that vow, I offer this." Lifting her hand, he kissed it, then slipped a ring onto her finger.

She trembled. Never had she seen anything like it. A swirl of gold cradled a triangular emerald, reflecting and warming its brilliance. The effect was mesmerizing.

"It's beautiful, Gray." She stared at the ring for a long minute before meeting his eyes. "Where did you find an emerald this shape?"

He smiled, seeming relieved. "One of my captains bought it in the Caribbean. It suits you, for you are also unique. I had the ring made up this morning."

The statement stunned her. He must have paid a fortune for such service. Of course, he could easily afford it, and producing so special a ring added credence to their courtship.

"Thank you, Gray. I will cherish it always."

He stood, drawing her into his arms. Last night's excitement returned, though he didn't kiss her. His cheek rested atop her head, and his hands caressed her back, making it harder to lean passively against him. But she must never forget that his actions were designed to protect them both from censure. So far, he was hiding his anger at fate's latest blow, but he could not like it.

She stayed in his arms a long time, drinking in his warmth even as she schooled herself to stillness. But her calm vanished when he swayed.

"Sit down before you collapse," she ordered, sliding her arms around his waist to hold him upright. He was exhausted—again. Illness, injury, and lack of sleep drove grooves across his face and painted shadows under his eyes.

"In a moment." He pulled her closer. His shoulder was warm under her cheek. When his hand traced a line down her neck, she wanted to purr. Her body trembled under his touch, drawing a blush.

She thought his lips brushed her hair—or perhaps he sighed. But before she could decide, he released her.

"The ring is not the only reason I needed to see you," he admitted when he'd seated her next to him on the settee. His expression was serious. "I spoke to the cart driver this morning. As you expected, he was hired to knock me down."

"What did you do?"

"Nothing." He shrugged. "This was the first time he had accepted such a commission, and I doubt he will ever do so again. But his description matched Turner."

"As I feared. Turner doesn't know that gossip is unreliable." She paused, but Gray needed to know everything. "He truly hates you. He sent me a vitriolic letter this morning, accusing you of the most vile deeds. I fear he is even more unbalanced than I thought."

"He mentioned the letter." He scowled.

"You spoke with him? Dear Lord, he could have killed you!"

"Shh." He patted her hand, but his expression lightened. "It's all right, Mary. I took Nick along."

"Nick?"

"Nicholas Barrington, my closest friend."

"Did you convince Turner that the gossip is wrong?"

"Gossip is not the problem. Constance sent him letters describing our fictitious courtship. He believes every word."

Mary frowned.

"He will change his mind only if I can convince him that she lied—not an easy task, for he all but worships her. The only sure proof is to produce the man who seduced her."

"Difficult. If the culprit had any honor, he would have come forward three years ago."

"True." Releasing her hand, he paced to the window overlooking the garden.

Mary joined him, touching his arm. "Who were Miss Turner's particular friends that Season?"

"I have no idea. After that first night, I avoided any gathering where she was a guest. When that failed to discourage her, I retired to my estate." He pulled her against his side as if absorbing her warmth. Tremors rippled through his arm.

Only now did she realize how unusual it was for him to discuss this with her. Most men considered openness to be weak, or they believed ladies were incapable of understanding. To be fair, most ladies did not want the responsibility of facing trouble, so they discouraged disclosure by suffering vapors over any unpleasantness. But Gray was treating her as a partner. The implied trust nearly stole her breath. "Did she mention any friends to her brother?"

"He did not say. Why?"

"Because if anyone knows her secrets, it would be her bosom bows. The seduction had to have occurred long before she met you, probably in the country."

"True, but London friends would hardly know whom she'd met in Yorkshire." He shuddered.

"Not necessarily. When did you meet her?"

He frowned. "Early May, though I don't remember the exact date. I was late returning to town that year."

"Did she pursue anyone else before fixing on you?"

He shook his head. "Not to my knowledge. Nick claims she was an observer rather than a participant in the Season. As far as I know, she didn't flirt and rarely danced. That was why I—" He broke off.

"That was why you partnered her that night. You feel compassion for those who are ill at ease."

"I certainly have no compassion for her," he snapped, twisting away.

She followed. "Of course not. But you discovered too late that she was neither shy nor nervous. She must have expected to wed her lover, so she really was an observer in town. And she probably knew that exertion would cause dizziness or nausea. Catherine was miserable for months while carrying Sarah, and it was even worse with Max." Blake's heir was now six months old. Catherine's morning sickness had kept them at Rockburn last Season. "The problem was bad enough for someone like Catherine, but for Miss Turner, any hint of illness would have brought disclosure and censure."

"Then why dance with me?"

Mary paced to the door and back. "Something changed. I suspect her paramour repudiated her when she informed him she was increasing. Thus she needed a husband immediately."

"Lucky me," he muttered. "But it's true that she hung on me after that set ended, even following me onto the terrace at one point. At first I thought she was terrified of her first London ball. I tried to discourage her interest and left as soon as possible. It wasn't until later that I learned she'd been in town for weeks and rarely spoke with gentlemen. When the next day's rumors claimed we were old friends, I was furious. That's when I decided to avoid any gathering she graced."

"And you quit speaking to innocents entirely, confining your attentions to matrons and courtesans."

"Gossip has always exaggerated my deeds." Fire flashed in his eyes. "The wildness it describes lasted less than a year. And I never pursued married women, no matter how many lies claim otherwise. I refuse to follow in Rothmoor's footsteps. The man is disgusting."

"I know that." She laid a hand on his arm, but refrained from sharing her own conclusions of his motives. He might take insult.

"There is only you now, Mary," he vowed, drawing her closer.

His eyes warmed her clear to her toes. But the vow confirmed that his honor was unique. Even a forced marriage to a near stranger would not cancel an oath he must have made many years earlier—which told her even more about his childhood.

"Thank you." She squeezed him, then returned to business. "Even if Miss Turner ignored gentlemen, she would have had friends. But since you avoided her, I must discover their identities elsewhere."

"Where? I don't want you taking risks, Mary. Turner is obsessed by her death and determined to avenge her. He may strike at me through you."

She smiled. "Lady Beatrice can answer my questions. Turner can hardly be surprised that I call on her. It is only natural that I verify his claims, and Lady Beatrice prides herself on knowing everything."

"Clever. I knew you were. May I see the letter?"

"I consigned it to the fire. But you surely know what it said. Every charge Lady Horseley makes, plus some rather venal speculation about your motives and preferences." She blushed.

"Damn his hide," he muttered, drawing her closer. "I would have spared you that."

"I am not a fainting violet, Gray." She looked up at him.

"Thank God."

She sighed. "I heard worse imputed to me when our neighbor tried to destroy Catherine. He understood that his most effective tactic was attacking her family."

"Why did he hate her?"

"He'd killed our father and Catherine's first husband—not intentionally, but his conscience was uneasy. Though everyone assumed it was an accident, he feared she knew the truth and meant to make it public."

"And now I've placed you in a new scandal."

"Hardly. We will prove you innocent."

"You really believe it possible?"

"I know we can. Since everyone accepted your guilt, they never questioned the evidence. I will make them do so. And that's a vow." She looked deep into his eyes, willing him to believe.

He shuddered. Then his mouth claimed hers in a kiss more searing than last night's. She melted against him, awed at the strength of his passion. And he had pledged all of it to her—

The front door opened. Voices floated up from the hall, followed by feet clattering on the stairs. Gray jumped back and straightened his coat.

Mary forced herself to breathe slowly. Thank heavens they had been interrupted before she did something stupid. "Catherine and Laura have returned." Her voice sounded hoarse.

"Then I must leave. I've no wish to meet your sisters today."

"Understandable. I will let you know what I learn."

"Until Almack's, my dear." He kissed her lightly, squeezed her hand, then left. Catherine entered moments later. Laura's half-boots continued loudly toward her room.

Mary sat, retrieving her cooling tea. She'd not yet explained her friendship with Gray to either Blake or Catherine, so she must do so now. To give her nerves a chance to settle, she gestured toward the stairs. "She sounds angry."

"She is no longer in favor." Catherine helped herself to tea and sighed. "Blake told me about last night. I cannot believe she expected forgiveness after that. She has completely lost her wits. I knew she was vain and arrogant, but where does she find these delusions? Even after she received eleven cancellations at breakfast, she expected to walk into Almack's tonight and find her usual court."

"What happened, Catherine?"

"What didn't?" She set aside her cup so she could massage her temples. "The crowning touch was Lady Jersey, who not only cut Laura dead—after greeting me warmly—but crossed the street so she didn't share a walkway with her. And she made sure Laura knew you'd received permission to waltz."

"Ouch."

"But no matter." She straightened. "You should not meet Grayson alone. I know you are betrothed, but the circumstances raise questions. Any hint of impropriety can harm you."

"He was here only for a moment," protested Mary. "And we left the door open. He brought me this." She held up her hand.

Catherine gasped. "Gorgeous. Where did he find that emerald? Or it is some other stone?"

"It's an emerald. One of his captains discovered it. Gray had the ring made up this morning."

"Really? That is most unusual, even for a love match."

"I know. He is a most unusual man. We will deal well together." She described her meetings with Gray and her conviction that his reputation was undeserved, though she left out Turner's campaign. It would stop as soon as they proved Gray's innocence—tonight, or perhaps tomorrow. But soon. Once she forced people to think, they would acquit him.

"I'd no idea," said Catherine when she finished. "But you are right that we can claim a courtship, unconventional though it might be."

"He could hardly seek me out in public," said Mary piously, then laughed. "Your expression!"

Catherine chuckled.

"In truth, he is a good man. I am content, except . . ." She hesitated, but this was as good a time as any. And it would deflect further questions. "I must find my own maid. Now that everyone is watching me, I can no longer dress myself. Laura will never give up Frannie, even if she is confined to the house."

Catherine bit her lip. "I should have thought of that weeks ago. Frannie is too loyal to Laura to do you justice."

"Dressing me is a waste of her talents."

"Hardly. Her talents are limited to creating tight curls and to lowering necklines. Those styles don't suit you."

"I will not argue the point. For the moment, can Wilson help me change? I need to call on Lady Beatrice, but Frannie will be busy with Laura."

"Of course. Will you be out long?"

"An hour at most."

"Then take Wilson with you. I can do without her for now, and she will lend you more countenance than a parlor maid. When you return, we will leave for morning calls."

Mary groaned, but it couldn't be helped. She owed it to Gray to play the role of a well-bred lady delighted with her betrothal. Nodding, she headed upstairs to change.

"You wished to see me?" asked Lady Beatrice when Mary was ushered into her private sitting room. It was even shabbier than the drawing room, but more comfortable, with footstools and deeply padded chairs. An exquisite piece of needlework protruded from a sewing bag at the dowager's side.

"If it isn't t-too much trouble." Mary took a chair. Her hands shook. Seeking out Lady Beatrice was the hardest thing she had done in her life. And now that she was here, she couldn't find the words to begin.

"What an unusual ring," said Lady Beatrice.

"Lord Grayson had it made for me," Mary admitted, offering her hand to provide a closer look. She'd slipped it over her glove.

He trusts you, whispered her dreamer. *And he needs this information. You can't let him down.*

"That takes time." Lady Beatrice nodded. "Have you known him long?"

"Long enough. Though his illness kept him from calling this past week, we have spoken often—suitably chaperoned, of course."

"No secret assignations?"

"Never!" Mary tried to sound shocked, though her claim was true, for they had never planned to meet. "That would be most improper and reflect p-poorly on the Rockhursts. I could never cause them distress. But Grayson and I wanted to make our decision without the distraction of gossip and well-meaning friends. His reputation makes the usual courtship difficult."

Lady Beatrice held her gaze. "I believe you will do well together," she announced at last. "You share a number of interests. Birds, for example." She smiled at Mary's surprise. "These old ears hear much. For example, while many know that Lord Wendell lost yet another fortune at Watier's last evening, only I know that he cannot cover his vowels this time. He will be fleeing London by nightfall, unless he chooses a more permanent escape."

"Men. Why do they risk what they cannot afford to lose?" murmured Mary.

"Men are not the only ones who take absurd risks. Your sister is another. She also risked everything last evening—and lost. Like all gamesters, she did not expect to lose, so she ignored potential consequences." Lady Beatrice shook her head. "Now what can I do for you, child? I do not flatter myself that you seek idle gossip."

"Not idle," Mary admitted. She drew a deep breath and plunged ahead. "I had t-two purposes, my lady. The first was to ask you not to blame Rockhurst for Laura's behavior. I know he sponsored her, but he did not realize the extent of her willfulness. None of us did."

"You flatter her. Last night surpassed willful," said Lady Beatrice sternly.

"I know." Mary twisted a handkerchief between her fingers. "She deserves rebuke, but not Rockhurst. And even Laura does not deserve to be p-permanently ruined. Perhaps you can someday forgive her."

"Perhaps. It will depend on her future conduct. Personally, I doubt she will warrant redemption. Nor will she thank you for intervening. I have seen many girls make their bows to society—from kind to cunning, naïve to scandalous. She is the sort who will blame all her troubles on others. And because she never admits fault, she will not change her ways."

"I know. But I hate to see others pay for her indiscretions."

"They won't. Now you told my butler that you needed information."

Mary nodded, speaking slowly to control her tongue. "I know Grayson well enough to know he is not the blackguard rumor paints him, particularly with Miss Turner. Her condition existed before she arrived in town."

"Quite true," agreed Lady Beatrice. "She was nearly four months with child when she died."

"Thank you. I was sure it must have been that advanced. So why did everyone assume Grayson had seduced her?"

Lady Beatrice examined Mary's face closely, then nodded. "She paid little attention to gentlemen that year. When Grayson finally returned, he immediately sought her out. She welcomed him with the fervor of a lover. But after a walk in the garden, his attitude changed. He cut her quite cruelly and left. That must have been when she revealed her condition. I cannot abide a man who ignores his by-blows. Even worse is one who seduces a lady of quality."

"I agree with both points." Mary braced to challenge the formidable dowager, fingering Gray's ring to keep up her courage. "But Grayson describes the evening quite differently. He had just returned to town for the Season and noticed a girl sitting apart, shy and without a chaperon to supply her with dancing partners. Hoping to ease her fears at what he thought was her first ball, he shared a set with her, then moved on to talk to friends. To his surprise and consternation, she threw herself at him, clinging to his side and even following him onto the terrace. He told her to mind her manners, then left, but she persisted, finally driving him from town."

Lady Beatrice sighed, but said nothing.

"I believe him," continued Mary. "He had barely returned to London when they met. She had been in town for weeks and in Yorkshire before that. So how could he have seduced her? His feud with Rothmoor has kept him from Yorkshire since he left school."

Lady Beatrice's eyes sharpened. "An astute observation, my child. Would you care to elaborate?"

Mary sagged in relief. "I rarely indulge in gossip, but I hear a great many things because people seldom notice me. Grayson has been a frequent topic of conversation since he returned to town. Many know he divides his time between his Sussex estate and his import business. I doubt he has been ten miles north of London since founding that business, let alone two hundred."

Lady Beatrice nodded.

"I've heard condemnation of Miss Turner's half brother, who allowed her to run wild for years with limited supervision. I know that her Season in London was the first time she'd left Yorkshire in her life, for she did not even attend a school for gently bred girls. So who fathered her child?"

"Hmmm. Have you an answer?"

"Not yet, which is why I am here. As you noted, she

paid little attention to potential suitors. That tells me that she considered herself betrothed. I believe that shortly before Grayson's return, she learned that her paramour had no intention of wedding her. Imagine her shock and desperation. She could not hide her condition much longer. So she had to find a husband immediately. Grayson had the misfortune to approach her soon afterward. His reputation made him a good target, for people believe anything of a rake. His ties to Yorkshire made him seem perfect. So she made up tales of clandestine meetings and passionate trysts, hoping that pressure would force an offer. But it was fantasy from start to finish. He never encouraged her. Now I must prove it."

"Because you don't want a husband of questionable reputation?" Her voice had hardened.

"Not at all. I believe him innocent, which is all that matters on my own account. But he deserves better, especially now that Miss Turner's brother has arrived. Mr. Turner was so furious when Rockhurst announced our betrothal last night that I thought he would call Grayson out. I fear he will not allow the man he blames for his sister's death to find happiness."

"A grave charge."

"And perhaps unfounded," she lied. "But I cannot bear to see Grayson hurt. The best way to avoid trouble is to discover the truth. To that end, I hope you remember who Miss Turner's particular friends were. I know they would have spoken up if they could name her lover, but it is possible that they might recall clues to his identity."

"I am pleased at your loyalty," said Lady Beatrice slowly. "And this explains your sister's pique. Beauties take offense when those whom they deride make brilliant matches, particularly love matches."

Gray would be relieved that Lady Beatrice accepted their story. And if she thought Laura had acted from envy, the scandal would fade sooner.

Lady Beatrice frowned for a moment. "Perhaps we wronged Grayson. I know he was innocent of the imbroglio with Miss Irwin. Her father was a scoundrel who schemed to attach a wealthy son-in-law from the moment he set foot in town. She was more than willing to help. In the end, she actually believed her own lies. Irwin would not have backed down unless Grayson could prove their claims false, so the incident was no more than a nine-days wonder. But the Turner case was different. Grayson's denials carried little weight against the note blaming him for her condition."

"It actually named him?"

Again she frowned. "I don't remember the exact wording, but it was something like, *Grayson refuses to offer. How could I have thought him honorable?* She went on to describe his flight from London. Then she said, *He has utterly ruined me, leaving me no choice but death. My only request is that someone avenge my honor.* It seemed quite clear."

"Not rambling in any way?"

"Most such notes ramble. Those with clear minds rarely choose to end their lives."

"Then she undoubtedly wrote only part of her thoughts." Mary stiffened her back, meeting Lady Beatrice's eyes. "She probably spent hours on that farewell. Her emotions would have progressed from yearning to anger to despair. Grayson had fled town, leaving her plot in shambles. It was too late to find another beau. She could no longer hide her condition. After decrying her untenable situation, for which she blamed Gray—like Miss Irwin, she had described their fictitious courtship so often, she may have come to believe it—her thoughts probably turned to her seducer. She still loved him, perhaps possessively. Yet he had ruined her. She faced expulsion from society and the fury of a half-brother who bore her no love. He would hate having her on his hands forever and might even repudiate her, casting her into the workhouse. Death would save her from such disgrace, but she also wanted revenge against the man responsible for her troubles. Unfortunately, in her distress, she didn't name him."

"That is possible," admitted Lady Beatrice. "But few will accept the theory without strong evidence. The other tale is too entrenched. And some would explain away the discrepancies—a secret trip home to beg forgiveness from Rothmoor, a new argument, a drunken revenge in which he forced himself on a girl he thought was Rothmoor's tenant . . ."

"I can hear Lady Horseley propound that very theory," agreed Mary wearily. "But to find evidence, I must have a starting place. And that means identifying Miss Turner's friends."

"Very well. She was not well liked, for she remained by herself much of the time, and though her father was a baron, no one knew anything about her mother. However, two girls spoke with her most evenings and even accompanied her shopping once or twice. Elizabeth Cunningham was the friendliest. She married Sir Harold Twickham and remains on his estate awaiting childbed. Their second."

"I will write. Where is Sir Harold's estate?"

"Cumberland. Even if she replies instantly, it will take two weeks to receive an answer. So speak with Penelope Osham first, now Lady Sheffield. She is in town this Season and would recall Miss Turner. And I believe Miss Turner's maid now serves Miss Derrick."

Mary hoped she would not have to speak with the maid. If the girl was anything like Frannie, she would remain loyal to Miss Turner and resent any questions. Lady Sheffield was another question mark. She made a point of speaking graciously to everyone, no matter how shy. But that did not mean she exchanged confidences with society's misfits.

Thanking Lady Beatrice for her assistance, she headed for Sheffield House.

Lady Sheffield was at home and was not entertaining— a surprise, for the lady was reputed to hate solitude, welcoming friends even before formal calling hours. After again explaining her mission, Mary plunged into her questions. "Did you ever see Lord Grayson encourage Miss Turner?"

"No. Several people commented on that. The consensus was that she was clinging to an earlier courtship he wished to abandon. Few approved her behavior until her reasons became clear. Of course, by then it was too late." She sighed. "I cannot blame her for exaggerating their liaisons. She was desperate for him to do the right thing. I know he acknowledges your betrothal, but you must be careful that you do not end like Constance."

"There is no danger of that. Did she ever mention other men?" asked Mary.

"No. The only name that crossed her lips was Grayson's."

"You say she exaggerated. How?"

"Several ways. Despite her claims, anyone could see that he felt only anger and disdain, not love. She followed him like a persistent puppy, hanging on his arm and intruding into conversations. Each time he cut her, she would laugh, claiming a lover's spat. And she described a tryst in the gardens at Marchgate House on the fifteenth of May that could not have occurred. Grayson won five hundred guineas from Sheffield at Watier's that evening. I am sure of the date because Sheffield had arranged to speak to my father the next day. I was furious that he had risked so much. His fortune was not large, and the tale made Father doubt his suitability. We had to plead for days before he finally granted permission to wed, and even then he tied up my dowry in a trust for our children." Anger snapped in her eyes.

"Lady Beatrice claims Miss Turner was four months with child when she died, meaning someone seduced her before she came to town. But Grayson has not set foot in Yorkshire in ten years."

"Four months?" Lady Sheffield frowned. "That might explain that swoon, but I was sure she'd been seduced here. Grayson often comes to London on business without attending social events."

"Lady Debenham's ball was the first time he'd seen her. What swoon?"

"It was at Lady Plodham's at-home—about a month before Miss Turner died. She was quiet, as usual, but she seemed relaxed until Lord Roger Duncan arrived."

"I haven't met him. Is he in town this Season?"

"He lives here, but is unwelcome in society, which is why his appearance was such a shock. Horrible man. Quite unscrupulous, but he is Lady Plodham's cousin, so she still receives him."

"What has he done?"

Lady Sheffield shrugged. "Just about everything. His raking puts Devereaux to shame. One of his lesser scandals found him in Lady Torson's bed before she'd produced an heir. On another occasion, a seventeen-year-old innocent found him coupling with a rather dashing widow in the ladies' retiring room at Almack's."

"Good Lord!"

"That incident lost him entrée to society. He is credited with eight duels against outraged husbands and fathers. Darker rumors hint that he enjoys force, particularly against young ladies, and that he will do anything on a lark, including treason."

"Yet he walked into Lady Plodham's drawing room during calling hours."

"She wasn't pleased. Not with a room full of respectable ladies. Nor were others. Lady Cunningham left in outrage lest Elizabeth be tainted. Three others followed. Those remaining hurled vulgar charges at Lord Roger. Quite graphic, really. Lady Wharburton was so furious she forgot that innocents remained in the room and described the incident that had banned him from the courtesan balls a few months earlier. That raised Lady Wilkins's ire—she always had a soft spot for Lord Roger. I suspect they were lovers at one time."

"I suppose she defended him." Mary shook her head. Lady Wilkins usually did the opposite of what people expected. She only remained welcome because her husband was a powerful figure in society, and she managed her own liaisons with reasonable discretion.

"Of course. She reminded everyone that his life had been ruined by a scheming fortune hunter who tricked him into marriage at the tender age of twenty. He banished her to Scotland the moment she produced an heir."

"Hardly an excuse to harm others," snapped Mary.

"I agree. As I said, Lady Wilkins has always defended

him. One of Lord Roger's pleasures is inciting scandal. His visit that day was no accident. He never calls on Lady Plodham when she is alone—but I've drifted from my point. The room was full of shouts, curses, and even fear. The uproar overset Constance, who fainted dead away. Afterward, she blamed the heat—it was quite warm that day. We wondered why she had to justify the swoon, for most of us felt giddy to some degree. But if she was already in a delicate condition, I can understand it. She feared we would ask questions."

"Yes, heat does pose a problem in such cases. Was that before or after Lady Debenham's ball?"

"The same day. I was surprised that she attended, for she remained quite pale. But perhaps she expected Grayson. Her behavior changed completely after he returned. She had always been content to sit with the chaperons, dancing only an occasional minuet. Afterward, she chattered about him constantly, describing fetes she had attended at Rothmoor and many meetings with Grayson."

"I doubt Miss Turner or any innocent attended Lord Rothmoor's gatherings," said Mary tartly. "Even Grayson avoids them."

"That bad?" Her eyes sparkled.

"Deplorable." Thanking Lady Sheffield for her time, Mary headed home.

Lord Roger Duncan. He had to be the villain. It wasn't his sudden appearance that had sent Constance into a swoon—she'd probably believed for one glorious moment that all would be well. It was the revelation that he was a cad who was already married, an uncaring rake who seduced innocent girls, then abandoned them without a qualm. Had he even remembered her three months later?

In a desperate bid to avoid the consequences of her indiscretion, Constance had thrown herself at the first man to show any interest. Fate presented Rothmoor's heir, the perfect substitute. So she claimed long acquaintance and secret liaisons. She hadn't cared that the tales cast doubt on her own virtue. Her reputation would be gone the moment society recognized her condition.

But she'd miscalculated. Gray despised force. And he'd had sufficient credit to resist it—then.

She sighed. Unfortunately Miss Turner's suicide had destroyed that credit. So he'd been forced into marriage after all.

Squaring her shoulders as the carriage rocked to a halt, she headed for her room. She would do everything in her power to make him happy, starting with exposing Lord Roger. Perhaps one day he would cease regretting their fate.

Chapter Thirteen

Gray reached Almack's on the stroke of eleven, barely nipping through the door before it closed.

He'd meant to sleep after giving Mary the ring. He'd certainly needed it. Weariness had clouded his judgment, as proved when he cut Laura dead on his way out of Rockhurst House. Like it or not, she would be family before long. And she might retaliate against Mary, who must share a roof with her until they wed. But it was too late to undo any possible damage. And he'd been too tired to care.

He also should have driven Mary in the park during the fashionable hour. But he hadn't offered, unsure whether he could drive on three hours of sleep. In the end, fate kept him from bed, and by the time he'd finished that business, he'd slept so deeply that Jaynes couldn't wake him for dinner. Then an overturned carriage had blocked King Street, so he'd ended up walking from St. James's Square, barely reaching Almack's before the porter locked the door. Mary must be dying by inches. Society's cruelest tongues would have spent the last three hours regaling her with prophesies of doom.

And that wasn't his only fear. Despite Lady Jersey's gesture last evening, he wasn't sure of his welcome. Three years of censure made assumptions dangerous.

He reached that hurdle at the top of the stairs. Lady Jersey was waiting at the door.

"About time," she said tartly.

"Snarled traffic." He lowered his voice to imply shared secrets. "An overturned carriage carrying Mr. Beasley and Lady Gwendolyn Harte, both in greater dishabille than an accident would explain."

"You don't say!" Her eyes gleamed.

"I do say. His waistcoat was unbuttoned, and his cravat gone. Her hair was down, and though she was wrapped in his cloak, her skirts were dragging on one side—an unpinned bodice unless my eye is completely out."

"Wicked man." She tapped him with her fan. "How can I ignore you after such a delicious tale?"

"You would welcome me even if I arrived taleless," he said daringly. "As a favor to my lovely Mary, if nothing else."

"Perhaps." She shook her head. "Just don't betray my trust."

"Never. It would hurt Mary." He raised her hand for a courtly kiss.

"Very well. Go rescue your betrothed from Lady Horseley. The woman annoys me. She's been predicting scandal all evening."

"Then she will be disappointed." He spotted Mary across the room with several of society's naysayers. She was stunning tonight in an emerald gown trimmed with golden flowers. Her ring gleamed.

Joining her took several minutes, for he had to accept felicitations, respond to ambivalent greetings, and ignore hesitant cuts—Lady Jersey's acceptance did not fully restore him to favor; too many were shocked that he'd passed these sacred portals without bringing the roof down.

He avoided questions, smiling graciously to one and all, but he was cursing himself with every stride. Mary's pale face raised every one of his protective instincts. She had probably been surrounded since the moment she'd arrived, something he could have buffered if he hadn't overslept. He knew how much she needed solitude.

Only after he drew close enough to meet her eyes did he relax. They lit with pleasure, sending an arrow straight to his groin. She was lovelier than she realized.

"Sorry to be late, my dear," he said, dropping a kiss on her brow. "I overslept."

"I feared—" She stopped.

That he had already jilted her? Fury swept him, aimed directly at Lady Horseley and her ilk. "We will dance."

The next set was a waltz. Probably Lady Jersey's doing. "Did you really think I might break my vow?" he asked gently as he led her out.

"Never! I feared you dead," she blurted, then blushed crimson. "Turner might grow desperate now that you know of his plot."

"Nay." He pulled her closer, marveling at her softness. The sprinkle of freckles across her shoulders begged to be kissed. But that was for later and might require some gentling first. He'd noticed how she pulled back each time he kissed her. "Turner would not dare attack now, for others also know his dishonor."

"Perhaps, but horrid images have plagued me all day."

"Tell me."

She sighed. "My imagination is often lurid. It conjured visions of you sprawled on the floor with a bullet through your heart or your face black from poison, crumpled in the wreckage of your carriage, bloated and bobbing down the Thames, blackened by fire—"

"My poor Mary," he said, interrupting the gruesome recital. "I should have told you that I have men watching him—not that I expect further attacks. Already doubts are plaguing him, though he cannot yet admit he is wrong."

"Sometimes doubts make people lash out to still the voices they do not wish to hear. And people can be quite destructive when thwarted. Consider Laura."

"I would rather not. Have people warned you against me all evening?"

"Some."

"I presume Lady Horseley was particularly venal."

She hesitated, as if fearful of admitting anything unpleasant, but finally nodded miserably.

"That is yet another reason to convince Turner. Promise me something." He waited until she met his gaze. "Don't ever lie to me, my dear. Not even by silence. We have both suffered the slings and arrows of vicious gossip, so we know that only truth and trust in each other will do."

"I do not wish to hurt you, Gray. You have suffered so much already."

"Truth may not be pleasant, but ignorance leaves us vulnerable." He waited until she nodded. "So what happened?"

"Lady Horseley, as you surmised. Like others, she warned me to break off this ill-conceived betrothal lest I face Constance's fate. But she is amazingly insistent, clinging to my side all evening to exhort me with tales of your dishonor. I cannot escape her. And she will not hear a word in your favor."

"Hardly a surprise. She is cousin to the Turners."

"What?"

"Cousin. And as tenacious about protecting family as you."

Her eyes widened.

"I know you better than you think, Mary. Ignore Lady Horseley for now. She will admit the truth eventually."

"Perhaps."

Gray sidestepped Miss Cunningham, who had tripped on the uneven floor, pulling Lord Bankhead off balance. "Is anyone else bothering you?"

"No. Other than Lady Horseley, the evening has been quite remarkable. Lady Jersey is being kind, and even the fiercest patronesses smiled. I've danced every set. It is truly amazing. I doubt I've danced two sets a night all Season until now."

"There is nothing amazing about it. You merely crept out of the corner so people can see you. That gown is lovely, and your hair is different tonight." That hint of gold turned out to be sunstreaks—she probably forgot her bonnet when bird-watching. They animated the brown waves framing her face. The style suited her well.

"Thank you, but don't exaggerate. Most of the attention arises from curiosity about this oddity who wishes to wed you."

"Never an oddity. You are an original," he said sharply.

"As you say. But we have more important matters to discuss than my dress and dance partners. I have identified Constance's paramour."

"You did?" He stumbled. "Amazing. Who is he?"

"Lord Roger Duncan." In a low voice, she described her inquiries. He pulled her closer so he could hear, then found that her scent distracted him.

"The timing is perfect," she concluded. "She discovered he was married and swooned. I do not believe her condition was responsible, for those early symptoms would have been fading by then. Panicked, she tried to attach a husband."

He swore, then quickly apologized.

"I feel the same. I hope to speak to her maid tomorrow."

"No. I doubt the girl would talk. She must have known the truth, but speaking now would endanger her current position. No one wants a dishonorable servant. And seeking her out could endanger you."

"But my evidence will never convince Turner. He will attribute her swoon to pregnancy, not shock, just as Lady Sheffield did."

"I know. But now that I have a suspect, I can find out when he visited Yorkshire."

"Excellent idea."

They danced in silence for a time. Her eyes glowed green tonight, reflecting her gown, which was more stylish than others she'd worn—perhaps because this was Almack's, with its many archaic rules. It was the only place besides court where she still had to wear knee breeches. But he hoped she had dressed for him.

He had claimed to know her, yet in many ways she was an enigma. Her unhappiness with this match showed in the way she held back, despite her vows to make the best of it. She had wanted to wed for love—her only remaining dream. Laura had destroyed her other illusions, leaving her pragmatic and more knowing that most ladies her age. Now fate had stripped her of the last one.

Ironically, he wanted her more each time they met. And it wasn't just lust, though kissing her kept him burning for hours afterward. She was intriguing and already a good friend. They shared many interests. He trusted her even with his weaknesses. Perhaps she could come to love him, provided he didn't frighten her. But that meant moving slowly—like coaxing a bird to his hand.

She was very protective of family, which hinted at other dreams she had yet to share. Maybe she would respond to having one of those realized. It was worth a try, and there might be time to manage it. He would look into the possibility when he returned home.

"You seem warm," he said, dancing toward a window. "Shall we step onto the balcony for a moment?"

"I would enjoy that."

The balcony was small and overlooked the mews. No one else had ventured forth, for the night was cold, with fog beginning to build. Gray led her to a corner out of sight of the door, then pulled her into his arms. Just one kiss, he promised himself. Light and coaxing.

But the moment his lips met hers, he lost control. Her taste exploded in his mouth, triggering needs that ran deeper than enjoyment of a willing woman. She was soft in his arms, with delightful curves and a scent that made him dizzy with desire. He knew he should stop, but he couldn't help himself.

Drawing her tight against him, he teased his manhood with caresses he couldn't complete. Only when his hand touched her hair did he pause, groaning, for he could not leave her disheveled.

That moment of sanity made him aware of another problem. She had responded at first, but now stood stiff in his arms.

Fear. It was clear in her eyes. His unexpected assault frightened her.

Cursing, he gentled his touch, pulling the threads of his control taut. "Can you be ready to wed by Tuesday?"

"So soon? I thought you said we needn't rush."

Her question chilled him to the bone. Had he frightened her into second thoughts about this match? She was an innocent who knew nothing about the marriage bed.

"I may have been hasty," he admitted, lightly stroking her back. "Our betrothal is attracting more attention than I expected. The pressure to jilt me before I ruin you will increase, as will the warnings against my wickedness." The betting book at White's had contained twenty-three wagers on the match by the time he'd left last night. Their number would swell with each passing day. Too many of those wagerers would press her to reconsider.

"Will haste not prompt even more speculation? People will assume that I am with child."

He flinched. "Blunt, as usual." When she tried to protest, he laid a calming finger across her lips, clinging to his conviction that they would deal well together once they got past the initial discomfort. "I would not have you any other way, my dear. I want there to be complete honesty between us. And you are right. Such speculation already exists." With wagers in place. "It will not cease until nine months pass without a child."

She blushed. "So we will be a nine-months wonder."

"To some. I can do nothing about that, but we can reduce the other talk. The only reason for waiting was to remain in town. That problem is now solved. I bought a house after leaving you this afternoon."

"No wonder you overslept. You must not have reached your bed until after dinner."

When she laid her head on his shoulder, he relaxed. Perhaps he had not terrified her after all.

Her arms crept around his waist. "How did you find a house so quickly?"

"Luck. I had offered to buy it a year ago," he admitted. "So when the owner decided to sell, he sent for me. You will like it—a six-bay exposure on Berkley Square, large garden, stabling for eight horses and four carriages, ample space—we will be in town half the year because of business. The drawing room is shabby, and the library needs enlarging, but it should suit us very well. Comfort without ostentation." And as different from Rothmoor Park as possible. He had always felt stifled at the family seat, with its massive furniture crammed into tiny rooms. His first act when the title came to him would be to tear it down and rebuild.

"So that is how Wendell is recouping," she murmured.

"You know of his trouble?" He didn't know why he was surprised, for all London must have heard by now.

"Lady Beatrice mentioned last night's disaster at the tables. She claimed he was completely done up and implied he might put an end to his existence."

"Then for once, she exaggerates. He is not destitute. I gave him a good price for the house and advised him to invest the excess in his estate. He can rebuild his fortune if he avoids playing cards while in his cups." He kissed her nose. "So is Tuesday acceptable?"

"Are you sure you want to go through with this?" Her voice trembled, slicing him to the core. "I know you were not seeking a wife, particularly one as lacking as I. Once the truth about Miss Turner becomes public, you could find a more suitable match."

"What nonsense is this?" he demanded. Was it Lady Horseley's warning that had scared her rather than his lovemaking? "You will make an admirable wife, Mary. I knew you were special from the moment we met and had already been considering this step." He hesitated. "Or do you not wish to wed me? Is your determination to redeem my reputation a plot to be rid of me?"

Mary gripped his arm. "Of course not. I am trying to keep you alive. I can't think of anyone I would rather wed. But I fear you will come to regret this bargain."

"Never. We will do quite well together, Mary." He pulled her closer. "Trust me. I promised never to lie. You suit me very well, my dear."

"I will always trust you, Gray."

Smiling, he kissed her again. Heat flashed even faster than before. And this time her response made him wish he was anywhere but Almack's. She opened her mouth, sliding her arms around his neck to pull him closer. Her breasts flattened against his chest, driving him wild. In imagination he saw her hair spread across a pillow as he feasted on her nipples, his hand sliding down to tangle in the folds and curls guarding her secrets. His manhood strained against his breeches, grinding against her in a vain attempt to escape. He groaned.

"Mary." He trailed kisses across her face, wishing the wedding was behind them. "My wonderful Mary. Next

Tuesday. I will call on Rockhurst in the morning to make the arrangements."

"Tuesday."

The music stopped. Laughter penetrated the door, reminding him of their location.

She released him and straightened her gown. "We had best return to the ballroom, Gray, or we will both lose our vouchers. Lady Jersey is enjoying the romantic tale we've woven, but she will soon tire of bending rules for us."

"So true." He stole one last kiss. "Later, my dear. We will finish this on Tuesday. I look forward to it."

Laura stopped pacing when Frannie returned. Not that she was calm—even destroying everything in the house would not relieve her fury—but she could not admit her pain to a servant. Not only had her sniveling, bluestocking sister stolen the man she had wanted, but twenty hostesses had now retracted invitations. No doubt they accepted Mary's lies so they could exclude the Season's diamond, increasing their own insipid offsprings' chances.

Catherine had refused to take her on morning calls or allow her in the park during the fashionable hour, treating her as though she were back in the schoolroom. Blake had forbidden her attendance at Almack's tonight. When she had finally convinced Catherine to go shopping so she could escape the house for a while, three ladies had cut her dead on Bond Street—barely acceptable ladies at that, the jealous cats. Then that appalling modiste had informed her in a fake French accent that she could not make up new gowns just now. *The press of work, mademoiselle. So many very important clients. You must wait your turn, n'est ce pas?* Then when she'd arrived home, Grayson had cut her dead on the stairs of her own house!

She'd shed stormy tears for more than an hour. It wasn't fair! She should be planning the wedding of the Season instead of being shut away like a dirty secret. How could Mary betray her? She'd always been such a quiet mouse. Who would have thought she could be so bold?

A voice in her head urged her to face facts, but it sounded too much like Blake, so she ignored it.

New tears had fallen after Mary slithered off to Almack's, rosy from Blake's compliments, though he must know that green was a ruinous color that made one look quite bilious. And that gown was too plain to be fashionable. There wasn't a ruffle or bow in sight, only a modest ribbon under the bodice and a few flowers around the hem. Watching them leave from her perch on the third landing had made Laura feel like a child sneaking peeks at adult fun.

The analogy had started a fresh round of tears. Unable to face an evening alone, she'd wracked her brain for anything that might promise amusement. It took half an hour to recall Dr. Sparks. She'd sent Frannie out to discover the details.

"Well?" she asked when Frannie halted just inside the door.

The maid extended a card. "The Society for the Investigation of Electricity, Spectral Phenomena, and Ancient Legends welcomes visitors to their meetings. Tonight they are testing an electricity machine across the square. It sounds dangerous. Lord Rockhurst would not approve." She sounded shaken—and defiant. Never before had she invoked Blake against Laura.

"If I remain here, I shall expire of boredom," said Laura sharply. "Since Rockhurst refused to take me to Almack's, I must choose my own entertainment. But you need not fear. The society has many members from Polite Society—how do you think I learned of it?" Again she stifled the voice reminding her that none of her informants actually belonged, and Miss Pepperidge had mocked Dr. Sparks sharply. But anything was better than staying home alone.

Frannie sighed. "I do not wish to see such a contraption."

"You need not. I am sure the other maids are enjoying themselves in the servants' hall. Come. We can walk."

"Miss Laura—"

"We will take a footman." She stalked toward the door. "My pelisse, Frannie. Now, or I will go without you. Perhaps you would be happier back in Devonshire," she added, glaring. The threat would whip the girl in line. She'd been carrying on with a footman at Rockburn Abbey and never wanted to see Seabrook Manor again.

"I'm coming."

Laura had no idea what to expect. When Miss Pepper-idge had mentioned the meeting—giggling behind her fan to Miss Connors—she'd described ghosts and machines that made hair stand on end. She'd known little else, for she had heard the tale from her brother. It sounded rather exciting—certainly more exciting than sitting at home with only servants for company.

But her first impression was disappointing. The house was narrow, with a dark-paneled entry that seemed dingy in the light of a single candle. A shuffling butler ushered her into an equally dingy library.

Eight people crowded around a table, whispering. They didn't notice her entrance.

"When we have amassed a large enough charge, we will test your theory, Lady Spectre," said a gentleman.

"How much longer?" Lady Spectre demanded. "It is half past eleven already."

"Soon. There is plenty of time."

"Miss Seabrook," announced the butler.

Five men and three women turned to stare. Laura stared back.

"I am Dr. Sparks," said the leader. "This is Lady Spec-tre, a noted spiritualist. Miss Watson. Mr. Showalter." He continued around the circle. As they parted ranks to allow her closer, Laura caught sight of the apparatus on the table.

A servant was vigorously turning a crank attached to a large metal disk. As it rotated, it rubbed against wool pads, producing occasional sparks. A wire ran from the disk's center to a metal ball atop an enormous glass jar, whose lower half was covered with metal sheeting.

"Carry on," Dr. Sparks ordered the servant, then led Laura closer. "This is the world's largest Leyden jar, Miss Seabrook. We are filling it with electricity."

"Why?"

Lady Spectre beamed. "You are about to witness the culmination of years of study. Spectral phenomena—

ghosts, to most people—are produced by souls trapped between this life and the next."

"Like poor Uncle Harold," sobbed Mrs. Jones, sniffing into her handkerchief.

"And my great-grandfather, Alfred," added a white-haired gentleman.

"Exactly." Lady Spectre's voice turned seductively soft. "I have investigated hundreds of spectral hauntings. Hundreds, Miss Seabrook. And I have discovered that every one was the product of a violent death. Every one. And that is the secret of spectral phenomena. Life imbues the soul with energy, Miss Seabrook, very like the electricity Dr. Sparks captures in this jar. When a person dies a normal death, that energy propels the soul into the hereafter." She flung her hands toward the ceiling, fingers spread.

Mrs. Jones gasped.

"But violence and emotional distress drain that energy, robbing the soul of its ability to move on." Her arms collapsed. "It is doomed to wander in a formless state forever."

"Forever?" Miss Watson's thin voice cracked.

"Until now. Through the magic of electricity, we can now restore that lost energy, propelling the soul into the hereafter to reap its reward."

"Thus tonight's experiment." Dr. Sparks curtly cut off Lady Spectre's mesmerizing voice. "My Leyden jar holds a larger charge than has ever before been amassed. By releasing it into the spirit, we can complete its journey."

"Isn't that dangerous?" asked Mrs. Jones.

"In the wrong hands, it can do great damage. But I understand and control its power." He continued his exhortation, but Laura lost track of his words as she watched Lady Spectre.

The spiritualist resumed her preparations by unrolling a pair of wires. "You say the ghost always appears in this chair?" She glanced at their host, Lord Roger Duncan.

"Yes. The spirit was once Mr. Cavendish, who owned this house until he broke his neck falling down the stairs. He began appearing a month ago, which is why I called on you. I cannot have him upsetting my servants. I've already had to replace two maids and my cook. The housekeeper has threatened to leave unless something is done."

"Irritating," agreed Dr. Sparks. "The uneducated do not realize they have nothing to fear from these lost souls. The deceased is asking for help. Rest assured, we will respond. He will meet his Maker by morning."

"How can you tell how much electricity is in the jar?" asked Laura, intrigued despite herself.

"I feel it boiling within." Dr. Sparks touched a bare fingertip to the metal ball. "Come. See for yourself."

Laura studied the jar as she removed her glove. The knob narrowed to a thin rod that penetrated a wooden stopper, then supported a heavy chain that dangled to the bottom of the jar. More metal sheeting coated the lower inside.

She extended a finger to the knob, hesitantly at first, then more firmly. It tingled. The fine hairs on the back of her neck stirred, awakening more excitement than she had felt in days.

"How do you release it?" She turned as she spoke, brushing her other hand against the metal sheeting. "Oh!" Lightning blinded her, throwing her backwards. Only a pair of strong hands saved her from sprawling.

Voices rose on all sides.

Someone cursed.

Lady Spectre screamed that the experiment was ruined, pounding on the table as she raged.

"Are you all right?" asked Lord Roger, holding her upright.

"I don't know." Her hand burned. "What happened?"

"You discovered how to release the electricity," said Dr. Sparks, gesturing for silence. "But there is no harm done. We will merely start anew. The ghost is not due until midnight, so we have sufficient time." His eyes pinned Lady Spectre, willing her to silence.

Laura backed away from the machine, unwilling to touch it again. Miss Watson and Mrs. Jones were whispering in the corner—probably laughing over her clumsiness.

The servant cranked at high speed. Dr. Sparks lectured on the properties of electricity, urging everyone to handle objects that had been exposed to it. Most emitted brief shocks when touched by a gloveless finger, but nothing as large as the Leyden jar.

Lady Spectre subsided as the jar collected a new charge, delivering observations on spectral phenomena as she elaborated on her theory of energy transference. Laura stayed well away from the table, hovering in the shadow of a bookcase.

"Your finger is red," murmured Lord Roger, reaching over her shoulder to lift her hand. The motion brushed his chest against her back—and a muscular chest it was. "I hope it will heal."

"I am convinced of it, sir." The mark had already begun to fade. Yet she did not protest when he rubbed it lightly. His bare hands produced tremors of excitement along her skin similar to those she'd felt when touching the knob.

"Is electricity a regular interest, Miss Seabrook?" He led her farther into a corner so they did not disturb Lady Spectre's lecture.

"No. But this demonstration sounded intriguing. And the location was convenient. I live across the square."

"You do not mind visiting a gentleman's house?"

She frowned, but his voice seemed teasing rather than critical. "I did not realize that it was a gentleman's house until I arrived. But it hardly matters since the gathering includes ladies."

He was still massaging her finger, sending ripples of heat up her arm. Lord Roger was a man in his prime, broad-shouldered, long-legged, confident. Not for him the rigid disapproval of narrow-minded gossips. He hadn't turned a hair upon hearing her name. Nor was he averse to newfangled notions—like using electricity to rid him of an unwanted ghost.

So she had found adventure after all—and an adventurer. The rasp of his fingers made her warm all over. When she lifted their joined hands to see what he was doing, he smiled, tightening his grip as his thumb traced circles on her palm. His dark eyes gleamed with pleasure, clearly entranced.

"Why aren't you at a ball this evening, Miss Seabrook?" he murmured into her ear. They had drawn behind the bookcase, out of sight of those clustered about the table. Dr. Sparks was approaching a critical point in the experiment, but Laura no longer cared.

"My sponsor is annoyed that I outshine my sister, so he refused to take me to Almack's. Lady Cunningham followed his lead," she said, stretching the truth. "She wants me banned so her daughter can snare a high-ranking lord."

"Banned. Such a strong word."

"But true." She sighed most tragically. "People are jealous that men vie for my favors."

"How unfair. Perhaps I can change their minds, my dear. As your champion, I can slay these silly society dragons. Have you plans for tomorrow?"

She shook her head. Lady Edmondson's note withdrawing the card to her rout had denounced her in scathing terms. Perhaps it was time to carve a new niche for herself in the wider world of adventurers. Her mistake had been to expect such men to waste time on frivolous parties with their rigid rules and disapproving eyes.

His other hand stroked down her arm. "The electricity society will meet again tomorrow. Dr. Sparks wants to repeat the treatment to make sure the spirit is truly gone and not merely stuck at another point in its journey. Join us. We can discuss your situation. I should have devised a remedy by then."

"How chivalrous, my lord. Thank you." A hand brushed her cheek, light as gossamer, but she felt the touch clear to her toes.

"It will be a pleasure, my dear. So charming a lady as yourself deserves only the best. And I will see that you find it." Those gathered at the table gasped in anticipation. "I believe it is time. Come." A clock began to strike midnight.

"Hold hands to confine the spirit to the corner," ordered Lady Spectre.

As the group formed a semicircle, Lord Roger's thumb continued to caress Laura's palm, quickening her breath into shallow pants. She met his glittering gaze before reluctantly turning her eyes to the corner, where a light mist was gathering. Her heart raced.

"We are ready."

Lady Spectre had fastened her wires to the chair. Using wooden tongs, Dr. Sparks raised the other ends.

Miss Watson fainted as the mist wavered, shrinking into a form that might have been human. Laura gasped. Lord Roger pulled her against his side, sliding their joined hands along her waist to steady her.

"Now!" ordered Lady Spectre.

Dr. Sparks touched one wire to the knob and the other to the jar's base. A blinding flash ripped through the room.

"Oh!" gasped Laura, burying her face in Lord Roger's shoulder.

"It is quite all right, my dear," he murmured, brushing her breast as his arm tightened around her.

She could barely breathe for the excitement coursing through her veins.

"Success!" declared Dr. Sparks.

Laura forced her eyes toward the corner. The mist was gone. The smell of singed wool hung heavily on the air—and something else she couldn't name, though it made her scalp tingle.

Lord Roger remained at her side for the remainder of the meeting. Dr. Sparks concluded his demonstration by forming the group into a circle, again with joined hands. He grasped the wire while the servant cranked furiously. Electricity tingled from one person to the next, heightening the sensation of Lord Roger's bare hand against her own.

By the time she reached home, Laura glowed. Lord Roger had insisted on accompanying her, proclaiming that a maid and footman were insufficient protection so late at night. He left her with another of those butterfly touches and the promise of even more excitement tomorrow. She could hardly wait.

Chapter Fourteen

Mary smiled as she headed for her room. Almack's had been exhilarating. And she would be wed in less than a week.

For the first time since her sudden betrothal she considered her wedding night. Gray's kisses had been different this evening, more demanding and certainly more exciting, awakening urges she'd never felt—which was probably good. While many ladies considered the marriage bed an onerous duty, those who admitted enjoyment seemed closer to their husbands.

She chuckled softly. How many frank conversations had she overheard because people rarely noticed her? Far more than the average miss.

So Gray would likely appreciate a wife who could enjoy his touch. After all, he had vowed fidelity, so he could not seek pleasure elsewhere. And he wanted her.

With their bodies pressed close, she had felt the changes that proved his interest. At first, they had startled her. Before she had worked out what had happened, he had diverted her with news that he'd bought a town house.

But the second time, there had been no mistaking his intent.

The knowledge was heady. No one had ever wanted her. Few men even noticed her, for Laura's beauty drew every eye. But even that first day before they even knew each other's name, Gray had treated her with respect. Their shared interests made them friends. Now she knew that he also desired her.

Weakness again washed over her as she recalled that

embrace on the balcony. He had rubbed against her, breathing heavily as he murmured her name. A hand on her bottom kept her from pulling away. His tongue had tasted, explored, then devoured until she had to cling with all her strength to keep from melting at his feet. Her breasts still tingled every time she recalled those brief moments.

Six more days. The wonder weakened her knees. Gray had partnered her for a second waltz, stayed by her side between sets, and played the besotted fool all evening. It was no more than she had expected, considering his determination to convince society they'd planned this match. But perhaps it was not all pretense.

Don't confuse dreams and reality, cautioned her conscience. *That is how Laura comes to grief. Just because you lo—*

She could not complete the thought, even in her mind. Yes, she was eager for this match. He cut an amazing figure—sleek and confident—putting other man to shame the moment he entered a room. His clothes were elegant, but not extreme. His manners faultless, lacking the affectations so many dandies espoused. His form owed nothing to artifice, nor did his speech. He was a man who created his own fashion rather than followed others. And in the process, he spoke directly to her soul.

Yet she could not abandon caution. Friendship was fine, for he had welcomed it. But until he wanted her heart, she must restrain it. Besotted females had hurt him more than once. She must never add to that pain.

"Home at last?" asked Laura, rushing into the hallway as Mary passed her door. Mary frowned. Laura was wearing her favorite walking dress, and her eyes glittered with excitement.

"I am surprised to find you still awake." It was nearly two, and Laura's expression could only spell trouble. Where was the anger that had flared at dinner or the boredom that should have replaced it?

"I only returned half an hour ago." Her mischievous smile raised new fears.

"From where?" Even Mrs. Burton had canceled Laura's invitation for tonight. The Burtons were mushrooms willing to accept any connection to the polite world, so their cancellation had thrown Laura into hysterics.

"The Society for the Investigation of Electricity, Spectral Phenomena, and Ancient Legends. Their meeting was more interesting than Almack's, with its stale cakes and undrinkable orgeat."

"Really?" Mary's wariness increased. Laura heaped scorn on anything intellectual. The day Almack's bored her was the day the family had better look out. She might be exaggerating to soothe her pride, but Mary did not believe it. Alarms were clanging on all sides.

"Yes." Laura couldn't stand still, picking up item after item from tables as she paced the hall. "Dr. Sparks demonstrated his electricity machine. It is a powerful force, able to bind the oddest objects together. He stored vast quantities of it in a Leyden jar, then released it to banish the ghost haunting the library."

"A ghost?" That might explain the excitement, though Laura had never evinced interest in ghosts, either.

"The previous owner. You would have fainted dead away, as Miss Watson did. It started as a wisp of fog, then thickened and twisted into human form."

Mary shivered.

"Fortunately, Lady Spectre knows how to handle ghosts."

"How many people attended?"

"Nine." Laura's eyes narrowed. "If that scowl implies disapproval, you should know that Frannie and a footman accompanied me. Three other ladies were also present, so there is no need to preach of impropriety."

"I was not implying anything. I was merely surprised that you would enjoy a scientific gathering. You have demonstrated no interest in the subject previously."

"I did not know what I was missing. Electricity is marvelously energizing. I've not had such fun in years." Cunning flashed in her eyes. "The gentleman who owns the house is quite handsome—and eminently proper," she added as Mary opened her mouth. "He was appalled at my plight and promised to restore my standing in society. As a duke's son, his credit is very high."

"Then he does not understand your situation. I doubt the Regent could help you at the moment. Tonight's condemnation sent even Catherine into the vapors."

Laura flinched, but recovered quickly, examining her hand as if she could not meet Mary's eyes. "The rumors will soon fade. Lord Roger promised to restore me, and he is a most chivalrous man. Even Lady Beatrice will listen to him."

"Lord Roger?"

"Lord Roger Duncan." With the uttering of the name, Laura's excitement spilled over, sending her dancing along the hallway. "Handsome. Charming. Quite the most wonderful man I've ever met. You would not believe how he makes me feel."

The blood drained from Mary's head. She opened her mouth, then closed it without uttering a word. Laura's mood was more fey than ever. Even in the best of times, she rarely listened to advice. Informing her that Lord Roger was a scoundrel who had already ruined at least one innocent would merely pique her interest. There was no telling what she would do. Even revealing that Lord Roger was married might make no difference.

But perhaps she could make Laura think. "Why have we never met him?" she asked carefully. "He has attended none of the Season's parties, not even the one at Hartleigh House graced by the Regent."

"He has more important interests than frittering away his time in ballrooms. Besides, he moves in higher circles than we do," claimed Laura airily.

Higher? Mary stifled a sigh. Arguing would harden Laura's determination. Yet she had to try. No matter what Laura's faults, she was still her sister.

"Who introduced him?" she asked.

"Dr. Sparks, but he is also a gentleman. A younger son, I expect. He reminds me of Mr. Billows." Billows was a neighbor in Devonshire who dabbled in science.

Mary gritted her teeth. Another adventurer. Sparks's character was probably as false as his name. "One cannot

e too cautious. A formal introduction from someone
ou know is the only defense against scoundrels."

"Which makes one wonder how you know Grayson,"
napped Laura in one of her lightning changes. "Who
ntroduced *you?*" Retreating to her room, she slammed
he door.

Mary blushed. She'd stuck her foot in her mouth that
ime. Mentioning proper introductions was truly ironic.
he had yet to be formally introduced to Gray, the man
ho had kissed her senseless only three hours ago, and
he man she would wed Tuesday morning.

She sighed. She had to warn Blake, though she hated
earing tales. And Gray.

Mary slept poorly, awakening with a throbbing head-
che. She had hoped that ostracism would force Laura
o change her ways, but instead it was pushing her into
orse indiscretions. Not that society would care. Laura's
rrogance had annoyed too many people. Now that she
ad handed them a weapon against her, they were
ielding it with enthusiasm. Last night's gossip had
een brutal.

Even worse, it looked like Laura had invented the tale
bout Miss Norton's elopement with the dancing master.
ord Norton swore on his honor the story was false.
Most now believed him, accusing Laura of fostering the
e so she could steal Miss Norton's court. Miss Norton
ad unpacked her trunks and headed for Almack's the
oment she heard. While she reveled in a return to
avor, whispers accused Laura of spreading other lies,
o.

Mary would never have believed Laura could stoop so
ow, for she knew how painful lies could be. But there
as no denying that Laura knew how to manipulate
pinion. She had learned the art from a master. And she
ad never been one to tolerate rivals.

Now Laura faced permanent ostracism. Lady Beatrice
ad vowed to watch Laura closely, so she would know
bout her call on Lord Roger. Mary shook her head.
What had possessed the girl? It didn't matter that he was

hosting a society of electricity enthusiasts. His reputation was so bad that even calling accompanied by one's entire family would draw censure.

Sighing, she dressed in a simple gown, pinned her hair in a tidy knot, and went downstairs. It was nearly eleven. Blake and Gray should be in the library.

"Is this import—" Blake abandoned his question the moment the light caught her face. "What is wrong, Mary?"

"Laura."

"Did she attack you again?" Gray leaped up to take her hand. He sounded furious.

"No." Mary squeezed gently to calm him. "She is too busy with her own plans to waste time on me."

"Plans?" Blake stiffened.

Gray led Mary to the couch and settled her by his side. "What now?"

She leaned into Gray, grateful for his protection, though Blake's anger was not aimed at her. "She sought out the Society for the Investigation of Electricity, Spectral Phenomena, and Ancient Legends last evening."

Blake's brows rose. "I'm not familiar with it. Grayson?" He turned to Gray.

"Nor am I, though I know most legitimate science organizations." He met Mary's gaze. "You are concerned."

She nodded. "The group is probably harmless. Its demonstrations attract young men looking for mystery and excitement. Garbled reports reached some of their sisters—which is where Laura heard of it. Miss Pepperidge and Miss Connors were giggling about them one day. Their leader calls himself Dr. Sparks. He has an electricity machine and makes a great show discharging Leyden jars and such."

"That does not sound like something Laura would find interesting." Blake frowned. "In fact, I cannot imagine her enjoying such things."

"Not in the usual way, but Dr. Sparks's partner is a spiritualist who calls herself Lady Spectre. Their current business is exorcising ghosts. That might well have caught her fancy."

"Good God," said Gray in disgust.

"She said nothing about leaving the house last evening."

"The meeting was across the square. She took Frannie and one of the footmen to maintain propriety."

"Then what is the problem?"

"The house's owner. She was bursting with excitement when I returned from Almack's. Now that Gray is out of reach, she has formed a new infatuation for Lord Roger Duncan."

"Damnation," muttered Gray.

"It will go no further," vowed Blake, rising.

"Wait," begged Mary. "Think before you approach her. She is beyond fey this time. In her present humor, she will do the opposite of what you demand."

Blake slumped. "Again?"

Mary nodded.

"What?" asked Gray softly.

"Laura can be willful to a fault," Mary replied. "In certain humors, she reacts very badly to suggestion."

Blake sighed. "Yet I cannot let her see him. Merely speaking with him could ruin any chance society might welcome her back."

"He would not stop with speech," pointed out Gray. "Mary discovered that he seduced Miss Turner three years ago. I've a runner investigating his activities, and even the preliminary report makes horrific reading. Not only is he willing to ruin innocents, he actually enjoys it. In his twisted way, he sees it as retaliation against the society that rejected him."

Blake swore. "I have to stop her."

"Agreed. But how?" asked Mary. "This is her worst attachment yet. I asked Lady Beatrice about him last night. She can talk for hours about the man, all of it bad. But from her description, I fear he is bored."

"Bored?" Gray stared at her.

"Think about it. He has been ostracized by his own class—not censured, as you were, but completely cut off, even from the clubs. Only two other scoundrels will even speak to him. Yet his birth prevents the lower classes

from accepting him." She leaned closer to his side. "He
has no conscience, and breaking society's rules does him
no harm. So when Laura throws herself at him, he won't
refuse. And she will do just that, for she finds his aura
of danger exciting. Unfortunately, while he knows exactly
what he is doing, Laura does not. She believes that he is
a powerful member of society, eschewing Marriage Mart
events because he is engaged in more important matters
and moves in higher circles."

"My God! Has she lost her mind?" demanded Blake.

"Sometimes I think so," admitted Mary.

"At least we can disprove that notion," said Gray.

"Not easily." Mary pinched her throbbing temples.
"Laura never listens when in the throes of fantasy. If she
decided the sky was green, she would ignore evidence to
the contrary. She has already spent an evening in his
house. What is to keep her from returning—and not in
the company of her maid? If you post a guard, Lord
Roger would relish the challenge. As would Laura."

"Are you suggesting that she learn this lesson the hard
way?" Blake demanded incredulously. "I cannot allow
it. She is in my charge. By the time she admits the truth,
her virtue would be gone."

"Not if you control the circumstances," said Gray
slowly. "Let him start his seduction, but keep men close
at hand to step in before it progresses too far."

"Impossible," snapped Blake.

"Is it? Suppose they arranged a clandestine meeting
during Lady Wharburton's masquerade tomorrow. When
she joined him, you could discover them, then accuse
him of seducing Miss Turner—a disaster that left her
with child and led to her suicide. Finish by asking after
his wife. He can hardly deny he has one."

"I don't like it," put in Mary. "Too many people
would be near at hand. You cannot expect Laura to behave reasonably when her plans go awry. Look what she
did at Lady Cunningham's. And Lord Roger would not
care. He is safe from aught but a duel and would likely
cheat at that. I doubt he even remembers Miss Turner,
but he might create enough clamor to attract notice, thus

ruining Laura forever and dragging the rest of us down with her."

"Have you a better suggestion?" demanded Blake.

Mary nodded. "We cannot send her to the country. Lord Roger would follow her, and there are too many places they could meet unobserved. But exposing his affair with Miss Turner might work. Gossip would recall his other misdeeds, including his marriage. If Laura hears tales about him from people who do not suspect her acquaintance, she would be more likely to listen."

"That would require that she remain in society," said Gray.

"Private entertainments aren't the only places to hear *on-dits*."

Blake nodded, pursing his lips as he thought. Gray drew Mary's hand between his palms, then kissed her fingers one by one. That treacherous weakness again settled in her legs.

"We will attend the theater tonight," decided Blake at last. "And Lady Wharburton has not yet canceled Laura's invitation—an oversight, I am sure, but I will prevail upon her to allow Laura's attendance. If we keep her occupied, she cannot meet the rogue. Is your evidence compelling enough to convince Lady Beatrice?"

"No," said Gray.

"It might be by tomorrow, for she is already half convinced," countered Mary, turning to Gray. "Have you studied old newspapers yet? The society pages should show where you were. Since you avoided entertainments she attended, they should refute her claims."

"I've not had time, but I have a friend who collects papers. I will bring them here this afternoon. We can read them together."

Nodding, she left him to explain his own problem—or not.

Laura was heading for breakfast. "Who called so early?" she demanded, eyes shining at the murmur of voices from the library.

"Gray. He and Blake are discussing settlements."

"Oh." All excitement faded.

"Blake has devised a plan to put this unpleasantness behind us. He is taking us to the theater tonight, and Lady Wharburton agreed to welcome you to her masquerade tomorrow."

"Theater." Laura scowled. "I must decline. I promised to attend the Society's meeting."

Mary grimaced. "You had best tell Blake immediately, then. But he is in no mood to humor you. He was not happy about last night's rumors. People are claiming you made up the tale about Miss Norton."

Laura paled. "As you wish. Tell him I will attend the theater." She swept into the breakfast room.

Mary frowned. Laura had refused to meet her eye. Very shifty. Was she planning to slip out after they returned home?

Gray returned to Rockhurst House at two, his carriage crammed with newspapers. One of his odder friends was a scholar writing a history of England's war with France, from the death of Louis XVI in 1792 to the end, whenever that occurred. To aid his research, he had accumulated more than twenty years' worth of newspapers and journals. They filled his house, leaving him little room to maneuver, but this treasure trove was at Gray's disposal.

"Heavens!" exclaimed Mary, pausing just inside the door. Stacks of newspapers littered the room.

"Your idea has merit, but it will not be easy," said Gray, dropping a kiss on her cheek. "We must find every mention of Lord Roger, Miss Turner, or me. Are you sure you are up to such a task?"

"Stop teasing, Gray. It cannot be overwhelming. We need read only the society pages. Let's hope that the attendance lists are extensive. And we already have one discrepancy. Miss Turner claimed a tryst with you in Lady Marchgate's garden on the fifteenth of May, but Lady Sheffield knows you were at Watier's that night. You won five hundred guineas from Lord Sheffield, jeopardizing his suit for her hand."

"She blames me?"

"Of course not. It was Sheffield's fault for risking so much."

Her words warmed him. Never had he known a lady who was so adamant in his defense. Most demanded attention. If they didn't get it, they resorted to megrims or pouting. But Mary cared more for his welfare than her own.

Or was she hoping redemption would cancel their betrothal? She had denied it, but despite her response to his kisses, she remained calm and aloof the rest of the time. Maybe they should stay with the original wedding date. If she wanted to be free of him, he would agree. He could not force her into marriage.

"You take the *Morning Post*," he suggested. "I'll start with the *Observer*. Then we can move on to the *Times* and *Life in London*. *La Belle Assemblee* and *Ackermann's Repository* carry provincial news. We can check Yorkshire for any mention of the Turners."

"Excellent plan." She drew out paper and quills, then took her place on one side of a large library table. Gray sat on the other.

Two hours later, Mary closed the last copy of *Life in London*—the one reporting Miss Turner's death—and switched to *La Belle Assemblee*. Gray's name appeared often. As heir to an earldom, his presence was usually noted. It was harder to track down Miss Turner, for she was the undistinguished daughter of a minor baron. If she attended at all, she was one of the anonymous faces that qualified a gathering as a crush. But they had found six evenings in which Gray was clearly not with Miss Turner. And *Life in London* had noted his retreat to Shellcroft, wondering if Miss C—T——had driven him from town. With luck, these incidents would contradict enough of her claims that Turner would admit she had lied about everything.

But so far they had found nothing about Lord Roger. After fifteen years of total ostracism, the papers no longer noted his activities.

"Here is another interesting note," said Gray—he was still perusing the *Times*. "Under *New Arrivals,* they list me reaching London the day before Lady Debenham's ball."

"Wonderful. You cannot have met her until her condition was well advanced."

He squeezed her hand. "I wish I had thought of this three years ago. It would have saved me much trouble."

"Perhaps. But thinking is rarely clear in the heat of the moment. You were probably sunk in blue-devils."

"True, though that shouldn't have mattered."

"But it does." She pulled his hand between her own. "Serious blue-devils affect everyone who has suffered a severe shock—like Catherine after her first husband died, or me when Father was killed. Surviving each day is such a challenge that you have no energy left to analyze your troubles. By the time the blue-devils leave, you've accepted the explanations of others and no longer question anything."

"Like whether I could prove my innocence?"

She nodded. "Or how Father really died." She released his hand, then picked up the next *La Belle Assemblee*.

Gray had barely returned to the *Times* when Mary laughed.

"I found it. Look, Gray. I found it." She thrust it into his hands. The words leaped from the page.

Yorkshire: 20 January. A pack of hounds decimated the poultry yard at Turner Hall, having been seduced from a scent trail by a disturbance involving two cocks. The dogs—mostly pups—were captured by their owner, the Earl of Rothmoor, ably assisted by Lord Shipley, Lord Turner, Lord Roger Duncan, Mr. Bridges of Parsing Downs, and Mr. Gillow of Upper Stoning. The victims included three dozen pullets, seventeen geese, and one cock.

"That's it. Dear Lord, Turner was right. The culprit came from Rothmoor Park. Rothmoor always holds a house party when he starts training the next pack. It often lasts a month."

"You are free, Gray. No one can ever blame you again."

Gray couldn't respond. Restoration of his honor left him speechless. He had never truly believed that redemption was possible. And it was all due to Mary.

Pulling her across the table, he kissed her. She consumed his senses, teasing his nose with the lightest of fragrances as she murmured his name over and over. With each new touch, the heat rose faster and higher. She was made for him, her skin soft as a rose petal, her breasts the perfect size for his hand.

His palm closed over one soft peak and gently squeezed. The nipple hardened, pressing against him, begging to be tasted. His shaft strained against her thigh, wanting the freedom to probe her yielding depths.

She was perfect. He could not have found a better wife had he searched England from end to end. And she returned his ardor with complete abandon. Excitement built. He wanted nothing more than to bear her to the floor and make her his.

But this was not the time. He was so close to restoring his honor that he could do nothing to jeopardize it. With a groan he pulled back and smiled. Discovery would pitch them both into the fire, casting new stains on their marriage. But honor was hard—very hard.

"We'll finish this on Tuesday," he panted, nipping her earlobe before releasing her.

"I will look forward to it." Her eyes had gone hazy with desire, making it even more difficult to return to work. Her passion matched his own. Yet even as she opened the next paper, it was gone, leaving the aloof woman in its place.

He cursed, but this was no time to demand an explanation. He might consider their proof conclusive, but he wanted every scrap of evidence he could find. Turner was as stubborn as Laura when it came to admitting fault.

Chapter Fifteen

"Aren't you ready yet?" Mary asked, rapping on Laura's door.

"I'm coming!" yelled Laura.

"Not fast enough. Blake will fetch you himself if you don't hurry. Lady Wharburton wishes to speak with you before the first act. If we are late, she may cancel your invitation for tomorrow."

Laura uttered a curse that would have made Andrew's foot soldiers wince. "Does he want me to arrive at the theater in my shift?"

"Catherine says that if Frannie can't dress you in time, she will send Wilson to help."

Frannie yelped.

"One more minute," vowed Laura, then lowered her voice. "Not that fan, Frannie. The one with the painted roses." A drawer slammed. "And see that you take care of that other matter tonight."

"Can't it wait until morning?"

"No. Take a footman if you are afraid of the dark. But don't fail me." Laura jerked the door open. "Don't just stand there, Mary. Let's go."

Mary shook her head as she followed Laura downstairs.

Two hours later, she stared blindly at the stage where Kean's Hamlet was debating suicide. The sense of wrongness that had been teasing her mind all evening suddenly swam into focus.

Laura's instructions to Frannie.

The shops were closed, and Laura had no invitations demanding responses. Had she sent a note to Lord

Roger? There was no honorable reason to do so. A meeting of the electricity society was not an event requiring regrets.

Mary opened her fan to hide her expression. Half the audience was watching the Rockhurst box. Some wondered about Gray's betrothed. Others stared at Laura, hoping she would create a new scandal for their entertainment.

She considered sharing her suspicions with Blake, but she feared his reaction. His temper was precarious tonight. Laura had first delayed their departure, then insulted Mr. Martin and stuck her tongue out at Miss Sanders in the middle of the lobby. Her tone with Lady Wharburton implied that she was granting a favor by accepting the invitation.

Blake had been purple with fury by then. It hadn't abated much by the first interval when Laura regally commanded him to fetch her a drink. He had yet to return.

The door opened. Mary turned, expecting Blake, but Gray entered instead. Relief swept over her. Gray would know what to do. He was calmer than Blake, for he had no responsibility for Laura, allowing him to see her more clearly.

Gray squeezed her hand as he took the chair at her side. "Sorry I'm late again."

Mary shielded her mouth with her fan, glad that Laura sat beyond Catherine. "We may have a new problem," she murmured softly.

"What?" He shifted closer.

She could feel eyes on them, but the intimacy of their pose fit their public image. "Laura might have sent a note to Lord Roger this evening. Perhaps it contained regrets at missing the meeting, but I doubt it. She ordered her maid to deliver it rather than a footman. She may have arranged an assignation."

"Has she no sense at all?"

Mary shook her head. "Not when her will has been crossed."

"What does Rockhurst think?"

"I just realized the significance of her instructions. But Blake is so furious with her that I would rather not accuse her without evidence. And I cannot discuss it with her. She is already bursting with indignation. She used to control her temper in public, but that has changed. One more incident could cause a catastrophe."

"Relax, Mary. I will deal with it." He patted her hand. And as his fingers smoothed her glove, she did, indeed, relax.

Gray stared blankly at the floor as his carriage turned into Jermyn Street. Nick sat silently beside him. With any luck, all problems would resolve today—Turner's plots, his own reputation, Laura's infatuation with Lord Roger. He couldn't believe he was trying to save her worthless hide. But Mary's loyalty to family was not tied to behavior. He'd always wanted a family who supported him completely. But support had to work both ways. Thus he had to help even those he didn't particularly like. At least Laura was the only Seabrook who fell into that category. Rockhurst assured him the rest of the family was fine.

He had sent his groom and a footman to watch Rockhurst House overnight. Laura had made no attempt to slip out, and judging from the traffic at Lord Roger's house, he had been too busy to see her anyway. Perhaps Mary was wrong, or perhaps Lord Roger had turned down Laura's suggestion. He might avoid riling Rockhurst. Or he might have lost interest when he discovered Laura's eagerness. She offered no challenge whatsoever. It wouldn't be the first time her judgment had proved faulty.

At least he would be done with the Turner affair today, though he had changed the plan slightly. Naming Lord Roger as Miss Turner's seducer would divert Turner's obsession to a new target. Gray couldn't do it. Turner needed to consider his own future instead of wallowing in his sister's past.

So Nick would show Lady Beatrice the evidence that proved Miss Turner had lied about Gray. That would be enough to restore his own credit. Rockhurst would tell Laura about Lord Roger, citing his marriage and three other seductions the runner had found, then send her back to Rockburn. Only if Laura remained obstinate, would they reveal the Turner situation—it was the only one that had utterly ruined the victim; the others had managed to hide their indiscretions from society.

Gray hoped it wouldn't come to that, because he feared what Turner would do if he learned Lord Roger's identity, but he would rather make the entire truth public than see Mary unhappy. No matter how venal Laura was, Mary would mourn if Lord Roger ruined her sister.

The carriage pulled to a halt. Nick collected the pertinent newspapers and followed Gray to Turner's rooms.

"You again?" demanded Turner.

"You wanted proof that I did not seduce your sister," said Gray. "Have you compiled her schedule for that Season?"

"Yes. She was very clear about where she went, what she did, and whom she saw," said Turner, lips pressed into a firm line as he tapped a selection of Constance's letters. "Nothing you say can counter that."

"I would never expect you to believe me," agreed Gray. "And I am sure she attended most of the affairs she reported. But I did not."

Turner glared down his crooked nose. "Since your word is suspect—as is the word of any friends you pay to support you—this exercise is pointless." His body tensed as if expecting a blow.

Gray stifled his pain. The insult was hardly a surprise. "I will not argue the point. But as a man of honor, you are bound to consider evidence from disinterested, tamper-proof sources." He gestured to Nick, who stepped forward to lay the newspapers on the table.

Turner paled. "Very well, my lord. Let us see this so-called evidence."

"When did she first mention my name?"

"A letter dated the third of May." He picked it up. "You danced with her at Lady Debenham's ball. She was thrilled. Though you had spoken several times, she had given up hope that you would ask her to dance. You were most particular about whom you partnered, preferring conversation."

"She is right that I was particular. But we had not spoken before that night."

Nick opened the first paper, pointing to the *New Arrivals* column. "Grayson reached town on the second of May. The reporter expressed surprise at the delay, but noted that a project in Sussex had occupied his attention."

Turner frowned, his eyes shifting from the newspaper to Constance's letter and back. "She swore you ran a business in town."

"I do," said Gray. "But my manager handles much of the routine. I only visit the office when I have ships in port. Three years ago, I had fewer vessels. None docked before July."

"He spent the winter and spring in Sussex," continued Nick. "County papers mention his name often, for he was collecting funds to repair the parish church. And he was engrossed in the project mentioned by that reporter—establishing a hospital for wounded soldiers."

Gray gestured for silence. His charitable activities had no bearing on this matter. "I danced with her once at Lady Debenham's ball. She seemed so lonely perched on a chair near the dowagers. Without a chaperon to introduce partners, no one noticed her. I thought she was new to London, but later learned that her chaperon divided her time between eating and playing cards, avoiding ballrooms because the chatter and music gave her megrims. Everyone remarked on her neglect."

Turner flinched.

"If I had known she had been hiding in corners for six weeks, I would not have approached her. I did not do so again." His raised hand stopped Turner's protest. "I will remind you again that I did not approach anyone more than once that year, not even old friends or the Season's diamonds. I'd had trouble the previous year with a girl who read too much into a few kind words, and I did not wish to risk another such encounter. What else did she claim?"

"Three drives in the park. Dancing at four balls. Assignations in gardens, in an antechamber during a masquerade, and in various shops. You finally escorted her to Vauxhall, again seduced her, this time in the Dark Walk, then claimed you had no interest in marriage." His voice still accused, but a hint of uncertainty had crept in.

"And the Vauxhall date would be . . ."

Turner pulled a list from his pile. "The thirtieth of May. She took her life the following morning."

"Quite an imagination." Gray again stopped Turner's protest. "You've had your say. Now I will have mine. Many of her claims can be neither proved nor disproved. Her name rarely appears on guest lists, for newspapers name only the highest-ranking guests. I will concede that she attended most of the affairs she claimed, but I did not. For example, she said we danced two sets at the Cunningham ball on the eighth of May."

Nick produced the next newspaper. "From the society column on the morning of May the ninth. 'Among the fashionables crowding Harriet Wilson's box at the opera last evening was Lord Grayson, scandalously clad in pantaloons rather than breeches. Many, including the Almack's patronesses, decry the adoption of informal attire for evening wear,' et cetera, et cetera . . ." He handed the paper to Turner.

Turner frowned.

Gray waited until he had compared the article to Constance's letter, then continued. "She claims an assignation on the fifteenth. However Lord and Lady Sheffield swear I was playing cards at Watier's that evening. They recall the date clearly because Sheffield's losses caused trouble when he offered for her hand the next morning. Lady Sheffield was one of Miss Turner's friends and recalls her puzzlement when Constance mentioned our supposed assignation. She knew I could not have been in Marchgate's garden."

"Constance never mentioned Lady Sheffield."

"Your sister knew her as Miss Penelope Osham," said Nick.

"Oh."

Gray continued. "On the eighteenth, the newspaper lists Miss Turner at a ball honoring Miss Alice Maynard—she was one of the higher-ranking attendees. I was not there. You will note that I made appearances at Lady Jersey's rout, the Pierson ball, and Lord Hampton's card party that evening."

"Busy night," commented Nick as he passed the papers to Turner.

Gray waited until Turner finished, then continued. "Few people noticed her before Lady Debenham's ball, but her hoydenish antics in the weeks that followed attracted scorn in polite circles. Her most shocking escapade was described in *Life in London* on the morning of May the twenty-eighth."

Nick read, " 'Miss C—T——'s conduct reached a new low last evening when she sought entrance to White's. After a scuffle lasting a quarter hour, two footmen dragged her from the premises, kicking and screaming, still demanding to see Lord G——. A hackney finally carried her away.' "

"My God!" murmured Turner.

"That ruined her," said Nick. "By morning, her remaining invitations had been cancelled, Miss Pettigrew denounced her and quit her post, and the staff of her rented house vowed to leave if she remained in London. A carriage was engaged for the first of June."

"As to visiting Vauxhall on the thirtieth," continued Gray. "After the incident at White's, I concluded that she was mad. I left town the next morning." He proffered the newspaper that noted his departure.

Nick lifted the final paper. "Vauxhall opened late that year. The opening fete was held on June the fifth. On the thirtieth of May, the gardens were closed."

Turner shook his head. "Then why does everyone believe you destroyed her?"

"Many do not," swore Nick.

"Shock often obscures truth," conceded Gray. "I did

not return to London until three weeks after her death. By then, her dying words were on all lips. Everyone knew she was with child. They knew she'd named me. And they knew she'd taken her own life, despite your brother's claim that she had died in a fall. But few other facts were known. I only recently learned that her condition had passed the fourth month. Perhaps your brother did not realize that or thought it unimportant. Her maid said nothing beyond confirming that she died by her own hand. Even if she knows more, she could not now change her story without drawing attention to her own role in the affair, turning her current mistress against her."

Turner shook his head. "Lucy was always a deceitful creature. It was one of the few things Constance and I fought over." His voice cracked.

Gray shrugged. "Are you satisfied now? I will not tolerate another attack that might endanger my betrothed."

"I am satisfied." Turner poured wine while he fought to blink away tears. "But I still want the bastard who destroyed her."

"I doubt anyone will find him," said Gray. "They met long ago in a place far removed from London. Nothing will bring her back. It would be better to concentrate on your own future."

Turner nodded once, sharply. One hand slipped into a drawer. Turning, he looked Gray square in the eye. "I owe you an apology, Grayson. My behavior has been inexcusable. More than inexcusable." His extended palm contained two items.

Gray nearly revealed his shock. "So it was you." He slipped his purse into a pocket, then fingered his grandfather's watch.

"Yes. I didn't know you'd returned to town until I saw you at Lady Debenham's. I must have been mad."

"Grief can do that," agreed Gray, recalling Mary's words.

"How can I atone?"

"Leave the country?" suggested Nick.

Gray shook his head. "Go to Lady Beatrice today. Tell

her what you have discovered about your sister's death. If she accepts my innocence, we will be even."

If Turner presented the evidence, it would have a greater impact than if Nick did. London's chief gossip would soon spread the news.

Gray doubted that Turner could discover Lord Roger's guilt by himself. If Constance had mentioned the man, Turner would already have considered him a suspect.

Bidding Turner farewell, he dropped Nick at White's, then headed for Albany to inspect the repairs. He'd had no trouble selling his rooms—the waiting list for Albany was always long. And Wendell had already left for the country. Jaynes could start moving his things into Berkley Square, starting with the hoopoe. It needed peace.

Trilling softly, he examined its wing and gently removed the splint. The hoopoe raised its crest, stretching the wing slowly at first, then flapping faster.

"Hoop-hoop-hoop," it cried in obvious pleasure.

"A few more days, fellow," promised Gray. "As soon as your strength returns." But not until Mary met the bird. She would enjoy it.

Chapter Sixteen

Mary gasped at Lady Wharburton's ballroom. Even tales of previous masquerades had not prepared her for such magnificent extravagance.

Lady Wharburton had transformed the room into a fantasy forest glade, with trees stretching lantern-bedecked boughs above the dancers, banks of flowers and shrubbery in the corners, and a brook babbling across a grassy alcove.

Mary was dressed as a Tudor lady, her wine-colored gown fitted with trailing sleeves trimmed in sable. She had chosen the costume before meeting Gray, and as recently as dinner it had seemed silly. But a single glance spotted half a dozen similarly clad ladies. In fact, most of the guests wore elaborate costumes. Cleopatra strolled past on the arm of a highwayman. Socrates bantered with Charles II. A monk flirted with a shepherdess. Others were anonymous in dominos that disguised all but height and breadth. Everyone wore elaborate masks, making recognition difficult.

Laura had been suspiciously demure this evening, chatting lightly with Blake and deferring to Mary. Yet her eyes glowed with suppressed excitement. Catherine attributed it to the anonymity that promised a pleasant evening after the hostility she'd faced at the theater. But Mary didn't believe it. She'd seen that look before, and it always spelled trouble. She had already warned Blake.

Gray was waiting at the foot of the stairs. He bowed formally, then raised her hand to his lips. She trembled. He was dressed as an Elizabethan courtier, in a green velvet doublet with slashed sleeves, slashed gold and green trunk-hose, and thin stockings that displayed his well-formed legs even better than breeches or pantaloons.

"How elegant you are, my dear," he murmured, sweeping her into a quadrille.

"It is you who are elegant," she managed. He seemed different tonight, almost bursting with energy, as if he longed to romp through this forest like an ebullient child. One glance from those silvery eyes left her burning.

"I spoke with Turner this morning," he reported as they completed the quadrille's jetté figure. "He agrees that I had nothing to do with his sister's fate."

"Thank heaven." And that explained his excitement. She glided through a figure with a dashing pirate, then returned to Gray's side. "Will he tell society?"

"He already has. As satisfaction for his insults—one of which was attacking me disguised as a footpad—I demanded that he confess to Lady Beatrice. He must have done so, for Lady Wharburton welcomed me with unusual warmth, and Lady Horseley actually apologized. The tale is on half the lips in this ballroom—none of whom realized I was in their audience. A lesson if you are ever tempted to discuss secrets at a masquerade."

"Gossip can be an asset as well as a curse," she agreed, brushing against him on a pass. The contact burned through her gown. "Has Blake spoken with you today?" she added.

"Not since two. Is there a new problem?"

"There might be. Laura is excited, as though she knows some delicious secret. I told Blake to watch her carefully, but that will be difficult in this crowd."

"Very. Do you fear something specific?"

"She knew about tonight before she sent that missive last evening. What if she arranged an assignation here?"

"Logical, for it would be easier to slip past Rockhurst's guard here than at the house. She must know you told him where she'd been. My suggestion might play out after all." He shook his head. "Willful and headstrong do not begin to describe her. It would be far too easy for Lord Roger to slip through the garden. Or he could try the front door. The porter inspects only half the cards."

She nodded. "You will help watch her, I presume."

"Of course." The pattern separated them. When he returned, he smiled and squeezed her hand. "I can deny you nothing, my sweet."

"Do not tease. I will endeavor to make you a good wife, but I know this was not your choice."

"I wish you would cease denigrating yourself," he grumbled. "I am content. Devil take it, I am more than content. If this betrothal vanished in a puff of smoke, I would take immediate steps to reinstate it."

"You would?" She missed the next cue, throwing the set into disarray.

"Must be Miss Huntsley," growled a domino-clad gentleman, naming a lady noted for her clumsiness.

"Yes, I would," murmured Gray, picking up the pattern. "I had considered courting you even before you saved me from Laura's scheming, but my reputation made it difficult. So no more groveling."

Tears threatened, though Mary wasn't sure why. They separated once again.

"I will collect you at eleven tomorrow morning," said Gray when she returned to his side. "We will inspect the house so you can decide how you wish to decorate. It is on the west side of the square, three from the corner."

"I know. I've often admired the stonework around the door. And the ironwork on the upper windows is delightful. You have marvelous taste."

She floated through the rest of the set, hardly believing her luck. He claimed he would have courted her anyway. Could she believe him?

After the quadrille, she danced a reel with Gray's friend Nick and a country dance with Lord Justin. Neither set was conducive to conversation, but both men welcomed her as their friend's betrothed.

Several sets later, Mary was again on Gray's arm, admiring the brook—or pretending to. It was nearly midnight, and the supper dance was starting. If Laura had arranged an assignation, now was the time she would slip away. So they watched her in a mirror. Laura had turned down three partners for this set—another sign that mischief was afoot. At least the white gown of her Helen of Troy costume made her easy to spot in this colorful throng.

Laura glanced around the ballroom, smiled, and slipped onto the terrace.

"Stay here," ordered Gray.

"No. If you catch her with Lord Roger, she will need me to lend her countenance."

Gray sighed. "Come along, then. But be quiet and do exactly as I say. We can't draw attention."

Blake was also headed for the door. As was Nick. But could they protect Laura from harm?

"Relax," whispered Gray as they passed the fountain in the formal portion of the garden. "If Lord Roger is here, there will be two footmen nearby. Rockhurst assigned them to follow him in case Laura slipped out alone."

"I must thank him. He can have no love for her after all the trouble she has caused."

"That matters not. As long as she is under his care, he is honor-bound to protect her. Quiet, now. The folly is around the next corner. It is the most likely rendezvous." He draped an arm over her shoulders, drawing her close as he left the path. They slipped along a hedge until a break offered a view of the folly.

It was a small Roman temple, open on three sides. Clipped shrubbery hugged the base. A statue of Diana stood on a short plinth against the back wall.

But darkness obscured most of the details. No torches burned so far from the house. Laura's white gown shimmered like a ghost in the gathering fog.

Mary shivered.

Mask dangling from one hand, Laura traced the huntress's bow. Most observers would assume that she sought a moment alone, but to Mary, Laura seethed with disappointment and temper. Whomever she had expected to meet was not here.

Mary relaxed against Gray's side, absorbing his heat.

Perhaps there was no cause for alarm. Just because Laura had demanded a tryst did not mean Lord Roger would comply. This would not be the first time Laura had suffered a rebuff.

Gray's lips brushed her ear, distracting her. Trusting Blake to watch Laura, she slid her arm around Gray's neck, pulling his lips to hers. It was the first time she had dared take the initiative, and his response left her breathless. Passion exploded so fast she had no time to think.

Fire flashed through her body. He swallowed her moan, his tongue twining with hers in a dance that made her want to rip away his doublet. She crowded closer, crushing his trunk-hose between them. His hands raced over her back and hips, pulling her close and closer yet.

He wanted her.

She moved against him, crushing her breasts against that masculine chest, wantonly seeking something she could not define. This time it was he who moaned and she who swallowed the sound.

Longing settled in the pit of her stomach.

"Mary," he groaned, trailing kisses across her face. "How the devil am I to wait until Tuesday when I burn for you?"

"I don't know. I wish—"

"You came, my lord." Laura's voice was gay with relief.

Gray froze.

Mary whipped her head around, irritated at the interruption. Yet her heart also broke for Laura. There would be tears before this night was through. "Is that him?" she whispered.

Gray nodded.

"Helen of Troy," said Lord Roger, vaulting the steps to raise Laura's hand to his lips. He wore no gloves and no costume. "The perfect choice. You put the original to shame. Had you been present at the judging, there would have been no war, for none could choose another above you."

"You exaggerate," she said with a light laugh.

"Never, my love. Your beauty smites men blind. Such a face. Such a form. And so natural." The Grecian gown draped from one shoulder, skimming a body unconfined by a corset. Catherine had been appalled when she found out, but it had been too late. Laura's cloak had hidden the fact until they arrived at the masquerade.

Laura simpered, her mask fluttering as it dropped to the floor.

Lord Roger expertly flicked open buttons on her glove. "My life will be rendered sterile unless I touch your alabaster skin, my beauty. A finger. A palm. Or perhaps a wrist." The glove followed the mask.

"Flatterer," she charged, rapping him lightly with her fan. But she let him strip her of the fan and the second glove, then stroke her palms. "I vow you are quite forward."

"Oh, quite, my dear." He drew her arms up and out, feasting his eyes on the bosom molded by her thin gown—a bosom already firm from cold and excitement. His voice sank into seduction. "But you enjoy my boldness, do you not? It satisfies your need for adventure." His stroking thumbs smoothed her wrists. "For excitement." He brought one hand to his mouth. "For love." His lips sucked a finger inside.

Laura sighed.

His mouth trailed up her arm, the tongue laving the veins at her wrist and the sensitive skin inside the elbow. "So soft," he murmured. "So delightfully lovely. But I knew we would suit from the moment I saw you. I appeal to your nature, my beautiful Helen of Troy, as you appeal to mine. Surely you feel it, too, this connection that draws us together."

Mary tightened her grip on Gray's hand. She could see why Lord Roger seduced so easily. He mesmerized his victims. But beneath that soothing voice was a man far more evil than Mr. Griffin.

"So what is my nature, my dear sir?" Laura asked, breathless as she swayed closer. Her tongue traced her lips.

"You are a seeker, my dear." His voice thickened. "Of

excitement. Of challenge. Of passion." He drew her free hand to his cheek.

"I found excitement in your library." She traced his brow. "Tell me what happened last evening. I hated missing the meeting."

"It was flat without you."

"And the spirit?"

"Nearly gone. Only the faintest wisp appeared. I've no doubt the second shock did the job. Which is why I was free to join you tonight."

Laura shivered as he nibbled her shoulder. "I wish I could have seen it, but Blake insisted that we attend the theater. He is so very dull."

"We will not waste these moments on regret, my love. They are short enough already, for you will soon be missed. You would not wish to be discovered out here in the fog." His finger traced her neckline from shoulder to bosom. "I do adore Greek costume. So practical and free." His hand cupped a breast.

She gasped, swaying closer. "So you will not host the society again?" But the question turned breathless as her fingers lost themselves in his hair. She pressed against him.

"Ah, my beauty. I knew it would be like this from the moment you fell so gracefully into my arms. You wish to learn. And I have much to teach." He settled his mouth on hers, backing her against the statue.

"We must stop him," whispered Mary. "Can't you hear that undertone in his voice? He means to force her."

"Of course he does, but she does not yet understand. She thinks they merely play."

Gray's husky voice revealed that he was as affected as she by the scene they were watching. She felt guilty for leaving Laura in danger, even for a moment. Yet she wished she and Gray were alone, free to act on the breathless desire stirring in her heart.

Gray tensed, stilling the hand that had been stroking her side. "He will abandon seduction very soon. She is trapped, and he is not known for patience. Listen. In his

lust, he already forgets to play the suitor." His hand
rubbed the side of her breast.

"Then we must pay attention," she murmured, covering his hand so she could think.

"Ah, my dear." Lord Roger's voice roughened as a
twist on her gown freed a breast. "I've not had so lovely
a morsel in many a day. Sweet. Tender. And mine." His
teeth closed over it.

"My lord!" Laura tried to draw back.

"Do not pretend shock. I feel your response." Lord
Roger laughed. "You want to learn, my lovely lady. We
are too much alike to deny it. Unconventional. Wild.
Free." Again he suckled as his knee thrust between
her legs.

"Release me. You go too far," demanded Laura, trying to shove him away. But she was crowded against
Diana, with no room to move. Her strength was no
match for his.

"No megrims, sweetings. You knew what I wanted
when you sent for me. Why else would you play the
courtesan by leaving off your corset? I'll play at seduction if you want, but I'll not leave without taking my
pleasure. Go ahead and struggle," he added when she
redoubled her effort to pull free. "I love a lively wench."

"But you are a gentleman." Her voice trembled.

He laughed harshly. "I've not been a gentleman since
that she-witch trapped me at the tender age of twenty. I
take my pleasure where and when I will. And right now
you are my pleasure, lovely lady. I've dreamed of your
beauty, your soft skin, the way you melt at my touch. So
stop your teasing and let me in. If you turn cold like my
bitch of a wife, I'll have to hurt you. You wouldn't like
that." He ravaged her mouth when she opened it to
scream, then forced her hand to his groin and rubbed.

Laura was fighting in earnest now, clawing at his face.
But she was helpless. His shoulders pinned her in Diana's
arms as he jerked her skirts up.

"This has gone far enough," moaned Mary.

"Yes." Gray pointed. Blake, Nick, and two footmen
burst from the shrubbery and raced up the steps.

Blake tore Lord Roger away, knocking him to the floor. "You will pay for this," he growled. "You've ruined your last maiden."

"Are you challenging me?" Lord Roger tried to rise, but the others restrained him.

"Dueling is for gentlemen." Blake raked him from head to toe. "You, sir, are a cur and will be treated as one. As for you"—he turned to glare at Laura—"leaving the ballroom unescorted was the stupid act of a willful child. I am ashamed to have you under my care, for you have no more sense than a goose. There isn't a man in England who will offer for you after this stunt."

Laura burst into tears.

"That does it," murmured Mary. "He is too furious to remember where we are." She rounded the hedge and headed for the temple.

"M-Mary?" gulped Laura. "What are you doing here?"

"Trying to prevent a scandal. Cover yourself." While Laura tugged her gown back in place, she turned to Blake. "Save the scold for later. Not everyone is at supper."

Gray helped the footmen hold Lord Roger while Nick bound his arms, smothering his cries for help with the padded sleeve of his doublet.

Mary glared at Laura. "Stop crying. Do you want everyone in the ballroom to remark on red eyes? Your mask will not hide them."

"B-but he—"

"I am well aware of what he wanted. He is a rogue and a scoundrel, as everyone knows. There isn't a drawing room in London in which he is welcome. But when all is said and done, he stole only a kiss, like others before him. You are fortunate that Blake cares enough to intervene. Lord Roger wanted much more. And he doesn't care how he gets it."

Laura blanched.

"Now straighten your gown so we can go to supper. Whether you care about your reputation or not, at least behave for the sake of Blake and Catherine. If not for them, you would now be ruined in truth, with no one to whom you could turn. Lord Roger would never lift a finger for you. He won't even aid his wife, who is locked away somewhere in Scotland." She retrieved Laura's belongings.

"I did not know," wailed Laura.

"You did not ask. You never ask. Thank heaven your mask covers your face, or we could never manage."

Blake had himself under control. He thanked Gray and Nick for their help as the footmen jerked Lord Roger to his feet and forced him down the steps. Mary was following when Turner burst from the shrubbery, much the worse for wine, waving pistols in both hands.

"You killed my sister!" he shouted at Lord Roger.

"I sincerely doubt it," drawled Lord Roger. "I reserve killing for highwaymen and irate papas." He turned to Blake. "Who is this imbecile?"

"Leonard Turner," said Gray.

Lord Roger shrugged.

"Don't deny it," sobbed Turner. "Her maid told me everything. The lies. The secret meetings. The promise of marriage and fancy clothes and fine jewelry. You even gave her a ring, you bastard. Then you disappeared without a word, leaving her with child. God, my poor Constance." Tears ran down his cheeks.

Laura gasped.

"Constance . . . Constance . . ." Lord Roger frowned. "Oh, *that* chit." He shrugged. "You can't blame me for that. If you let her roam the countryside unescorted, what do you expect? And her clothes! I took her for a tavern wench. But she was eager for it, no matter what her maid claims. Passionate little devil. Didn't really expect it. Had a face like a horse. But her body . . ." He smacked his lips. "Much better than those whores Rothmoor collects. Poxed, most of them."

Turner fired, hitting Lord Roger in the shoulder. The footmen dove for cover. Mary ducked behind the rail, though it offered little cover.

As Lord Roger staggered backwards, a second shot rang out—from the same gun—nicking his arm. Laura screamed.

"Devil take it, he has those double-barreled pistols," exclaimed Gray, boosting Mary over the side.

Footsteps pounded toward the folly.

"He still has two shots," shouted Blake, tossing a shrieking Laura over the other side.

Nick tackled Lord Roger as Mary's foot caught on the railing, toppling her head over heels toward the ground. A third shot exploded through the night.

The world went black.

Gray's heart stopped when Mary went down. Chaos reigned behind him, but he barely took it in.

Lord Justin raced around the hedge and tackled Turner, wresting the pistol from his hand. Mr. Turlet arrived to press a cloth to Lord Roger's shoulder while Roger cursed, swearing vengeance on Rockhurst and Turner.

Turner's tears turned to hiccups. He rolled from Justin's grasp to vomit on Lord Roger's leg.

Gray leaped the railing, horrified to find Mary in a heap. For a ghastly moment, all he could see was his mother's body sprawled at the foot of the stairs, blood pouring from her head. But he managed to shake the memory away.

It was too dark to tell if Mary had been shot, but he feared the worst. She didn't move and seemed not to breathe. Scooping her up, he raced toward the house. The library window stood open.

She sagged like a corpse. When light from the first torch revealed a stream of blood rolling down her temple, he staggered.

"No! Not again!"

Spots crowded his eyes, making him sway. But he could not faint now. Mary needed him.

All his life this weakness had set him apart—which answered Mary's question about why he tried his hand at matchmaking. He had always felt out of place—reviled by his father for eschewing manly pursuits, mocked at school for his devotion to study, teased even by his friends for avoiding sports. He knew the pain of rejection well, so he could not tolerate seeing others in the same straits. They needed help to move into the world to which they belonged. And he needed to give that help so he could maintain his own tenuous tie to that world.

But his need for Mary went beyond any quest for acceptance. He needed her more than food or drink or air to breathe—more than life itself. If she were gone . . .

Staggering inside, he laid her on a couch, then tugged a handkerchief from his trunk-hose and wiped away the blood. The scent revived memories of every beating that had tried to turn him into a man, every swoon triggered by the resulting blood, every retch when Rothmoor forced him to watch butcherings. He tasted bile. The room faded as he fought dizziness. But he refused to succumb.

At least she had not been shot. There were no holes. But blood continued to flow.

He cursed himself for freezing after Turner's first shot, for pushing her out of the temple, for allowing her into the garden in the first place. He should have covered her, protected her. But his first reaction had been to escape. Run and hide lest he see blood and faint. Cower so society would not learn his weaknesses.

Tears escaped. Mary lay insensible, and it was all his fault.

"Mary! Wake up, love," he begged, chafing her hand. More blood welled. He wiped it away, fighting the spots swimming before his eyes. "Please be all right, Mary. I can't lose you."

Still she bled.

"My God, Mary! Wake up. I don't know how to fix this!" He dashed away tears with the bloody handkerchief, smearing his face.

"Gray?" Her voice was weak, but her eyes fluttered open.

Relief nearly overwhelmed him. "Thank God. Are you all right, love?" He wiped away another stream.

"Don't dab at it," she ordered. "Press firmly."

"I don't want to hurt you."

"You won't." She cocked her head. "How is it that you remain on your feet?"

"You needed me." He held her eyes. "I could not let you down. I love you."

"Truly?"

"Truly. I thought Turner shot you." He was shaking again.

"I caught my toe on the rail." She lifted her arms.

He scooped her into his lap, pressing his handkerchief against her temple. "Can you ever return my regard?" he asked, surprised to find that he was more terrified now than before she'd awakened. He'd never felt more vulnerable.

"Oh, Gray. I already do." She smiled. "I fell in love with you in Lord Oxbridge's library."

"Why? I was weak as a kitten that night. I could not even sit up properly."

"That matters not. You are intelligent, you care for others, and you never succumb to dishonor. Besides, you are the first man I've ever been able to talk to, and you've accepted me from the beginning."

"I loved you, too, though I didn't recognize it." He smoothed her hair. "But you've seemed so aloof these past days that I feared you regretted this match."

"Never." She sighed. "What I feared was giving you a disgust of me. You have too often been plagued by hoydens like Laura."

"I love you. I need you. Never fear to show me you care, my dear, for your caring is real." He kissed her, keeping the touch gentle lest he aggravate her wound. But passion flared. The handkerchief fell unheeded to the floor as Mary stroked his bare throat. He gave up and plundered, twisting until he sprawled atop her.

"I should know better than to start this when I can't finish it," he groaned some time later. "How can I endure four more days without you?"

"It will be difficult." Her fingers combed his hair. "Perhaps impossible. But we can't here. Blake and Catherine will find us soon. We cannot burden them with new scandal. They will have enough trouble surviving Laura's latest escapade."

He nodded, but did not sit up. "Are you sure you are all right?"

"Yes. Has the bleeding stopped?"

He nodded.

"Then it is merely a bump. No worse than the time I fell in the dairy, and far less than the broken leg I sustained at age ten. I will have a sore head for a day or two, but no more. And you?"

"Vastly relieved. A little dizzy from watching you bleed to death," he admitted freely. "I don't ever want to endure that again."

"That I can't promise, but we will survive whatever happens."

He nodded, indulging himself in another long kiss.

"What will happen now?" she asked when he pulled back.

"We hide our growing frustration, bid farewell to Lady Wharburton—who will doubtless be in shock that a shooting occurred at her very proper masquerade, though with luck we can keep Laura's part in it quiet—then see you home to bed. Alone, alas." He kissed her again.

"That isn't what I meant. What will happen to Mr. Turner?"

Sighing, he helped her sit up. "Transportation, if he is lucky. There is no way to save him, Mary. I tried. I told him no one could identify the culprit after all these years, for I knew he would transfer his obsession to Lord Roger. But he discovered the truth anyway. Now Lord Roger is wounded. He might be a cad, but his father is a duke, and Turner is merely the younger son of a baron and on poor enough terms with his brother already."

She sighed. "Poor boy. He does not deserve such a fate."

Gray agreed, but there was nothing he could do.

Yet they were wrong. By Monday morning, when they met to release the hoopoe in Hyde Park, Turner was free and Lord Roger was gone.

The Duke of Athland had settled matters personally. He had long deplored Lord Roger's vices. Allowing Grayson to bear the blame for Miss Turner's seduction was the last straw. The attack on Laura, which had become public knowledge thanks to Mr. Turlet, merely sealed his fate. Athland gave Lord Roger a choice—leave England forever or stand trial for assault. Lord Roger's courtesy title would not avail him at the Old Bailey, where he had no more privilege than the lowest knave. His arm hung in a sling when he boarded a vessel bound for the Caribbean.

Laura was also gone. The second bullet had grazed her cheek, digging a furrow that would leave a four-inch scar. Her hysterics had lasted two days. Laura defined herself by her beauty. Blemished, she could not even face her family. The moment Dr. McClarren allowed her out of bed, she fled London.

Gray's reputation was completely restored. Turner had credited him with tracking down and exposing Lord Roger, thus saving society's daughters from the ruin Laura and his sister had found. So Gray was now a hero.

Mary met him in the chapel of St. George on a sunny Tuesday morning. Only a dozen witnesses joined them, though Blake expected hundreds for the wedding breakfast. As Blake escorted her in, she scanned the faces.

Lady Beatrice beamed, as did Lady Horseley. Lady Sheffield sat with Mr. Turner—she had told him much about his sister's last days, helping him put her death behind him. Catherine was already shedding tears. Nick, Justin, Medford, Gray's manager, and—

She stumbled when she identified the last three faces—their presence compliments of Gray, no doubt: William, who must have broken speed records to make it from Devonshire on such short notice; Thomas, up from Eton; and Andrew, one arm in a sling. What fate had brought him back from Spain in time for her wedding? He could not yet have received her letter announcing her betrothal. Mary nearly burst into tears at the sight of her favorite brother.

But greetings must wait until later. Now she gazed into

Gray's silver eyes. His voice filled the chapel as he vowed to love, honor, and cherish her. Hers remained firm, with nary a stammer as she gave her life into the hands of a man who loved her so much he'd mastered a lifelong weakness because she needed his help.

"I love you," he whispered as he bent to kiss her.

"Forever." Her arms crept around his neck.

He made the witnesses wait a long time before leading his wife into the sunshine of their new life.